# *The* Thyssen *Affair*

## MOZELLE RICHARDSON

*Dedication*

*Special love to children Jerry, Judy, Susie and Rock*

For Christy
with great hopes!
6/1/'11
Mozelle

1980

Cane Eliot knew he was being followed before he reached the shuttle to *Lufthansa* for his overnight flight to Germany. It was the same thing that made the skin on the back of his neck crawl during the war when something was wrong.

Making a quick decision to try to lose whomever was tailing him, he called *Lufthansa* and cancelled his flight. Taking a taxi downtown, the shadow still with him, he got out at Rockefeller Center, and slipped through the restaurant near the skating rink to the subway. He found the small hotel he had known in the Village thirty years earlier and paying for the day, he carried his valise into the waiting elevator.

At the fifth floor he left the elevator, ran down two flights of stairs and ducked into the men's room at the end of the hall. He had to change his appearance and do it fast. The Stetson had to go. He stowed it deep in a swing-top garbage can, pulled off his boots and dropped them after the hat. Goddamn bloody shame to have to leave his old friends. For a minute he considered retrieving the rattlesnake hat band, but thought better of it. It takes years for a hat and boots to conform to a man's own brand. Well hell, he thought, I'll just have to start over in Colorado when this damn mess is finished.

He opened the valise and pulled out his straight-edged razor. Peering intently at his reflection, he twisted his lips first one way and then another. With a few clean strokes, he shaved off his moustache. He learned a long time ago that losing your identity was just part of the game. He ran his finger across his smooth upper lip and down the scar across his cheek. That brought back memories of a war that he'd just as soon forget. It is also as sure an identifier as a set of fingerprints.

Changing into a gray suit, white dress shirt, knotting the blue silk tie, putting on the black oxfords he'd seldom worn except to funerals, he shook his head. The unfamiliar clothes made him feel awkward and uncomfortable.

But a quick glance in the mirror, adjusting his tie and smoothing his vest, Cane admitted that a suit made a hell of a difference in his appearance. Securing the German skull with his jeans, jacket and cowboy shirt in the valise, he cursed under his breath. The satchel was a dead giveaway. But it couldn't be helped. How the devil had he been spotted so soon? Who was following him?

It must have been the man who passed him on the road to Cummings. Who was he? Well, for Christ's sake, he had to be KGB and that meant the Russians knew they had the wrong skull. It meant too, that they could move pretty damn fast. He opened his billfold, cut up his credit cards with the Lapis knife and buried them in the trash. That was a big mistake—using credit cards in Oklahoma City. He wracked his brain. Was there anything else to connect him with Cane Eliot? God, yes! The plane ticket from Denver to New York had been in his name! He had been out of it too long. Peter had made a goddamn poor choice for a Company man. He'd better shape up quick. This was not as simple as Peter had thought.

He opened the door slowly, satisfied he was alone, walked briskly down the hall. The damn valise. He had to get rid of it. Taking the stairs again, this time to the basement, he left through the alley door, walked several blocks, took a cab to a small residential hotel he remembered in the Bronx. The lobby was empty. He rang for the clerk and in a heavy German accent asked for a room and signed the register Wilhelm Schwartz. Well, by God that ought to take care of any snoopers!

He immediately called the number that would locate Peter and briefed him about the tail that had followed him from Oklahoma City. But not about his carelessness. He'd rather Peter didn't know about his getting a plane ticket to New York from Colorado via Oklahoma City in his own name. And then to rent a car—my God! Who would dream a cover would be needed before leaving New York!

Peter was silent for a minute, then in a tight voice said, "Chili, contact your friend at the Consulate in Munich as soon as you get there, so he can stay on top of things and keep me informed."

"Roger." Well, perhaps Peter didn't think this was such a piece of cake

2

*as he'd let on. Taking a bottle of Scotch from his valise, he poured half a glass, drank it in two gulps, ate a room service dinner, and went to bed. On his back, his head pillowed on his arms, unable to sleep, he considered the strange events that centered on a thirty-five year old skull of a German prisoner of war. Had it only been two days since Peter was at the ranch?*

# CHAPTER I

*LoBar Ranch, Colorado*
*Thursday, September 25*

C ane felt the tension in Peter's voice as soon as his call came at noon from Stapleton Airport in Denver. Since then the rancher had been waiting with the storm getting progressively worse. It was with a considerable feeling of relief that he saw the foggy lights and heard the automobile.

Standing at the open door, with the blizzard whirling about him, he watched as Peter Landis parked at the hitching rail, got out, greeted the barking dogs. He saw Peter pull a briefcase and duffle from the back seat, hunker down, duck his head into the blowing snow, and start toward the ranch house. Cane knew this was no social visit.

The screen door screeched back on its hinges as the dogs flew in, scattering snow. Cane reached to take Peter's bags.

"What the hell are you doing out here in the boon-docks on a day like this? You're supposed to be in Virginia."

Peter hugged the older man.

"Damn! It's good to see you, Cane! I called from Langley last night, but couldn't get through. It's been a hell of a trip. Thought I'd never make it—there have been jack-knifed semi's, campers blown off the road, and cars in ditches. " Cane helped him with his sheepskin jacket, shook off the snow and returned the hug.

"Whatever lucky or unlucky circumstance it took to bring you here— I'm glad! A drink is the first thing you need—hot rum or Glenlivet--?

"I'll stand close to the fire and have the Scotch straight, thank you." He took off his fogged glasses, breathed some steam on them, pulled a handkerchief from his hip pocket, polished and put them back on.

"And my belly sincerely hopes that there is some food in the kitchen!"

"You can count on it. There's a pot roast on the stove. What the hell is so important about this trip?" Cane was at the make-shift bar on the roll top desk, pouring generous servings of Glenlivet into kitchen glasses. He handed one to Peter and then lifted his in a toast. "It better be good!"

"Cane, you better believe it's good. Here, I've an article I want you to read first."

Cane rubbed his chin with its day old beard, and looked at Peter from under bushy brows, "You mean it's in print?"

Peter nodded as he thumbed through his briefcase, found the newspaper, and handed it to Cane.

"Read it and then we'll talk." Picking up his glass he walked to the sleet-glazed window that reflected the room—the fire, the books, the easy chairs. "Shitty weather," he said over his shoulder. An unseasonable blue-norther had paralyzed the Colorado valley with a freezing mixture of snow and sleet and cut-throat wind that surged around the ranch house with a frenzy that rattled the windows and shredded the trees.

Cane nodded absently, concentrating on the newspaper, standing in front of the fireplace. He finished the article, pitched the paper on the floor and joined Peter. They stood shoulder to shoulder looking at the bleak wintry dusk.

"Now, why the hell would anyone want to dig up a thirty-five year old Nazi skull? And why does it interest the CIA?"

"Hell, we don't know. But the Company is interested because the Russians are. Actually we know little more than what's in the paper. Two men were involved. They left their shovels and footprints at the site of the grave in Fort Reno, Oklahoma. It was a POW camp during the war." He took a satisfying drink of Scotch, then added, "The FBI was called in because the Prisoner of War cemetery is Federal property. Someone sent a skull trussed up in Sima film shield from a Richardson, Texas post office the following Monday morning. Richardson is a suburb of Dallas."

"Yes, I know. Who sent the package?"

"We don't know. The return was a vacant lot. But it was air-mailed to a research foundation post office in Zurich. We've had that under surveillance for some time as a suspected Red drop. For once, there was complete cooperation all the way around. The FBI swapped packages in New York, and we watched the post office in Zurich. Sure enough, you know who turned up to claim it?"

"The Russians?"

"Right!"

"What was in it?"

"A skull from Cornell Medical School."

"So the CIA has the original?"

"Yes, we have it. But that's all. We don't know what the hell to do with it. If the Russians want it, then they must have a good reason, so naturally it means we are curious. We want to know what that reason is. Here's something I want to show you." He zipped open his duffel and pulled out a round package. Carefully pealing the brown paper and film shield from the skull, he balanced it on one hand and bowed slightly.

"Commander Eliot, allow me to present Major von Stober."

"For God's sake!" Cane, shocked, gingerly took the skull in both hands, twisting it from side to side. The lower jaw and skull were wired together in such a way that the lower part dropped a little as Cane took it.

"Son of a bitch! And he was wrapped like this when you got him?"

"Yes. And we did the substitute the same way—film shield and all."

"Film shield—you know that is to protect film from X-rays in airport surveillance." Cane placed the skull in the center of the coffee table. "The paper was a little vague about the details. Fill me in."

"The facts are, Cane, the vandals found the casket had disintegrated so they took the skull and left. Soon after that it was mailed it to Switzerland. The AP picked up the story from the *Fort Reno Weekly*."

Cane nodded, sipping his drink. A warm glow of affection showed as he looked at his friend. Solidly built, there was a hard compactness about Peter, whose thinning sandy hair, ruddy complexion, eyes a serious amber behind horn-rimmed glasses, that made him look anything but a career intelligence officer.

Cane gave a long introspective look at the skull on the coffee table. Reflections from the fire made shadows come and go around the eye sockets, highlighted the steel bridgework around the molars and showed clearly enough the seamed articular joints in the curvature of the head. He pulled a pipe off a rack on the desk, packed it from a tin humidor, struck a match with his thumb nail, lighted it methodically.

"The hell with it, Major," he said. "All you need are some cross-bones! So make yourself at home. I'm going to read about you again." He picked the newspaper off the floor.

Switching on the floor lamp, after another quick glance at the skull, he settled himself into a battered leather chair, and stretched his boots over the coffee table to reread the article.

While Cane read, Peter busied himself with the dogs, scratching their ears, ruffling their fur, pausing occasionally to glance at Cane. His eyes softened; the affection he felt for this older man showed plainly enough. It had been a lasting and mutual regard since that first day when Canyon Eliot Jr., his son, had brought him to the ranch a week after they'd met in the freshman enrollment line at the University of Colorado.

That first weekend was followed by dozens more. And after Peter's parents died in a flu epidemic, the Colorado ranch became his home. It was Cane who turned Peter's interest toward the Intelligence Service while young Canyon went to Navy flight school. They were both in Vietnam, Peter with the CIA, Canyon a Navy pilot.

Peter returned to Colorado with Cane's son. He stood beside the older man at the funeral, had his hand on Cane's shoulder as a Navy bugler played taps. Young Canyon Eliot Jr. was buried beside the Mother he'd never known.

Since that time, between assignments, Peter would return to the ranch and they would sit up all hours over drinks discussing politics— the country, the Company, the economy and always the Russians. They were an ongoing problem—would they ever not be? He glanced at the older man, spotlighted under the old fashioned silk fringed lamp, absorbed in the newspaper article. His friend Cane, his surrogate father, was the toughest kind of survivor and it was etched in his face. It was as weathered as this rangy country he called home.

Peter knew that the language Cane had learned as a child was still a major part of his life. A daily record was kept in German, and his quarter horse responded to German commands. At over six feet, Cane had a broad shouldered strength and lean body that gave the impression of a stubborn intractable mulishness.

And that's not bad, Peter thought, for a quick character analysis. Bushy gray-black brows shaded eyes almost squinted shut from years of looking into the sun and wind and dust. But, occasionally when they looked at you sharp and quick, they were open and piercingly direct, blue green and ice cold. He was tanned to a leathery sheen. His hair, dark and crisp, streaked with gray, curled over his ears and collar. A matching mustache of noble proportions partially hid a hairline scar that reached from his nose to his jaw.

Faded jeans, timeworn colorless boots and a threadbare wool shirt showed years of hard wear. He looked exactly what he was. A man who belonged to this room with its Navajo rugs and beamed ceiling, with its great soot blackened fireplace and scarred roll-top desk that served as both office and bar. A room with a filled gun-rack and floor-to-ceiling bookcases stacked with volumes in four languages. Elk antlers by the gallery door held stiff oil skins, a sweat-stained Stetson with a rattlesnake band his own and Peter's sheep-skin jackets.

"While you're up, throw another log on the fire." Crossing his boots on the low table, careful not to disturb the Major, he rolled up the newspaper and pointed it at Peter. A flurry of sparks hissed up the chimney.

"Did you notice something here—the date the poor bastard died? It was after the cease fire. There he was all happy and jubilant, ready to go home and he died. Died by drowning. Where in the hell in Western Oklahoma is there enough water for a man to drown?"

"I know. Curious. Here's what we have on our Major from the POW records," Peter said, pulling out a sheaf of papers from his briefcase. "von Stober, Heinrich Friedrich August."

"Full German handle of the aristocracy."

"Quite. Date of birth, April 4, 1914, rank or grade, Major."

"Major—that means regular Army. The Wehrmacht as opposed to the Schutzstaffel—that is the SS."

"That's right. Certainly when you consider that his regiment was the First Para Corp, First Battalion Company, 65th Infantry."

"I knew that outfit," Cane said. "The Parachute Corps was the elite of the German Army. They fought in Eastern Italy under Kesselring."

"Right. And that's where he was captured September 18, 1944 in Rimini. Here's a photo a neighbor sent to the FBI when the news broke. He said he helped his wife with her garden."

Cane picked up the picture. "This is strange. Officers didn't go on work detail."

"No, but they could if they wanted to."

"Not a Wehrmacht Major, Peter. I know German officers—"

"So we have a full blown mystery."

Studying the picture, Cane said, "I'll be damned—the son of a bitch is working. At least he's holding a pitchfork." He looked at Peter, then back at the photograph. "And he looks arrogant as hell. Have you been to Fort Reno?"

"No, I came straight from Langley. But something interesting happened there about three weeks ago. An agricultural team from the Ukraine visited the fort. You know it's a state agronomy and cattle experimental station."

"I thought it was federal property."

"It is, but after the war it was disbanded as a remount station and Oklahoma took it over."

"I see," Cane nodded. "And so the Russians came looking?"

"They sure as hell did and they asked to see the POW cemetery as soon as they'd looked over the livestock."

"That's interesting. Now what was it about Major von Stober's grave that attracted their attention—?"

"Obviously his skull."

"But why?"

Peter shook his head.

"That's what we keep coming back to. It doesn't make sense."

"But it made sense to someone in the Kremlin. Did you examine it?"

"Yes and we took photographs." He handed Cane half a dozen 9x12 slicks.

Cane fanned them out and studied the pictures taken from every angle.

"He looks fairly clean to have been buried six feet under in Oklahoma clay for thirty years." He pulled one picture from the others, examined it, then picked up the Major's skull.

"Christ, Pete, you can't really appreciate dental work until you see it in a skull. Especially steel bridgework."

"Pretty gruesome, eh?" Peter reached over and took the skull in his hands. "Looks like he kept a dentist on a retainer."

"What about POW dental records?"

"None in his files. They probably didn't worry too much about dental records in the camp."

"But you'd think there would be an explanation of his drowning.

11

Did you look up the guard unit?"

"C Company of 113th Security Police. The dentist was Lt. Harvey Worth who died some years ago. The doctor was a Captain Ellis Benton who doesn't remember him at all."

"So our friend kept a low profile. What about a death certificate?"

"There's no death certificate in the file, Cane."

"I can't imagine that."

"Nor I. But we have a lead on him. The old man who owned the farm near the prison camp called the FBI when the story came out—he's the one who gave us the picture. His name is Jim Cummings, a pretty smart old codger, they say. He remembered von Stober very well, and said the Major was a personable guy, a little on the abrupt side, but he seemed to enjoy coming to the farm."

Cane reached for the snapshot and studied it again. Faded from age, a brown streak on one side, the image of the German officer was clear enough. His face was highlighted in the sunlight, his black hair slicked down, his arrogance shown clearly in the toss of his head, his eyes. It looked like an unposed shot—a faded garden in the background, a surprised expression.

"He looks healthy enough here. You can't help wonder what happened."

Peter stood up and walked to the fireplace swishing his drink absently.

"And why—now—did the Russians get interested in him after all these years?"

Cane ran his hand over the day-old stubble of beard, then rose abruptly and joined Peter in front of the fire. The heat felt good and the crackling blaze danced across his face.

"So what are your plans?"

Peter turned to face Cane

"I'm going to lay it on the line, Cane. I've come for a hell of a lot more than advice. For more than just your thoughts on this." He paused.

"I don't follow you." Cane frowned.

"We need you to quarterback this operation. To take the ball—hell, the skull—and go for touchdown."

"And just what do you mean by that?" Cane's eyes turned cold.

"We need you to go to Germany and find out what this Nazi skull is all about."

Cane looked at Peter a long second, his eyes narrowed to slits, then said calmly, "You've lost your cotton-picking mind."

"Cane, hear me out—we've got to try to get a lead on why the Russians want the damn thing. Because, there has to be a reason they are so determined to get the skull and for that reason alone *if the Russians want it then by God so do we!* There has to be an explanation and we need to know what it is."

"No way, Peter. I've been out of it too long—and I don't want to get back in."

"Cane, believe me, it will be an interesting trip. With weather like this in September it's going to be a nasty winter. So you have a nice prepaid vacation in Germany. The whole thing will be fun—plain and simple."

"Shit! Nothing the Company does is simple. Forget it—I'm not your man." Cane finished his drink, walked to the desk-bar, poured another, stood looking at the dwindling fire. He shook his head repeating, "No way."

"You're the only person who can pull it off, Cane. You speak German like a native, you can go as a friend of the Major's—meet his wife and friends. Find out what he did in the war. A Major—it must have been important to have the Russians so determined to have his skull. So find out what is so damn valuable about his head."

Cane shook his head. "Peter, I don't know how I can make it plainer—I don't want to get back in. I had it up to here in the war. You're working on the wrong man. There has to be someone my age who was in the OSS and still around."

"Cane, even if you don't give a damn about Munich or the Oktoberfest, there's simply no one the Company has with your qualifications—speaking excellent German, the right age and who looks the part. You could go as a wartime buddy of the Major's who was in the POW camp with him. His widow would be happy to see you."

"The hell she would. She's probably been married a couple of times since then and has forgotten him by now."

'Damn it all! Go and find out. We need to get someone on this immediately. For God's sake, Cane, I know you are a patriot! Your country needs you. Aren't you the least bit curious about the goddamn skull?"

"How long would I be gone?"

"Not more than a couple of weeks. Depends on how much time you spend at the Oktoberfest."

Cane burst out laughing. Slapped Peter on the shoulder and said, "The hell with it. I'll go. Now let's eat!"

Working on the dining table that night, after big bowls of pot roast, with the skull between them, Peter made their plans. The operation, he said, would be called Tamale. Cane's code name, Chili. His control was a veteran CIA officer named Hastings whose cover was a minor clerk in the Munich consulate.

Cane sat quietly, not speaking and letting Peter make the plans. Occasionally, the younger man glanced at him, knowing that disapproval clouded his face. But finally when he looked at him, Cane smiled.

"By damn, my arm is near broken from the job you've done twisting it."

Peter winked and let his hand rest on the older man's shoulder without speaking.

He packed Cane's World War II valise with the skull, his seldom worn black oxfords, his three-piece gray suit, a dress shirt and blue silk tie, because, he said, you can't go to Europe looking like a cowboy. He also added three passports.

"Three? And you said this was just a simple operation—nothing to it. Just deliver the damn thing to Germany and meet the Missus. Christ....."

Peter grinned and went back to examining the passports, passing them to Cane. One in the name of Carl Becker, a chicken farmer from Arkansas, who would be an ordinary tourist, another in the name of Wilhelm Schwartz, naturalized citizen, former member of 65th Infantry, 1st Paratroop Division, a wartime chum of Major Heinrich von Stober, and the third—a worn Austrian passport, well thumbed and stamped, in the name of Josef Cranach, a freelance writer. To go with them was the identification—driver's licenses, credit cards, Social Security, insurance, family photographs. There were also confirmed reservations at the Boarshead Inn—The Eberkopfhaus—on the Altenbruckstrasse in Schwabing near the English Gardens in the name of Wilhelm Schwartz.

Cane looked at Peter sideways with raised brows. "You sure as hell were pretty damn positive I'd be available...."

"Now Cane— you know you'll enjoy a trip back to Germany."

The last item to go in the valise was a small aerosol canister of tear gas that Peter insisted on his taking—because you never know what the hell you might need it for.

They talked most of the night. Peter suggested that Cane fly to Oklahoma City, spend the night, go to Fort Reno just outside the city, visit the cemetery and the old man, Cummings, who had known the German Major and get his views on the man and then continue on to New York.

After very little sleep, Peter left, following a snow plow to the interstate and then to Denver Stapleton Airport to return to Langley as soon as possible.

Cane, still unhappy about being involved, knew that he would do exactly as Peter asked. Some affairs had to be settled before he left and he set about that morning taking care of them. By evening everything was done. Now he looked at the open valise on the dining table with narrowed eyes.

Pulling a leather pouch from his pocket, he opened it. Inside was a talisman given him by his grandfather before the war. A lovely lapis lazuli carving of a Chinese princess—very old and very rare. From the curve of her head with its tiny topknot to the hard slant of the shoulders flowing down her body to the tapered spread of the fluted folds of her robe, it was an exquisite work of art. Only he knew it concealed a sharply honed, double-edged switchblade triggered by the topknot. The handle, with its delicate carving, was shaped to fit a man's hand and the weight was perfect—heavy enough to slice a man's ribs, slender enough to leave little blood. He replaced her in the leather pouch, laid her carefully in the valise. During the war she had saved his life more than once.

Closing the valise slowly, he carried it to the car, stashed it on the back seat, and stood for a long minute with his arm on the door. *What the hell is Peter getting me into!*

# CHAPTER II

*Fort Reno, Oklahoma*
*Friday, September 26, 1980*

Cane parked the rented Mustang he'd driven from Oklahoma City in front of the two-story white stone building facing the parade ground that had been company headquarters for the old Ft. Reno Cavalry Unit. Cottonwood trees that shaded the CHQ then shaded it still. A broad flight of stairs led to a recessed veranda.

To the south as far as Cane could see were barns, corrals, and autumn-yellowed pastures. A sign, "Post Cemetery," at the corner of the parade ground pointed in the direction of the barns.

The only hint of life was a vintage white Chevrolet pickup angled through two parking spaces in front of the old post hitching rail. A golden Indian summer morning, the air crisp, the cottonwoods just beginning to turn, it was a far cry from the freezing blizzard with its drifts of windblown snow he'd left in Colorado.

He took a last draw from his cigarette, pitched it over the balustrade, sighed and pushed open the door. Taking off his hat, he smiled at a middle-aged secretary.

"I'm Canyon Eliot, ma'am. Do some ranching in Colorado. I was just passing through, and wondered if I could look over your operation here. Experimental breeding, isn't it?"

"Oh, yes sir. Let me call Mr. Mayhugh, he's the director, he'll be glad to show you around." Mayhugh, a thin stoop-shouldered cowboy/scientist, came out of a back office, hand outstretched.

"Howdy, howdy—glad to take you over to the station. Could we use your car? My pickup's loaded with feed front and back."

For the better part of two hours, a genuinely interested Cane followed Mayhugh through the cattle feeding and breeding programs.

From the calving barn, he saw the Post Cemetery. It was a quarter-mile or so distant in the middle of a pasture, enclosed by a white stone wall that held a solid growth of evergreens with a stand of golden cottonwoods just beyond. A herd of black Angus yearlings grazed the dry pasture grass by the cemetery wall. Cane casually asked what it was.

"Oh that?" Mayhugh answered, "that's the old Post Cemetery. You wouldn't believe the traffic we've had through here lately. About ten days ago, a couple of weirdos stole the skull of a German prisoner of war. The Associated Press picked it up, and since then it's the most popular spot around here. There's a car going there now. Want to see it?"

"Sure," he answered, "why not?"

Cane watched the car stop by the entrance to the cemetery. He was surprised to see a woman step out of the sedan, shoo away the cattle, unlatch the iron gate, and disappear inside.

It was a good fifteen minutes later after Mayhugh had finished his tour of the experimental station that he motioned for Cane to park beside the other car. The director spoke affectionately to the cattle crowding them, while he held the gate open.

There was no sign of the other visitor, and Cane asked, "Where did she go?"

"Oh, probably over the stile into the POW section. That's what everyone wants to see—where the German was dug up and lost his head." He gave Cane a quick summary of the vandalism as he closed and latched the gate behind them, then added, "This older part of the cemetery is interesting. It goes back to the Indian scout days. Sign our guest book here." He pulled a waterproof ledger from an opening in the wall. Cane signed and then thumbed through.

"See there," Mayhugh pointed out. "That was a bunch of Russians came through here with an interpreter. But that was before all the excitement. Who in the world would be crazy enough to want the skull of a POW buried thirty some odd years ago?"

"God knows. It's sure enough strange." Cane followed Mayhugh. It was a pretty cemetery filled with firs, pines, and cedars as old as the oldest grave. Cavalry officers, soldiers, wives, children, unknowns—so many of them—all had the familiar curved headstones found in American military cemeteries around the world.

Cane glanced up as the other visitor came back over the stile. There was no railing, and she stepped carefully down the metal steps. He looked at her with interest. She was older than she'd appeared from a distance. Her hair was dark and thick, combed back from a widow's peak across the top of her ears into a loose bun. Small gold hoops dangled by her cheeks. The brown leather collar of her coat was turned up and framed a finely chiseled face with shaded eyes, high cheek bones, and dark sharply defined brows. When she reached the ground, she looked at the men and smiled.

"Morning," Cane said. Her smile broadened and her eyes twinkled.

"Good morning," she answered. Her voice had a trace of accent that was hard to place. It was low and intimate. Cane wanted to keep her talking. He noticed a small dimple at the corner of her mouth, her softly rounded chin.

"Sure is a nice day," he added ineptly, and doffed his hat with a slight bow.

"Yes," she answered, "it is indeed." And flashed a dazzling smile as she passed. Both men turned to watch as she walked through the cemetery, pausing occasionally to read a dim inscription. Her coat swung gracefully with each sure-footed step. A brown leather bag hung from her shoulder. At the gate she turned, caught Cane's eye, and waved. He saluted her casually with his hat, then pushed it to the back of his head.

"What would a pretty girl like that be doing in a POW cemetery?" he asked, almost to himself, but Mayhugh answered him.

"Since the news of the vandalism, everyone comes. But she sure was a looker, wasn't she?" Cane didn't answer.

"Would you like to see the POW section?"

"Might as well since we're here." Cane couldn't push the woman out of his mind. What was she doing here? Would she really be that curious about a POW whose grave had been vandalized? She was more handsome than pretty—in a wholesome, fresh sort of way, and she wasn't a kid, either. He guessed she was in her forties. He followed Mayhugh up the stile and then down into the well-kept treeless appendage to the old Post Cemetery. Like the other, it was walled with white stone. Along the west side were graves of the German soldiers, on the east, those of the Italians. All had died in prisoner of war camps in Oklahoma, Texas, or Kansas.

"Here's the grave." Mayhugh pointed to a headstone that read:

MAJOR HEINRICH VON STOBER
1ST PARA CORP
1ST BATTALION CO.
65TH INFANTRY
D. MAY 20, 1945

The red earth, disturbed where the vandals had dug, was raked over. Grass wouldn't cover the scars until next summer.

"It sure would take a sick man to dig into one of them graves," Mayhugh said, kicking a clod aside.

Cane nodded. Poor guy. Buried in a foreign country and then, years later, to lose his head. But the irony of it all, Cane mused, is the fact that his skull was headed home.

~~~~

Anya Vasilievna Petrovna latched the gate of the cemetery, her mind on the bleak grave. How could this supposedly simple operation have taken such a wrong turn? Reaching her car, she watched as the two men climbed over the stile. When they were out of sight, she opened the door of Cane's car. Nothing there but a trench coat. Going through the pockets quickly, she found a package of cigarettes, a pipe, a tobacco pouch, and matches—wooden matches. Smiling, she thought that he looked the type of cowboy to light a match on the seat of his trousers.

Flipping open the glove compartment, there was a Hertz car envelope with a name and address on the rental form. Taking a notebook from her shoulder bag, she wrote down Cane's name, address—LoBar Ranch, Eastern, Colorado—and driver's license number. His signature was tight and controlled but with a fast swing to it, as if he couldn't waste time making the same letters match. An interesting script. Replacing the papers in the envelope, she put it back into the glove compartment then checked the back seat and the trunk. Nothing there and the trunk was locked. She drove directly to the Oklahoma City airport.

For two days Anya had covered the city, checking newspaper files, reading and rereading the account of the grave robbery. Two trips to the cemetery did no good. Her visits to the library to do research on POW camps in Oklahoma had not helped. It was almost as if the camps' history had been erased completely when they were closed. The only thing left of the hundreds interned here was this small cemetery where the prisoners had buried their dead. As much as she hated failure, Anya would have to report that her trip to Oklahoma had accomplished nothing in the way of locating the skull or who had made off with it.

She could only guess where it might be. Had it been switched at the post office in Texas? Had it been screened in New York and the skulls exchanged there? Well, she could only hope Professor Belyakov would know something when she talked to him tonight in New York.

~~~~

21

On his way to the airport, Cane mulled over what he had learned from Jim Cummings. The old fellow, although more than a little deaf, was sharp as a tack. Cane had found him sitting in a porch swing reading a newspaper, his head thrown back to use the lower part of his bifocals to best advantage. He was shriveled with age, had sparse white hair, and wore a faded gray coat sweater buttoned to the neck. Cane parked the car and walked to the porch without attracting his attention. He shouted.

"Howdy, Mr. Cummings."

The old man looked up, startled, then broke into a smile. He got to his feet slowly.

"Mighty fine, mighty fine—come in, come in—don't have much company drop by. Pleasure, sir, pleasure. Sit down, sit down."

Cane pumped his hand vigorously and introduced himself by mumbling a name—any name—as a journalist doing a story on the German Major whose grave was vandalized, then joined the old man on the porch swing. His watery eyes had brightened at the opportunity to talk and have a listener. Cane heard about the farm, the son George, the daughter-in-law Louise, the grandchildren and, finally, the POW camp and the German Major.

Cane asked if he had any pictures of the German. Cummings shook his head.

"Sure sorry. I had one, but the FBI wanted it. You know," he slapped Cane on the arm, "it was funny but the Major didn't want his picture taken at all. Got real nasty when Mae snapped it unexpectedly."

"Mae was your wife?"

"Oh, no. Mae Bush was a friend of Ella, my wife. She took the picture. She worked, still does, on the weekly newspaper. It was Ella's fault, I guess. She asked Mae to take a picture so we could have it—a sort of keepsake. And he wouldn't let her. No, sir! He said he didn't want his picture taken, and he meant it."

Cane nodded, giving the old man his complete attention.

"But that Mae was determined. If I'd known she was going to

surprise him like she did, I'd have stopped her. But after it was done, I couldn't let the Major take after her. He was real upset. Showed a mean, nasty temper. He didn't come back after that. It was in the spring sometime, about the time the war in Europe was over. We figured they'd be going back to their homes so we called the camp to tell him goodbye. And, sure enough, you know what—they told us he was dead."

"Did they say what happened—an accident or illness?"

"No. We asked, but they wouldn't tell us anything. We felt real bad."

"Where can I find Mae Bush?"

"In town at the *Fort Reno Weekly* office. It's west, across from the courthouse square."

Cane eased away the best he could, shaking hands, saying goodbye several times, with the old man still talking as Cane put the car in gear. He headed for the newspaper office to see Mae Bush.

Before he reached the highway, a car going the opposite direction passed him. It was a gray late-model Chevrolet with a bare-headed man at the wheel. Cane wondered about it as they passed. The road dead-ended at Jim Cumming's place. Almost had to be his son.

In Fort Reno, Cane found the *Weekly* closed for the rest of the day. At the corner drugstore, he called Mae Bush at home, but there was no answer. Deciding it wasn't worth missing his plane to interview her, he headed for the airport. But he had something to think about. Why did von Stober object so strenuously to having his picture taken?

# CHAPTER III

*Fort Reno, Oklahoma*
*Friday, September 26*

The first place Magen Ben-Yanait, Israli Mossad Special Agent, went in Fort Reno was to the newspaper office where he struck up a conversation with Miss Mae Bush, the septuagenarian office manager, women's page and obituary editor of the *Fort Reno Weekly*.

"Well, I certainly do know about the vandalism of the grave! It's the most shocking thing that's happened around here in years." Then, "Oh my, yes. I remember when they had the POW camp here. It was out on the highway across from Fort Reno. The government, you know, owned all that land. I remember the day the first ones came in by train. Half were Italians and the rest Germans captured in North Africa. It was a sort of elite camp for officers."

"That's interesting," Ben-Yanait interrupted. "I didn't know they separated enlisted men from officers."

"Well, I don't know, except that they did here. However, they didn't allow any reporters out there, and we never had any news about the camp. But I did meet this Major von Stober, the one whose grave was vandalized."

"You met him? How did that happen?" The Israeli's eyes brightened with interest.

"It was at the farm," Miss Bush continued, pleased with her audience. "You know, officers didn't have to work unless they wanted to. Some of them did, though, just to get away from the monotony

24

of the camp. So von Stober worked at Jim Cummings' farm almost every weekend. I think he did it mostly for Ella Cummings' food. She was the best cook hereabouts. I went out there one day to get some news about a Home Extension meeting. This German was working in her garden. She invited me to stay for lunch, and nobody in their right mind ever turned down an invitation from Ella to eat. We all sat around the kitchen table. I talked with the German, von Stober, who turned out to be a Major. He spoke pretty good English in a formal sort of way."

Ben-Yanait nodded. "Go on," he encouraged her.

"Well, I needed to get a picture of Ella for the paper, and afterwards she asked me to take one of the Major. But he didn't want his picture taken. He was very stiff-necked about it. When I asked if he wouldn't like one to send to his wife, he said 'No!' His parents? 'No!' again. But," she added with a sly smile, "if there's anything that gets my dander up, it's a bull-headed man. After he turned back to the garden, I set my camera, then called to him— just as he looked up I took the picture. He was furious! Acting as if he wanted to smash my camera. He would have if it hadn't been for Jim. Ella was upset, and I decided I'd better come back to town. I thanked her for the lunch and left. When the pictures were developed, I sent the Cummings one. I have some more around here somewhere in my files."

"I'd like to see one if you could find it. Did you know when he died?"

"No," she answered, "not until Ella told me. The Cummings didn't even know until they called the camp. It was after the victory in Europe, we expected them to be pulling out. Ella called the camp hoping she could tell him goodbye, and they said he was dead."

"Who did she talk to?"

"My goodness, I don't know. Whoever answered the phone, I guess."

"Is Mrs. Cummings still alive?"

"No, but Jim is. His farm was right next to the camp. He still lives there, although his son farms it now. Jim's getting mighty old, way up in his eighties. Let me see if I can find that picture. I think I know right where it is." She went into a back room, while Magen looked around.

How was it possible she could find a picture thirty years old in the clutter that filled the office? Yet she was back in minutes, darting around the desk and handing him two photographs. Magen didn't need to look at them closely to know the man was exactly who the Russians said he was. Otto Adolph Thyssen. Thyssen in Ella Cummings' garden. Thyssen, whom Adolph Hitler had looked upon as a son. Thyssen, who controlled the finances of the SS-- the Schutzstaffel , the Special Security force of Germany—and their resources in the Reichsbank, and who was responsible for sending a large part of it to Argentina to help those Nazis who fled Germany. Thyssen, who in his own self interest, had hidden somewhere a fortune in jewels, currency, and gold. No wonder, he reasoned, Thyssen didn't want his picture taken.

Magen Ben-Yanait's smile widened. He could have been any age from thirty to fifty. With hazel eyes, angled cheekbones and a vertical crease highlighting the planes of his face, newly pale, because the night before in an airport restroom he'd shaved off a full beard, he looked the part. His brows were uneven, his hair unruly. A sublime smile, warm and intimate, was his trademark. He could kill a man and smile the same. His accent was pure Midwestern when he wanted it to be, or German, or French, or Italian. He spoke them all, plus Yiddish, Hebrew and Russian. This was no common man.

He had been one of those children left to wander in the years of the war's aftermath. Bright, cunning, he slipped from one Displaced Persons' camp to another, always searching—neither understanding nor interested in the restless drive that pushed him. Nimble-fingered, light-footed, a master of artifice, a scavenger. Remembering no parents, he had no curiosity about his nationality, picked up quickly any language he heard, and successfully mimicked any dialect if the reward was food. In his wanderings he met a Jewish teenager and together they hiked across Europe headed for Israel.

At a kibbutz he was given, besides his name, a thorough training in guerilla warfare. He carried messages and ammunition through Arab sections of the Old Town. He learned to climb ropes, jump from moving vehicles, surreptitiously break into houses—to take a Sten gun apart and put it back together, to hit a moving target with a revolver. To toss a hand grenade with deadly accuracy, and master night fighting. He learned to think like an Arab and to speak the language as fluently.

When Israel became a nation in November, 1948, Magen Ben-Yanait was twelve years old and he joined the excited throng who danced a wild and happy Hora in front of the King David Hotel the whole night through.

But that was long ago. What he learned then had stood him and his country in good stead. A colonel with the Israeli Intelligence Service—Mossad—code named Jasmine, he had a wife and two children in Tel Aviv. He still was ready for any duty. Looking at the picture he held in his hand he smiled. This could be a rare assignment.

General Alwar Chaim, head of Israeli Intelligence, had called him in Beirut to drop what he was doing and go to Oklahoma, USA, immediately to check on a POW skull the Russians had dug up. Reputedly it had a hollow tooth which was supposed to hold a micro-dot film map of the treasure taken from the concentration camps. Oh, yes, it is the real thing. A Mossad agent had bugged the Russians' hotel room in Zurich. When the Russians unwrapped the skull sent to them—it wasn't the right one. So count the Americans in, but it's doubtful they know what they have. So his new assignment—find who has the skull and get it!

He looked at the picture in his hand, and smiled his signature smile.

"May I have one?" he asked. "I'd like to have a copy made for my own files."

"You're welcome to it. Did you say you were a writer?"

"Well, a historian, so to speak, of World War II prisoner of war camps in the States. Where is this POW cemetery—and the Cummings' farm?"

She gave directions. " When you see Jim, tell him hello for me. I don't get to see him often."

Magen Ben-Yanait took her hand in both of his.

"Miss Bush, you're a sweetheart! I can't tell you how much I appreciate the time you've given me." He kissed her on both cheeks. "Goodbye, now."

As he was going out the door, she called, "Will you send me a copy of your article when it comes out?"

He nodded and waved.

He missed Cane Eliot by ten minutes at the Fort Reno Cemetery. And he missed him by five minutes at Jim Cummings' farm. Their cars passed on the blacktop road.

~~~~

On his way to the airport, the Israeli grinned with satisfaction. The old man had been a mine of information. Really keen on talking about the journalist who had just been there and about the Major and Mae Bush. For an old man who had outlived all of his friends, it was a red-letter day when he'd had two callers. But it was the journalist, his previous visitor, who held Magen's interest.

He'd been in Europe during the war, the old man's visitor told him, and now he was doing a story about the German Major. Jim couldn't understand why so dang much was being made of the POW's grave. So his head was stolen—just an early Halloween prank. Boys will be boys. No, didn't get the guy's name. We just talked. Then the old man laughed.

"Well now, sir, to tell the truth I think mostly I talked. Don't get much of a chance to talk out here by myself."

The Israeli sat with Jim Cummings on his front porch swing until he barely had time to make his plane.

Magen gripped the wheel with both hands and ignored the speedometer needle climbing into the red. That son-of-a-bitch cowboy! No point trying to find him in Oklahoma City. Better to return to New York as planned and turn the organization loose on him. They'd locate him. And Magen Ben-Yanait knew well enough he would recognize him if he saw him again. He'd had a glimpse of him as they'd passed on the road. Rolled brim Stetson. Then the old man's description. About six feet, dark hair, wiry with a little curl. Moustache to match. Jeans, Cowboy boots? Well now, that the old man hadn't noticed. But he wore a faded jacket over a yellow print cowboy shirt. For an old man with rheumy eyes, he saw a hell of a lot. Question now on tap—is he FBI, CIA, or even KGB? They have a splendid assortment of local spies in every country, and they are smoothly polished in the USA! But for any kind of agent, he sure made no effort to be inconspicuous.

Magen Ben-Yanait's smile lit up his whole face. He turned in the rented Chevrolet and rushed into the TWA lounge just as the flight was called. Hurrying to the counter, he picked up a boarding pass and then relaxed. That was when he saw the cowboy. It had to be him. He watched as the man stood up, picked up his valise and overcoat, and stepped into line. Goddamn!—it's him, still wearing the Stetson a little the worse for wear— could that be a real rattlesnake band? And that valise—plenty large enough to hold a skull. He didn't take his eyes off Cane as he entered the plane behind him.

~~~~

Anya Vasilievna Petrovna had been in the TWA lounge half an hour when Cane walked in. With time to kill, she'd picked up a

*New York Times* in the gift shop and was reading it when she looked up and saw the man from the cemetery. He was dressed as he had been there, but now he carried a valise and the overcoat she'd gone through in his car. She watched him present his ticket, heard him say "smoking," then saw him stick his boarding pass in his shirt pocket. Her eyes were still on him when he pulled a package of cigarettes from his jacket, methodically selected one, and lighted it slowly from a match folder. He took a seat, his back to her, facing the runway where the Boeing 707 was rolling up the apron.

The flight was called.

Stooping to pick up her bag, she almost collided with a man rushing to the ticket counter. She looked at him, annoyed, then caught her breath. In a quick reflexive action she turned away, walking to the back of the waiting room. *My God, it's impossible!* What in the world is Magen Ben-Yanait doing in Oklahoma City? Could it have anything to do with the skull? *Everything* to do with the skull? Safely out of his sight, she watched as he dropped his ticket on the counter, received his boarding pass, and took a place in line. Good God! He must not see me. She was watching Ben-Yanait when Cane stood up, stretched, and picked up his valise, swinging his overcoat across it.

She still had not taken her eyes off the Israeli when she saw the astonished look that flashed across his face when he noticed the cowboy. He certainly hadn't expected to see him, that was evident. But that he recognized him was obvious. Ben-Yanait moved so that he was behind the rancher, watching him as they entered the plane. For some reason Magen Ben-Yanait knew Canyon Eliot, but Canyon Eliot didn't know Ben-Yanait.

Certainly, she didn't want either man to see her. She knew that, very likely, Ben-Yanait would recognize her, as she had him, from surreptitious pictures taken on the job, undercover. It's a rare long-time agent who is unknown to the opposition. She had seen his picture in a dozen different situations flashed on the screen in the viewing room in the KGB building at Two Dzerzhinsky Square. He had been in living color with and without a full beard. She felt a tightening in her stomach. Was he after the skull? *You better believe it!* The man was dangerous. Slipping on dark glasses, she tied a scarf over her head, and was the last passenger to enter the plane. She took her seat and opened a magazine. Though she turned the pages, she didn't see a word of print; her mind was spinning with the news she was bringing back. Her trip to Oklahoma had been far more successful than anyone at the Center could have imagined.

# CHAPTER IV

*New York City*
*Saturday, September 27*

C ane woke with an unpleasant feeling that bad news was piling up. Hopefully his shadow was gone. Who in hell could have followed him all the way from Oklahoma? His uneasiness didn't go away until he'd had two cups of coffee and a full Colorado ranch sized breakfast. The damn valise! How to get rid of it. After breakfast and checking out, Cane took the subway back to Manhattan and a cab to the Plaza Hotel. The itch at the back of his neck was gone. Still, he had coffee in the Garden Room where he could see everyone who came in.

Scratching his head, running his hand through his hair, he really missed his hat. It must be a security thing, he thought—a hat was as necessary to a cowboy as his left hand, so crossing the street to Bergdorf-Goodman he bought a gray fedora. With his hat cocked at a jaunty angle Cane took a cab to the Museum of Modern Art, still carrying the valise with his trench coat over it. After spending an hour at the Museum, he took a cab to FAO Schwarz where he bought a soccer ball, a net bag and a tube of rubber cement. Then taking a bus downtown to 48th Street, he walked to the Lexington Hotel. Still using his German accent to good advantage, he checked in for the day and paid in advance. In the room, he took the lapis knife and cut through the soccer ball. Padding the skull well with film shield and newspaper, he fitted it into the soccer ball and cemented the halves together.

While it was sealing, Cane took his Chinese knife and ripped all manufacturing and laundry tags off the clothing he'd worn from Colorado. These tags he flushed down the toilet. Then repacking the valise, he stripped off all identification and placed the extra passports with their identifications in his inside pocket. Pushing the valise deep on the top shelf of the closet, he took the soccer ball, dropped it into the net bag and, swinging it casually, walked to the elevator.

Downstairs in the bar, with a Scotch and soda he watched the door. He had a strong feeling that his shadow was gone. Well, he'd soon find out. After lunch, he took a taxi to LaGuardia. Satisfied that he had not been followed, he bought ticket to Boston, then using Carl Becker's passport, flew to Montreal and spent the night. The following day, Sunday, in an airport shop, he bought a carry-on bag, a sport coat, shirts and slacks. That afternoon he boarded an SAS plane for Copenhagen and spent the night. The next morning he flew to Rome, switched passports and, as Wilhelm Schwartz, old friend of Major von Stober, he caught the next plane to Munich. And Peter had insisted this would be a simple operation!

~~~~

# CHAPTER V

*New York*
*Saturday, September 27*

**M**agen Ben-Yanait lit a cigarette and walked slowly down Fifth Avenue. Well, damn! He'd lost the fellow masquerading as an American cowboy. After following him through Rockefeller Center, in and out of restaurants to his hotel, even to his room, the man had disappeared. He'd tried the old bellboy routine; it didn't work.

So, who was this guy? Certainly he was a pro to catch on so quickly that he was being tailed. And the way he lost him. There was no question in the Israeli's mind but that here was a first-class agent. KGB? CIA? FBI? That valise he was carrying—just the right size to hold a skull. Taking a last thoughtful draw on the cigarette, he flipped it into the gutter while waiting for the light to change. If he was KGB, why would he be running all over New York to avoid an unknown tail? He would have headed directly to Long Island, and would have left his shadow outside the gate of the diplomatic mission there. If he had the skull, he wouldn't give a damn about being followed. He'd just want to get it on an Aeroflot plane for Moscow.

Ben-Yanait crossed 54th Street with a stream of pedestrians, then stopped abruptly, almost knocking down an old Jewish rabbi. He apologized profusely in Hebrew and Yiddish, then ran to flag a taxi. One thought was curling in his mind—if the man wasn't KGB, he had to be CIA or at least an American, and *they didn't know the skull was Thyssen's.* So they would naturally head for Munich to find someone who knew Heinrich von Stober.

It was necessary to send a coded telex to Tel Aviv, then catch the first plane for Frankfurt, and a commuter flight to Munich. He had a definite feeling he would see the cowboy again.

*Enroute to Munich*
*Sunday, September 28*

On the last leg of his journey, Cane settled back in his window seat with a copy of *Der Spiegel*, satisfied he had lost the shadow who tailed him from Oklahoma. The flight was smooth, high above a thick cover of cumulus clouds until shortly before they landed in Munich, when the clouds opened to show a full vista of snow-capped, sawtoothed Alps—and the past was with him.

Cane knew these mountains. He closed his eyes remembering. Those times when he'd been hunting or fishing or just plain hiking in them.

Then he wasn't over the Alps at all; he was weathering a winter storm as a Navy ensign on a minesweeper in the North Sea. Battling seasickness, fifty foot waves, frostbite and frozen lungs; it was a hell of a duty tour. Then he was reassigned. Someone in Washington had noticed that the Eliot lad had grown up in Austria, had a flair for languages, had camped all over the Bavarian Alps and knew the country inside out. A natural for the OSS—Office of Strategic Services—the newly formed Spy Service of the USA.

Cane's father, Hank Eliot, had been a roving reporter, freelance writer, and sometimes Chatauqua lecturer. He met George Canyon during the summer season of the Chatauqua in a small Colorado town, when he was invited along with the other entertainers to the ranch. At the ranch, Hank met Beth Canyon and began one of those instantaneous romances novelists write about. A whirlwind courtship developed from the moment they met, and George saw his only child swept off in the arms of a total stranger, to spend the rest of her life in Europe.

She returned home only once, so that her baby could be born in the United States and, especially, at the ranch. As soon as young Canyon, nicknamed Cane almost from birth, was old enough, he was sent back to the ranch during the summer. There he learned the business firsthand, working cattle—spending dusty days in the saddle, branding, cutting, and driving stubborn herds into loading chutes and cattle cars for the Kansas City stockyards.

When he was eighteen, Cane returned to Colorado to attend the University. That same year his parents were killed in a plane crash. Pearl Harbor came during his junior year. The day after Christmas, Cane kissed his girl goodbye and joined the Navy. He spent enough time at the Chicago Naval Base to receive his gold bar and an ensign's cap. He was twenty years old.

He flew back to Colorado, married Elizabeth, left her at the ranch, and went off to fight the war. His assignment to a minesweeper, he felt, left something to be desired, and was happy to be reassigned to an intelligence unit in London. He was in England a year and during that time made several forays into Austria and France, setting up sabotage teams. Then it was back to Washington where he trained other bright young men and women in the art of espionage. Elizabeth joined him there. When he was ordered back to London, she returned to the Colorado ranch with a strong suspicion she was pregnant.

For a year and a half he operated in Austria.

He kept in touch with London Control by couriers, who sent his coded messages through half a dozen radio contacts. It was as safe a method as could be found and, for that reason, with no direct contact with Control, he didn't know when his promotions came, when his son was born, or when his wife died. He didn't know that his grandfather suffered a fatal heart attack. He didn't know any of this until April 1945.

One morning, walking along a road near Schöngau, he met a group of Volkssturm guarding a bridge. They told him the road had been cut by Americans and that he would have to circle the woods to get through. Cane crossed the bridge, turned off the road, and then back as soon as he was out of sight of the Volkssturm. For a couple of miles it was strangely quiet. Then, at a crossroads, he saw an American tank. And an American soldier. Waving his hands and shouting, he ran to meet them. For the first time in a year and a half, he spoke English.

There were interminable debriefing sessions with Army Intelligence and the OSS, then finally the void he dreaded in Colorado. A void—that is—until he saw his son. Thinking back, Cane knew that when he came home from the war, he was older and wiser than he was now at fifty-eight. And he remembered his grandfather's saying, "The sweet breath of life that separates the quick and the dead is nothing more than the upturned thumb of the Devil."

The plane dropped to the runway and rolled toward the gate. So long ago. Cane sighed. He had survived then through the built-in defenses that exist in a well-trained agent's subconscious. That tingling itch at the back of his neck, the automatic distrust of strangers, the loneliness that sharpens wits and hones vigilance. And now he was in it again—and he'd better damn well remember!

Cane rolled up Der *Spiegel*, stuck it in the pocket of his flight bag. The plane came to a stop. He was in Munich. It was just dusk....

# CHAPTER VI

*Moscow*
*Saturday, September 27*

L ow-hanging clouds drifted fitfully across the city. Red Square was deserted. Streams of vapor smoked up from the sewer drains to be swallowed in the raw gray mist. At the Kremlin, two blocks away, the Bell Tower of Ivan the Great and St. Basil's onion-shaped domes had been blotted out. Street lights were regimented orange-fogged globes.

Anya Vasilievna Petrovna pulled the belt of her coat tighter and the brim of her hat close over her forehead. From across the Square, the seven-story Center blended with the mist and clouds until it was one with the sky. A gray forbidding building that shared a common wall with the Lubyanka Prison.

Anya asked the driver who met her Aeroflot flight at Moscow's Sheremetyevo Airport to stop across the Square instead of taking her to the courtyard entrance.

"I know it's a dreadful night, but after sitting for over half a day in an airplane, I have to have some fresh air and, wet as it is, some exercise. They'll call when I'm ready to go home. *Spasibo*, Sasha." She waved the driver off. The KGB car moved away from the curb slowly then, gathering speed, disappeared in the fog.

Ducking her head into the wind, she followed the sidewalk to the statue, then stopped. Here was the man who had started it, Felix Dzerzhinsky, who organized Cheka, the first Soviet security service in 1917 for Nikolai Lenin. Threads of moisture trailed down the bronze face

38

and cloak and granite pedestal of the old Polish Bolshevik to make tiny cascades of waterfalls around the triple-layered base. An occasional car passed, invisible except for wavering shafts of pale light, and trailing blurred irregular rosy afterglows reflected in the wet pavement.

Anya took a deep breath and exhaled slowly. There was much to tell, and if she hadn't located the skull, she had discovered that both the Americans and the Israelis were after it. How had the Israelis gotten onto it?

Turning her back to the wind, she adjusted her shoulder bag. The weather reminded her of Massachusetts in the late fall, when the rain and the bone-chilling fog rolled off the Atlantic. Those had been happy years at Miss Katherine's Academy. There were football games, ice skating, and New York at Christmas. Her mother had loved it, too. There was a richness to their lives that would be hard to explain in Moscow. That is, until her father defected. Anya's face tightened, remembering. He was the Soviet expert on American crops—wheat and corn, cotton and cereal grains. He had set up reciprocal trade missions and cultural exchanges for rural districts in the United States and the Soviet Union, and was held in high regard in Washington and Chicago. How could he have done it? How had the Americans persuaded him? Not a hint to her mother. Nor to her. And he had been such a special father. The fun they shared! The ball games. Ice skating. She would never forgive him.

The accident he had was good retribution! And the Americans! Neither would she ever forget or forgive.

Her grandfather had been one of the old-time Bolsheviks, a friend of Lenin, of Dzerzhinsky. One of the lucky ones who helped unite a country, who survived Stalin and died a natural death. He never forgave his son-in-law and Anya's mother was as unforgiving. They took her grandfather's name, Vasiliena adding the *na* for the feminine patronymic, and erased Ivan Rabichov from their lives. Had it not been for her grandfather, Anya reflected, they would certainly have been sent east to Siberia.

In Moscow, her studies at the University continued. Her aptitude for languages was encouraged and she was admitted to the Institute of Foreign Relations. Graduating at the top of her class, she was given a responsible position in the Foreign Office. That's when she fell in love with Yuri Petrova. Fell in love, married, had a child, divorced. A whole life wrapped up in one sentence.

Then her thoughts returned to her father—remembering her mother's hysterics—the hurried packing—the trip to the airport in the black limousine with their grim-faced escort—the rush to get aboard the Aeroflot Ilyushin and the long flight home. She remembered the birches, pines and firs along the road from the airport to her grandfather's dacha. Then came the years trying to forget. Impossible....

Anya enjoyed her work in the Foreign Ministry, and when she was approached through her supervisor to join the Intelligence, she was flattered. A position with either the KGB or the Army Service, CRU, carried status and special privileges.

She had been given, along with the code name Regina, a complete political indoctrination and schooling in radio, codes, surveillance, marksmanship, secret writing, the newest electronic techniques—everything needed by the modern spy. There was the little booklet she signed setting out the rules of conduct for Soviet citizens abroad. And she heard in full the lectures: *You are leaving your Motherland. You must understand that a heavy responsibility rests on you.* Anya had long since mastered the technique of answering provocative questions, turning aside awkward conversations with clever repartee and a warm smile. She expounded the Party line with charm. Not only had she been an apt pupil, she had been a disciplined instructor to others going abroad. Her loyalty was unquestioned. The subject of her father had never arisen. As a senior officer in the KGB, she had a freedom few Soviet travelers experience.

During her travels, she missed her daughter and mother, but when she was home the time they spent together made up for the separations. Gifts from elegant Fifth Avenue stores or toys from Harrod's, holidays in notable resorts along the Black Sea, a well-furnished flat in the heart of Moscow, a dacha of her own in a wooded suburb by the river, even an old couple to maintain the grounds and cook. These were compensations both Natalya and her mother understood, the prestigious school Natalya attended, the special stores for shopping.

It was a good life.

While Natalya was at the University and afterwards, when she was working as an editor with *Literatura*, the Writer's Union Weekly, Anya traveled the United States with the Bolshoi Ballet, the Moscow Circus, and folk dance groups with various programs designed to entertain Americans. She was good at her job. Seeing and reporting things Americans never dreamed would interest Soviet Intelligence, her cover was secure. Speaking colloquial American English and understanding American humor, she laughed at their jokes and they laughed at hers. With her warm personality and stunning good looks she made a place for herself wherever she went, and wherever she went, she held the best interests of the USSR uppermost in her mind.

Her life had been an organized compact file of orthodox Marxian milestones. Along the way, her mother died. Natalya married, and made her a grandmother, divorced, she now had a promising career. Déjà vu, Anya thought. Their parallel lives! They were close—Anya and Natalya. They shared career gossip, the Moscow apartment, and the love of young Misha.

The last time Anya had been home, there had been a hint that all was not well with Natalya. She had left *Literatura* and was writing on her own. But nothing she'd shown Anya. She seemed unhappy with the Writer's Union and was far too open with her criticism of the Politburo. Perhaps they could have a good long talk tomorrow.

Anya shifted the shoulder strap of her bag. Her lips twisted into a wry smile as she looked back at the wet-slick bronze.

Natalya slipped from her mind. For the last year, she had been in New York with the Soviet delegation to the United Nations. Then had come this quick briefing and her sudden departure for Oklahoma City and Fort Reno. She gave a passing thought to the man she'd seen at the cemetery. What was it about him that had attracted the undivided attention of the Israeli agent? He seemed too innocent to be true. Had she felt that when she first saw him? Or was it when she realized he was the hunted and the Mossad agent was the hunter?

She frowned. Was it possible that the skull was in New York in the protective custody of a Colorado cowman? Had the skull been detected in post office surveillance in Texas or New York?

Shrugging, she gave the full-bearded Bolshevik an ambiguous smile and a careless salute with a gloved hand. Do you remember, Tovarich Felix, my grandfather, your friend, saying: *When you live close to the graveyard, you can't weep for everyone?* So let's get it over. Pulling her scarf closer under her chin, she crossed the street to the grim astringent building in front of her. On the left, the prison—to the right, the Center. The headquarters of the *Komitet Gossudarstvennoi Besopasnosti*—Committee for State Security—the Russian Secret Police, known around the world as the KGB.

She ran up the steps and showed her identification to the uniformed guard inside. The dry smell of the old building pinched her nostrils. There was a maze of cast-iron staircases, stone arches, and parquet flooring. Her steps echoed. The loneliest place in the world, she reflected, is the empty hall in the Center on a rainy fall day. Though it seemed empty, she knew that behind closed doors, the secret business of the country's Foreign Intelligence Service was continuing around the clock.

She took the brass elevator to the fifth floor. At a desk in front of the elevator was a *dejournaya* who proffered the official visitor's book for her signature. After signing it and adding the time of her arrival, she walked down the hall and opened a frosted glass door. A man and woman were bent over a green felt-covered table in the debriefing room of the First Directorate.

"*Dobri vechir*, Nikolai Ivanovich."

The elderly man turned quickly and held out his hand. "Welcome,

Anya Vasilievna, welcome home." He indicated the woman standing over a recorder. "This is Lena Makaroina, who will take the recording. Would you have coffee or tea, brandy or vodka?"

Major-General Nikolai Ivanovich Pugachev, head of the Politburo Intelligence Analysis section, was pale, sixty-plus, tall, spare, with thick white hair, marble-round blue eyes, and long arms, long fingers. He helped Anya with her coat, as she acknowledged her introduction to the clerk, a plain middle-aged woman with thick glasses.

"I'll tell you—I want coffee *and* brandy, to warm me before I get pneumonia!" She took her place at the table. "Have you heard from Comrade Belyakov? I'm sorry I didn't get to see him. He simply told me to return immediately, and here I am!"

She looked up, smiled, and thanked the clerk who placed a small tray with coffee and brandy in front of her.

"I'm sorry to be late. You can blame everything but me—the miserable weather, Aeroflot, and Sasha." She poured the brandy into her coffee, took a sip, and smiled.

Pugachev watched. He said, "Now we begin."

He looked at Lena and nodded. She switched on the machine and, in a monotone, said, "*Sintabr tritsati* (September 30), Regina arrived at twenty hours, Lena Makaroina at machine, Major-General Nikolai Ivanovich Pugachev official." Then Anya began her report. How she was contacted in New York by Comrade Nicholas Belyakov and told about the skull. That it had been switched en route to Zurich. Then she received her orders to go to Oklahoma City to try to determine what had happened. The long narrative of her trip, the follow-up visits to the cemetery, the fact-finding excursions to the library and the newspaper office took most of the evening. She told about the two men at the cemetery, one an administrator, the other a rancher from Colorado. With the recorder turning steadily, she related in detail how she recognized the Israeli agent, Magen Ben-Yanait and how, for some reason unknown to her, he recognized the Colorado rancher named Canyon Eliot. She followed them until Eliot lost them both, then the

Mossad agent slipped away from her on a one-way street mix-up.

"Did he know he was being followed?"

"I imagine so. But he's too clever to let on. That's when I called Comrade Belyakov, and he directed me to come to Moscow. I picked up my luggage and went directly to Aeroflot. They were holding the flight for me. And that's it."

General Pugachev had some routine questions, and the session went on an hour longer before Anya finished. "What now?" she asked.

"Comrade Belyakov thinks you should go to Germany. They picked up Ben-Yanait at Lufthansa on a direct flight to Frankfurt. We think it's altogether possible Eliot's going to Munich to locate von Stober's wife. We're also trying to find Thyssen's wife. The last we knew of her was an address in Berlin before the war. She's probably changed her name. Anyway, my dear Anya, you have your work cut out for you!"

"When shall I go?"

"Monday. Your cover will be a writer for an American magazine, *The Woman's Eye*. It's one of ours."

"Yes, I know."

"You'll do an article on the Oktoberfest, get interviews, go to restaurants—write anything young women will be interested in. Your passport and papers will be here Saturday morning. Your name is Marianne Mason."

Anya pushed back her chair and smiled. "A good American name." She glanced at the clock on the wall. Ten o'clock. It wouldn't be too late when she got home.

"Anya, you have done a good job," the General said, then added, "Oh yes, Niels Jannasen will be in Munich to back you up. We're not sure who you will be going up against. With Mossad in, the picture changes...."

Anya made a face. "Anyone but Jannasen. You know how he is about knives...."

"That's why he's still alive." He walked with her to the door. "Anya, this is a very sensitive project. We want that skull. It's a top

44

priority. That's the reason for Jannasen. There'll probably be a need for his special talents."

Anya nodded. "I understand."

"Also," Pugachev added, "Colonel Karuski will be in Munich with a Trade Delegation during that time. They will be at the Waldenhof, so reservations will be made there for you and Jannasen from the *Woman's Eye* New York office."

"That's fine," Anya agreed.

Pugachev opened the door, then touched Anya's arm. "I need a word with you about Natalya."

Anya felt an icy grip in her chest.

"Do you know she's been sending articles to the underground presses?"

She shook her head slowly. Her face felt cold.

"Can you talk with her? You don't need that." His eyes softened. He patted her shoulder, and they walked down the hall to the elevator.

"Dear, dear friend," she held his hand. "Yes, I'll talk to her—but it's like talking to the wind." Smiling, her face pale, she said, *"Do svidanya."*

"Goodnight, Anya." The General was proud of his English.

A car was waiting to take her to Natalya and Mischa. And that was the night she found Natalya's poems.

# CHAPTER VII

K eeping the Volkswagen just within the speed limit, Cane needed no map to guide him to the address he'd been given, Birkenstrasse 9 and Frau von Stober. The whole area was familiar. The great kidney-shaped park of Theresienwiese, which he was passing, was filled with workmen in full swing to open the next day—the first day of the Oktoberfest. This annual affair had been held since 1810, when Bavaria decked itself out in full regalia to celebrate Crown Prince Ludwig's betrothal to Princess Therese.

Cane knew he'd be back. He was tempted to stop now and look but he put such thoughts to the back of his mind. Business first, as it had been since he'd arrived Saturday evening.

The weekend had been uneventful. He was quite sure he'd lost his shadow. He had taken a taxi to the Eberkopfhaus, actually more of a pension than a hotel. Tucked away in a narrow street in Schwabing above a small tavern, the inn was identified with restrained enthusiasm by a gilded boar's head, no larger than a horseshoe, hung from a cast-iron bracket.

Cane, carrying his flight bag and protecting his soccer ball, threaded his way around tables and beer-drinking students to a stairway leading to the reception desk at the top of the stairs.

On the far side of the small office in the curve of the stairway was a cramped turn-of-the-century brass-scrolled lift. The narrow inn and its tavern reeked with an atmosphere of a different time, a different age.

The whole area had been leveled during the war, and Cane marveled that it had been so accurately reconstructed.

He followed an old porter to the third floor, Room 35, which overlooked an alley and a fire escape. Tipping the old man a little more than he should, he talked him into bringing up some beer, Bauernbrot, and Streichwurst, a fondly remembered combination of coarse whole wheat bread and sausage soft enough to spread with a knife.

Remembering Peter's instructions to reach his Consulate contact, he learned that Hastings was out of town until Wednesday. So that was that.

Succumbing to jet lag, he fell asleep reading *Der Spiegel*.

Sunday he roamed the area, had beer and Wienerschnitzel at a sidewalk café near the English Gardens. Memories of other days spent in Munich—both happier and sadder—drifted through his mind with a tantalizing nostalgia.

Early Monday, renting an ancient, black nondescript Mercedes he took care of the business at hand. It took most of the morning to camouflage the skull. Making half a dozen trips to sporting goods stores, so that none wondered at his purchases, he had the skull in its soccer ball cover nestled far back in the trunk of the car beneath an assortment of sports equipment including a pair of children's skis and poles, a tennis racket in its frame, a secondhand set of golf clubs and bag, an archery set. It filled the trunk.

Then there was the "paralyzer." Cane wired it carefully to the skis so that, if they were moved more than six inches, it would explode with a charge strong enough to immobilize a man for half an hour.

With the skull secure, and finding himself in the heart of the Oktoberfest, memories tumbled over memories. There was the time he came with his parents from Vienna, all of them dressed in Bavarian costume. The driver of a decorated wagon let him hold the reins of a team of matched strawberry roan Belgians as they made their way through the crowd delivering beer. The six-horse team wore wreathes of flowers around their necks and Tyrolean hats between their ears. He smiled, recalling a small boy's excitement. Later, he came with classmates, each trying to out-drink the other and to pick up the prettiest girls. Those were the good days, between wars. It was the Student Prince era. Only a pale shadow was cast of the Holocaust to come.

His thoughts slipped gently back to those early years in Colorado, bringing up his son—teaching him to hunt and fish and run a ranch, as his grandfather had taught him. And the college days with Peter and Canyon. The football games, skiing, camping in wilderness areas, rafting down mountain rivers. He shook his head. The memories were painful. Now he slowed the car and gripped the steering wheel a little tighter. Would he want to be young again? Oh, no! Not for God's good grace would he live any of it over.

Here was Lindwürmstrasse, and there was the gently contoured lane, Birkenstrasse. It was aptly named for the double row of amber birches, which cast piebald, hard-edged, early afternoon shadows across the postage stamp yards. Number 9 stood, one of a dozen like it, a united front of narrow stiff-bosomed exteriors plastered in beige and crisscrossed with brown timbers. Dormer windows were underscored with cascading flowers in their autumn flush of color, and steeply gabled red-tiled roofs angled against a blue and cloudless sky.

At No. 9 Cane parked, swung open the picket gate that matched the fence, winced at its warning screech, and followed the neatly bricked path to the front door. The pleasant odor of fresh-baked bread drifted around the corner. White boxes on either side of the walk spilled over with multicolored petunias and red geraniums. At his knock, the lace curtains at a front window were pulled back, a curious face peered out. Cane waved; the curtains dropped. A stout woman with a cloud of white hair and clear blue eyes opened the door.

"Ja?"

Cane introduced himself as Wilhelm Schwartz and asked if she were Frau von Stober. She smiled and nodded. "Once upon a time," she answered, "many years ago."

Cane explained how he had been a member of the 1st Paratroop

Division with von Stober, taken prisoner with him, and sent to America. Then, after the war, he returned to America to live and was now on his first visit back to the Old Country. He especially wanted to see the home of his old friend and, if possible, meet his wife.

*"Kommen! Kommen!"* She greeted Cane with warm hospitality, guided him into her parlor, and seated him on the horse-hair sofa that faced the window. He felt a sudden kinship to the man who had died in Oklahoma so many years before. This was a warm house with the same comfortable disorder he had in his own. She brought in beer, cheese, and warm black bread. "Now we talk!" she said, and sat down across from him smiling, nodding her head, folding her hands.

Her name was Lily Haupmann, and she was once again a widow. Dear Ludwig—she pointed out his picture—had died two years ago. But she wanted to talk about her handsome first husband whom she had hardly known. They were married a year. He hadn't had a leave in six months when he was injured in Italy, and she never heard from him again.

Cane looked at her sharply. "You never heard from him?"

"Nein—" She shook her head. "I know only that he was wounded in Italy and captured there. Nothing more."

"But that's impossible. He must have written to you from the prison camp. They allowed mail to go through the Red Cross."

"Nein—" she repeated. "Never did I hear until, after the war, I got a message he had died in Ok-la-hom-ah. I have a picture of Heinrich— at our wedding. I show you." Dropping to her knees she opened the chest. Reaching into folded linens, she brought out a box tied with a blue ribbon. She opened it, lifted out a framed wedding picture, and handed it to him. He saw a young man in uniform and a young bride, her thick blonde hair escaping from a veil. Neither of them smiling. Marriage was a solemn occasion.

Cane looked at it, stunned. The man in this picture in no way resembled the picture he had of von Stober.

What the hell kind of a mistake was this? Von Stober had a shock of blonde hair. His face was round, his eyes friendly. A complete opposite from the von Stober whose picture he had in his wallet.

Lily Haupmann reached for Cane's plate and refilled it with cheese and bread, then settled back in a chair, folded her hands across her lap, and smiled sweetly. "Now," she said, "you tell me all about Heinrich."

For the next hour, Cane sat with her trying to find answers to the questions she flung at him. How did he die? Was he sick long? Why didn't he write? Did he speak of her?

Cane wanted to get away. Christ! Did he ever have news for Hastings! He finished his beer, changed the subject as soon as he could, complimented her on her house, her fine-looking family, her cooking, and tried to escape without answering more questions.

When he returned to his car, he stood for a minute rummaging through his pockets for his keys, found them, then stood a minute more, rubbing his upper lip where he still missed his moustache. What do you know? Sonofabitch!

He drove slowly along the birch-lined street remembering everything Frau von Stober-Haupmann had told him. A strange turn of events. Who the hell is this guy in the photo from Oklahoma? Certainly a top Nazi officer. Someone important enough that he had to lose himself under another identity in a POW camp. One important enough that the Russians had stolen his skull. One that somehow or other had switched identities in Italy and allowed himself to be captured as a Major Heinrich von Stober. So what happened to the real Major?

Since he was wounded, he was probably in a field hospital. Had the unknown Nazi found him there, unconscious perhaps, decided they were the same size and, in the confusion of evacuating the hospital, taken his tags—his uniform, his name?

It had to be something like that. In the middle of a battle no one would be especially careful about pursuing identities. Certainly, if they found a sick soldier without tags, officer or not, they wouldn't go to any lengths worrying about who he was. Perhaps this Nazi had killed von Stober outright. All top-flight Nazis carried glass capsules filled with *Blausaure*—prussic acid, or *Zyankali*—cyanide of potassium, just in case. He wouldn't use it on himself unless his back was against the wall. But he'd certainly have no scruples against using it on someone else, if he needed a uniform and identification tags.

Cane bypassed the festival grounds, driving as fast as he dared, directly to the Inn. Parking was difficult, and he drove some distance to find a spot. Then he hurried back through the narrow crowded walks, entered beneath the boar's head, worked his way through the tavern, and ran up the flight of stairs.

In his room, Cane took a sheet of paper from his notebook and wrote rapidly in German: *Sehr geehrter Herr Hastings, I have just come from Houston, Texas, where your very good friend Jim Brown asked me to bring you two cans of Texas hot tamales and one of chili, for which, he said, you have a special fondness. I have them with me. I will be at the Eberkopfhaus, 58 Altenbrückstrasse, Room 35 at 7:00 this evening. Wilhelm Schwartz.*

It wouldn't do, Cane decided, to deliver it himself. Too many eyes watch U.S. Consulate and Embassy gates. He sealed the envelope, went downstairs through the tavern, walked down Königstrasse, across from the English Gardens, until he came to the pedestrian tunnel at the Consulate. He walked slowly down the steps then lighted a cigarette and waited. In a few minutes, a schoolboy passed on a bicycle. Calling to him, Cane asked if he'd like to make five marks delivering a letter. From the corner entrance, he watched the boy carry the letter to the Consulate and hand it to the Marine guard inside the door. So that was that.

Hastings had over three hours to change any other plans he'd made, and meet Cane. That is, if he were around to get the message. Cane strolled past Prinz Karl Palast, through the Hufgarten, past the Residenz, then on to the Marienplatz. He could only wait.

# CHAPTER VIII

The Isar was pleasant that late afternoon. Willows, gold-tinged against the autumn sun, dipped into their reflections and riffled the river above the Maximillian Bridge. Below the bridge a series of shallow cascading falls drowned the traffic sounds and would, as effectively, muffle conversation. Ben-Yanait sat on a wooden bench under a Linden tree, his feet half-buried in leaves, waiting. Once he looked at his watch. Five minutes yet. The Blocker had a reputation for promptness. When he appeared, the Israeli looked up at the oversized man with his rosy unlined cheeks and smiled.

"Ah, Herr Kruppel," he called, raising his hand in a casual greeting. "*Guten Abend!* Sit down, sit down." They shook hands.

"With pleasure. It's a lovely Wednesday evening. Very comfortable to get away from the Theresienwiese. It's too much of a good thing there. Too much food, too much singing, too much beer."

"Never that!"

"Ah, well. Winter will be upon us soon."

"That is true. Autumn sets and winter rises." With the prescribed preliminaries taken care of, the two agents shook hands again.

"How is the butcher business in Peiss?"

"Very well. And how are things in the Promised Land?"

"Warming up." Ben-Yanait pulled a pipe from his pocket, tapped it on the bench, then filled it from a plastic pouch. Taking his time lighting it, he gave his companion a sidelong glance. The Blocker wore standard Bavarian dress. His shirt was open at the throat, showing a triangle of black hair and straining the buttons across his barrel chest. A dark green Tyrolian hat with a brush of feathers dipped over one eye. For a while, the two men sat in silence.

"I will be glad to hear," Kruppel said, rearranging his large bulk on the bench. He gave the appearance of pure muscle and that image was accurate. Israeli emergencies often enough diverted him from his occupation as the well-known popular butcher of Peiss, to open doors, as it were, for the Israeli Mossad.

Issac Steinbine, code named "The Blocker," was known locally as Fritz Kruppel. He lived all his adult life in Peiss, but his childhood was spent with a Catholic woman in Munich, who saved his life and endangered her own by claiming him as her nephew when his parents were consumed by the Holocaust. No one looked less Jewish; no one felt his Jewishness more pridefully. His butcher shop, the Metzgerei, specialized in pork as well as beef and lamb and sausages, also processed messages from at least a half dozen Israeli agents. Kruppel made his deliveries in a fifty kilometer circle that included Munich. Early each morning he made his rounds in an old Volkswagen truck which, besides a refrigeration unit, had a sophisticated radio communications system.

Ben-Yanait took a long draw on his pipe and watched the smoke curl toward the river. "It seems that a certain Otto Thyssen, under an assumed name, died in an Oklahoma prisoner of war camp in 1945."

Kruppel shook his head emphatically. "No, Jasmine, you're wrong."

"It's true," the Israeli insisted. "The Russians found his skull but the Americans, with a clever bit of sleight of hand, purloined it. We think it is here with the secret of the concentration camp's treasure on a microdot film hidden in a tooth filling."

Kruppel looked at him in amazement, then shook his head again.

"I have a gut feeling you're mistaken."

"No, the KGB dug up the skull in August on the basis of a letter from the Italian dentist—a Russian sympathizer—who buried it in the tooth. It was mailed to Zurich, but it never arrived. We think the CIA intercepted it. Canyon Eliot, an old OSS agent, is here and there's a good chance he has the skull."

"How did you find him?"

"From the TWA manifold of passengers from Oklahoma City to New York."

"Under his own name! That's not very smart. So what do we have?"

"An interesting situation. A microdot hidden in a tooth filling in the skull of the Reichsbank officer in charge of the concentration camp's revenue. And you know what that means?"

"I do. It sounds like a movie script."

"Yes, except it's the real thing. The Russians have a letter from the Italian dentist, written during the war, telling how he did it. I followed Eliot completely unsure then whether he was CIA, KGB, or one of the South American Nazis, from Oklahoma to New York where he lost me. However, we know now he is CIA and our associates have located him for us. He's here in Munich and staying at the Eberkopfhaus. You know it?"

"Ja. I know it."

"I think you should check it out. With luck, he'll have the skull with him."

"Tonight?"

"Yes. Room 35. It's an inside room overlooking the alley. There's a fire escape in case you need it."

"No problem. I'll take care." He rose, stretched, then turned to the Mossad agent with a long icy look. "I'm glad," he said, "that the bastard is dead. But I wish I could have taken care of him in my own—my own special way."

"I think every Israeli feels the same. I'll meet you at five in the

morning at the coffee house near the Hauptbahnhof. *Mazel-tov.*"
"Shalom."

~~~~

The Marienplatz was crowded with tourists, students, local spillovers from the Oktoberfest, and itinerant musicians all waiting for the 5 o'clock performance of the Glockenspiel at the tower of the Rathaus. Cane found a chair in front of the Marienstatue, lit his pipe, and sat back to think about this sudden turn of events. Who was the guy buried in Oklahoma? And what was the secret of the skull that belonged to him? His eyes raked slowly over the crowd gathered in the plaza.

*It couldn't be!* He sat bolt upright, then stood. Impossible! That couple—there watching the tower—*it was the woman from the cemetery!*

The cathedral bells at St. Peter's began to toll, then the tower clock chimed the hour. Cane stared, unbelieving. Incredible! But there she was, wearing the same leather coat, carrying the same brown shoulder bag. Her hair was pulled back into the same soft chignon. Her profile was clear and true, as she watched the tower, her head thrown back. The figurines in the tower began to perform the Schaffler Tanz—the Barrelmaker's Dance, and he saw her touch her companion on the arm, laugh, and point.

He watched them with a lively interest. Who was that man? Her husband? Oh, no. He was much too young. Possibly a son. He was slender, a head taller than the woman, clean-cut with wire-rimmed glasses and thick blonde hair that fell below his collar. He looked like a tourist with his camera on an embroidered strap hung around his neck. Both were totally concerned with the revolving dancers.

She casually looked away from the tower towards Cane, and he caught her eye. For a second she froze—then smiled.

~~~~

For a full second, Anya Vasilievna Petrovna stood transfixed. It *was* the American. Even without his moustache and wearing slacks and a sport coat , it was the American agent Canyon Eliot, and he recognized her just as she did him. For only as long as it took to draw a breath did she stare; then she approached him. With a straight face and friendly smile, she spoke to him in German with a pronounced American accent.

"Mein Herr, I'm Marianne Mason with the American magazine *The Woman's Eye*. I'm doing a sort of citizen-in-the-street interview with German men about their views on the Oktoberfest, working mothers, Ludwig's castles, anything that might interest my readers in the States." She pulled a notebook from her bag and asked quite seriously, "May I interview you?"

"Fräulein Mason, it will be a pleasure," he replied in German, bowing. "May I compliment you on your German. For an American, it's excellent. I'm Wilhelm Schwartz, and I will be flattered to have you interview me. But see—" he pointed to the tower, "the tournament is starting."

Together they watched as the mounted figures below the dancers raced at each other until finally one fell back, mortally injured. The crowd laughed and the pantomime came to an end.

Niels Jannasen took some pictures, then, replacing his camera in its case, looked for Anya. He frowned when he saw her. She caught his eye and called to him.

"Niels, dear, you must meet my first interviewee. May I present Herr Wilhelm Schwartz. Herr Schwartz, my associate Niels Jannasen from Stockholm. He's mostly a fashion photographer, but today he's helping me. Will you pose for us, sir?"

Cane grinned self-consciously, holding his pipe. "I'd rather not. But I'll be glad to answer any questions, from politics to women in lederhosen."

"Now you sound like a chauvinist...."

"Ah Fräulein, I must admit—all German men are certainly that!

May I buy you a beer....?"

"Why, yes. Niels?"

"Marianne, we have an appointment...." Jannasen's voice grated with irritation.

"You go, dear. Tell him I'll be there in an hour. I do want to finish the interview with Herr Schwartz."

Jannasen's face turned red. "Marianne, you must come now! Make an appointment with Herr Schwartz for later."

She smiled sweetly and shook her head. "I'll meet you at the hotel. Now Herr Schwartz, what is your occupation?"

Turning her back on Jannasen, she saw the same grin on the man's face that she had seen in the cemetery when he had doffed his hat and spoken to her. She felt chill bumps tingle on her arms, and forced a genial smile. There was no question about it. Here is CIA agent Cane Eliot from Colorado, USA. Would he recognize her? He already has, she thought, but is not sure enough of himself to ask if she'd ever been in a POW cemetery in Oklahoma. That, or he's too smart. *Does he have the skull?* Yes. Or it's somewhere in safekeeping. All right, my friend, we'll play this game your way. Charades it is, but I make the rules.

She listened carefully, pencil and notebook in hand, as he answered with some dignity.

"At present, I'm a member of the Tourist Committee of the Oktoberfest, and one of our pleasanter duties is making our international guests feel the *Gemütlichkeit* of our Bavarian hospitality. Herr Jannasen, I would be honored if you would join us for a beer."

Jannasen gave Anya a dark look, then turned on his heel and left without answering.

"A disagreeable young man without manners. Did he say you had an appointment?" Cane touched her elbow, guiding her to an outside table at a tavern near the Rathaus.

"It's not that important. About you—if you're part of the committee for the Festival, why aren't you in Lederhosen?"

"Ah Fräulein, you see, besides being an important cog in our festival, I work at making a living, and judges take an unrealistic view of lawyers pleading cases wearing Leders."

She looked at him closely. Could she be wrong? Was he really a German lawyer, or was he as good a liar as she was?

Their beer came, and he lifted his stein. *"Prosit!"*

The steins clicked, and she repeated, *"Prosit!"*

The sun, low in the west, drenched the tower with light as they sat in its shadow. An old man with a fierce moustache and an accordion under his arm paused beneath the awning of the café and began to play a polka. A few couples left their tables and began to dance in the street. Then the old man swung into the Cuckoo Waltz, and more joined the dancing. Cane laid his pipe aside, stood and bowed.

"Fraülein Mason, if there's anything I can do and do well, it's the Cuckoo Waltz. Will you dance?"

"Yes, I'd love to," she answered, rising.

He guided her through the tables to the street. He had a strong sure lead, and Anya warmed to the feel of his arms and the rhythm of the old man's music. Thank heaven, she thought, Jannasen's gone.

The tension she'd felt since she realized the problems Natalya faced disappeared, and she danced with a joy she hadn't known for years. Anya knew that Cane felt this sudden surge of rhythm as the swing of her body blended with his. And, when the old man stopped to collect his marks, she was sorry.

"The song goes," she said smiling, "'I could have danced all night, and I shall write in my article that German men dance like dreams."

"No, Fraülein, you have it wrong. How you say, the cart she goes before the horse? It is you who dance like a dream. It made me feel young, and that is nothing short of a miracle!"

Anya looked at him again with a slight doubt. His German was so perfect, much better than hers. His English, on the other hand, was atrocious. Still....? She looked at her watch and stood up quickly.

"My! I had no idea it was so late. I must go. Jannasen will be furious with me. Thank you. I've had a lovely time."

"But what about my interview? The German man on the street and his views of women, the Oktoberfest, and the relation of that to the new crop of babies each June...."

"I can't do it now. Tomorrow?"

"One of my duties as Marshall of the beer drinkers is to show visiting journalists around. I shall call for you tomorrow at nine. We'll go to Nymphenburg Castle, then I'll take you to the Oktoberfest and you can interview me."

"Splendid! And Niels Jannasen, too?"

"Do we have to?"

"Yes. And be sure to go native, Bavarian all the way."

They shook hands with the old musician, then walked together toward the taxi stand behind the Neuen Rathaus. Cane opened the door.

"Where are you staying?"

"The Waldenhof. Do you know it?"

"Yes, of course. By the Bahnhofplatz?"

"That's it. I'll be looking for you tomorrow—at nine."

"Goodbye, Marianne Mason, American journalist." Cane lifted her hand to his lips, their eyes held. He closed the door. She waved as the taxi pulled away.

A darling man, she thought. *And an American spy!* She took a deep breath. It had been a long time since she had such a carefree time. Of course, I can explain it if I had to. Had she fooled him with her cover? She was fairly certain she hadn't, still she must see him tomorrow. She wanted to see him tomorrow. *Somewhere, he had the skull.*

~~~~

Cane watched the taxi until it turned out of sight. He reached for his pipe. It wasn't in his pocket—hell of a note. He must have left it on the table. He retraced his steps. The old man was gone, the table was empty. It was a favorite pipe. Well, damn! And the woman, who was she? Not American. He knew that. Not even Marianne Mason. Then he chuckled to himself. Between us, we've spun a provocative web of lies.

# CHAPTER IX

C ane crossed the Marienplatz slowly, his mind on Marianne Mason. *Who was she?* Certainly she was not the American journalist she claimed to be. And the man with her? Well, at least he looked like a Swedish photographer. But a hell of a surly guy! And what kind of weird coincidence was it that had her in the Fort Reno cemetery a week or so ago and in Munich today? Only one thing, by God! A German Major's skull.

Did she know the identity of the man whose picture he carried? So, who were they? A KGB team? Neither of them looked Russian. At least not his idea of what Russians looked like—thick-necked, broad shouldered ruthless men. And the women—well, the ones he'd seen in pictures, raking leaves in parks or carrying coal along railway sidings or shoveling snow off Moscow streets, didn't fit the image of this woman.

She was not only one sharp good-looking woman with her smoky-gray eyes, but she was a hell of a lot of fun. She'd felt like a feather in his arms. He smiled, remembering.

He scratched the back of his neck. The itch reminded him that *if* they were after the skull—and that was surely the explanation—then they were playing for keeps. Tomorrow both of them would be his guests at the Oktoberfest and that should be an interesting day!

A window display caught his eye. A family of mannequins dressed as they should be for Oktoberfest. He turned and entered the store.

"Ach! Nein!" an old lady cried, "*Ladenschlussl*—the shop is closed. The door was supposed to be locked...."

Cane turned on all the charm he could muster. To impress a beautiful girl, he told the old woman, he had to dress like a Münchener—and he would trust no one but such a knowledgeable saleswoman as herself to help him. In less than fifteen minutes he had the whole outfit. Hand-knit socks, *Lederhosen* that laced at the knee, a dark green Tyrolean hat with a white feather boutonniere in its band, an embroidered *Loden* jacket, soft leather boots—the works. In a diminutive dressing room he viewed himself skeptically and wondered if he would dare walk abroad in such a get-up. The main trouble, he decided, was that the clothes looked too damn new. They needed to be run over by a car or dragged along an alley. Maybe walking on them would help. He took the package, paid cash, thanked the little old lady and kissed her on the cheek. She blushed appreciatively. Stopping next door at a tobacconist, he bought a new pipe, then took the subway to the University station.

The activity around the small square and inside the inn had not subsided since Saturday night. It was noisy and friendly, smoke-filled and dark. Candles flickered on the tables. An accordionist in traditional garb was belting out drinking songs.

Weaving his way through the crowd, Cane ran up the stairs and picked his key off the board. The clerk wasn't around. Neither was the old concierge. With the inn filled, they had probably reasoned— why stay around? It had been at least three hours, maybe more, since he'd dropped his letter at the Consulate. There'd be the devil to pay if Hastings had called, and he wasn't in. He fumbled with his key, pushed open the door, and turned on the light. The man who had been sitting by the window in the dark stood up.

Cane stopped in the open door and stared, motionless, tense.

"Herr Schwartz," the man said, "I'm Hastings."

Damn poor judgment coming to his room unannounced. Suppose he was followed. Suppose he wasn't Hastings. Peter should have thought of something like matching parts of a bill or matchbook covers. Anything for a positive identification. His room key was still gripped between his middle and ring fingers—almost as good as brass knuckles in an emergency.

Hastings must have read his thoughts, for he reached into his coat and pulled out a wallet with his Consular identification, then asked, "You did bring my tamales?"

Eliot sized up the man before answering. Slender build, smooth parchment complexion with a dark receding hairline, intelligent eyes partially hidden behind heavy lids. He was all business and, slight as he was, looked capable of taking care of any situation.

"Yes, I brought them," Cane answered, then stopped in the act of putting his package on the bed when Hastings held up an envelope lettered in pencil. *The room is bugged. Keep talking naturally.* He nodded. "I hope you enjoy them," he said. "They are a little hot for my taste."

"Rather a different sort of W*urst*, eh?"

"Well, I've been gone for some time. But hot tamales are not my idea of any kind of *Wurst*—" How long can this inane conversation go on, Cane thought. "Here they are—"

He watched Hastings write on the other side of the envelope, *Meet me at the Platz in fifteen minutes. Bring a beer.* Cane nodded. This was more like it. Hastings struck a match to the envelope and watched it burn in the ashtray.

"How is old Jim? We used to play softball every Saturday. He's done very well in the poultry business, I understand."

"Ja. Very well. I sell him chicken feed. He's a good customer." A conversation for the sole purpose of convincing unknown listeners you are an innocent tourist is even more demanding than flirting with a beautiful woman who, you know, isn't who she says she is.

"I must go. Thank you, Herr Schwartz, for taking the trouble to bring me this gift from Texas. I hope you have a pleasant holiday. Goodbye."

"It was my pleasure, Herr Hastings, and also to meet you. I'll remember you to my friend Jim when I see him."

"Please do. *Gute Nacht.*"

"*Auf Wiedersehen.*"

Cane opened the door just as a large heavy-set man passed, heading for the stairs. He was dressed in Bavarian clothes and kept his eyes on the floor. The man continued down the steps. Had he been listening to the bugged recording? Had Hastings been shadowed? Or, he wondered, was he getting jumpy and the man was simply a neighbor?

Hastings, too, raised his eyebrows then shrugged. They nodded silently to each other. Hastings waited for the stranger to disappear, then walked to the stairs and went up. Cane grinned as he closed the door. Defensive precautions. Go up two flights and take the elevator down. Now, about the bug. Why hadn't he thought of that? Hastings had spotted it right away. Cane started looking. Where the hell was it? Damn—he was too old for this sort of thing! He wasn't as alert as he used to be. Surely not the telephone—that's where anyone would look first. But there it was. That's amateurish, Cane thought.

Taking the slender Chinese lapis princess from his flight bag he slipped her into his pocket. He emptied the ashtray into the toilet and flushed the burned remnants of the envelope. Just like 007. Efficient as hell! He fingered the cool lapis lazuli carving, then glanced at his watch. Time to saunter down the stairs, get a beer, and carry it across the street. He left the light on. Just as well to let the bastards watching think I'm still here!

The small Platz shimmered with light. Ornamental cast-iron pedestals holding incandescent bulbs lined the curb. A bronze fountain, green from oxidation, displayed a circle of small jets of water flowing smoothly from sea horses and turtles. Gravel paths led from corner to corner, outlining beds of red and yellow chrysanthemums.

The sound of an accordion drifted across the street from the tavern, and Cane remembered his brief encounter at the Marienplatz. Well, he'd see them in the morning and, until he had a clearer picture, he'd wait to brief Hastings about them. The news of von Stober was enough to spring on him in their first session.

The benches were filled. He lit a cigarette, missing his pipe, and remembered he'd left the new one in the room. Strange that someone would pick up an old, well-used pipe. He spotted Hastings in a far corner. Easing through a group of students, Cane asked if he could share the bench. Hastings nodded in a vague sort of way. Cane thanked him indifferently and sat down. They never looked at each other again.

Speaking softly, holding a beer stein in front of his face and moving his lips as little as possible, Cane told Hastings of the new developments in the case of the German skull.

"So there you have it. I don't know who the hell he is." He dropped his cigarette on the gravel path and ground it out with his shoe. "I have the picture, but I think the Company sent you a copy, right?"

"Yes. I'll get on it immediately. He could only belong to one organization that would make him anxious to conceal his identity, and that's the SS. He could be in any of a number of branches, but you can depend on it he was one of the regulars. Where is the skull?"

"Hidden in a soccer ball. I'll get it for you tomorrow."

Hastings stood up, stretched, stooped to place his beer stein beside the bench, and whispered, "Meet me at the Cornelius Bridge at five tomorrow evening. When I see you, I'll go down to the rose garden. You follow. I should know something by then. And I'll collect the skull." He rubbed his lip, then said, "Stay here for a few minutes to watch my back." He paused for an instant, then said quickly, "One more thing. Peter is in town. Don't be surprised when you see him." With his hands in his pockets, he sauntered off.

Cane sipped his beer, cradling the stein with both hands. Peter here? Splendid! Great to bring him up to date. He smiled, and his eyes softened. He felt a warm glow thinking about Peter. He's all I have and, by God, the only person I'd go out on this limb for! I'd like for Peter to meet this mysterious woman, to get his reaction.

He glanced over the small park. No one had followed Hastings. If a shadow was working him, he kept out of Cane's sight.

He left his empty stein under the bench, crossed the street, listened for a while to the accordion player, then climbed the dimly lighted stairs into the semi-darkness of the third floor hall. Before he reached his room, he knew something was wrong. A vague uneasiness—a gut feeling. Just as he approached the room, he saw the strip of light beneath the door go out.

Switching his room key to his left hand, he took the lapis carving from his pocket. Before he could insert the key, the door opened. In an instinctive automatic act, Cane hit the man as hard as he could under the chin and in that second recognized him.

"My God—Peter!" He reached to catch him, but Peter fell back hard, fast. His glasses flew off, his eyes opened in surprise, and he dropped to the floor unconscious.

# CHAPTER X

J annasen was waiting for Anya in the hotel lobby. His face was flushed with anger. "You made a fool of yourself over the German."

"He's no German," she said quietly.

"You heard him. He's an official of the Fair. You behaved like a—like an American whore!"

Anya's voice was low as she repeated patiently.

"He is no German. He's a CIA agent, and it's possible he has the skull." Anya watched Jannasen with smug satisfaction as she delivered her thunderbolt.

"You're mad."

"So you don't believe me," she shrugged. "Karuski will. Also I file my report tonight for Center. It is you, Comrade, who will look foolish when I have finished."

Jannasen motioned to a corner of the lobby where they could talk, then sat opposite her, a small table between them.

"All right," he said, leaning forward, "now tell me what it is that I don't know and you do."

"Wilhelm Schwartz is the cover for an American named Canyon Eliot from Eastern, Colorado. He has a ranch there. During the war he was with the OSS. We think he's probably with the CIA now."

"How do you know all this?"

"Center ran a tracer on him. They found that he was a top OSS agent during the war. He speaks idiomatic German, French, and Italian. He's been inactive since the war."

"Have you seen this man before?" It was hard for him to keep his temper in check. Why hadn't he been told of the variables of this operation?

Anya nodded. "Yes. In an Oklahoma cemetery."

"Fort Reno?"

"I was coming out just as he and the director of the agricultural station were entering. He had a moustache then, but I recognized him this evening—immediately. And he recognized me." She smiled thinly, then added, "So, my photographer friend, we are going to be his guests tomorrow from 9:00 AM on, and you are going to be gracious if it kills you!" She stubbed out her cigarette.

"What makes you think he has the skull?" His eyes never left hers.

"As soon as they discovered that the grave had been opened, the FBI was notified. Actually, Comrades Belyakov and Rintalen didn't handle it very well, letting the skull be discovered like that. If they hadn't been in such a hurry to get it to Zurich, it would have been better. *Nichevo!* You too were at fault. The Americans knew about the drop in Zurich. At any rate, now they have the Thyssen skull—and they have it right here!"

Jannasen, defensive, bristled. "No one ever saw me tend the drop! How did you find that Schwartz was—what's his name—Eliot?"

"I went through his car while they were in the cemetery. The car rental papers were made out to Canyon Eliot, Eastern, Colorado. It was simple enough to check out."

"That doesn't prove he has the skull." Jannasen opened a pack of cigarettes and offered Anya one. She took it for the peace offering it was, bent her head to get his light, then exhaled slowly.

"Early on," she said, "the Americans didn't know why we wanted the skull. So it would be natural for them to try to find out. To do that, they needed to have the skull with the agent where the answer could be found—do you follow me?"

Jannasen nodded. "Go on."

"The first time I saw Eliot was, as I said, at the cemetery. Then later that afternoon, I saw him at the Oklahoma City airport. We were on the same flight back to New York. And you know who was also on that flight? Magen Ben-Yanait, the Mossad Colonel. And guess who he was tailing? No one but our friend, Canyon Eliot—cover Wilhelm Schwartz."

"Does Center know all this?"

"Of course."

"Why in hell wasn't I briefed?"

"Because we haven't had time. I really never expected to see him again. We'll learn more tomorrow."

"Do you know where he's staying?"

"No. He's not that stupid. He's smart and he's clever. He lost Magen Ben-Yanait in New York."

"And Ben-Yanait is on it. Damn! How did the Jews know about the operation? Was there a leak in Washington?"

"Of course not. It was probably our lady dentist...."

"No, not her. She's not very bright, but she's loyal." He drummed his fingers on the arm of the chair, then asked, "Do you think he knows about Thyssen?"

"Ben-Yanait? Yes."

"I was speaking of Schwartz—Eliot."

"I'm not sure. He might by now. When he left the States, he only knew for sure that von Stober's wife lived here. That is, I'm sure he knew what was in the General Services file. Besides, if he's already met her, it's possible he knows who was really buried in Fort Reno."

"Where would he have the skull?"

Anya shrugged. "There is no telling. But he's a clever man. You can depend on it—it's well hidden."

Jannasen stood up. "We have to meet Karuski." He looked at his watch. "Damn, we're already late. You go on...."

"You have the photo session tonight. My interview is tomorrow

69

afternoon. He really gets a lot of mileage out of his agricultural committee."

"Anya, take my appointment now. I'll take yours tomorrow. When do you hit your drop?"

"At ten."

"You'll use the window signal?"

Anya nodded. "Yes, a light in the bathroom means to check the dead drop."

"Then I'll see you in the morning. I promise I'll be the perfect Swedish gentleman when I meet Herr Schwartz the Field Marshall of the Oktoberfest!"

"Where are you going?"

"I can't say right now. You go meet the Comrade Colonel. I'll see you in the morning."

With misgivings, Anya stood in the doorway and watched him leave. She could almost read his mind. He was going to contact their Munich control and try to locate Schwartz. The fool. For some reason she wasn't worried about the American. I think, she speculated, he can take care of himself. I'm not so sure about Niels—except, of course, for that knife he wears.

She watched until Niels hailed a passing cab and got in. So, when it came to a showdown between the two men, what would happen? Her chest tightened. The thought of the big Colorado rancher lying in a pool of blood, Niels standing over him withdrawing the knife that was his trademark, made her skin crawl. How would the American agent defend himself? She crushed out her cigarette vigorously. *Stop it!* she commanded herself. Of course he could defend himself. From the house phone, she called Karuski. "Herr Karuski, Marianne Mason here, from *The Woman's Eye.*"

"Yes, Fräulein Mason. We have an appointment tomorrow."

"I know, but if you have nothing better to do, perhaps you would have a drink with me in the lounge. It would be nice to meet you before our interview."

"Very well. You are in the Hotel?"

"Ja. I'll be waiting in the bar, Herr Karuski."

Over a glass of wine, Anya told Colonel Karuski the story of the American, then leaned back and smiled wearily.

"The stew is beginning to thicken," she added.

Karuski agreed. "I hope Jannasen doesn't do anything foolish."

"I'm to have my report ready by ten tonight. So I'll go now. Since we'll be with the American in the morning, I'll meet you tomorrow afternoon—say four o'clock? Afterwards, Jannasen wants a meeting."

"Good. I'll be at the Fair with the Agricultural Delegation. Perhaps I'll see you there."

"It's better not to be too obvious. Good night, Herr Karuski."

"Good night, Miss Mason."

In her room, Anya checked on the safeguards she'd left to be sure no one had searched it. Then she turned on the light in the bathroom and pulled back the curtains. Twisting the heel of her right shoe until it came off in her hand, she took the code book. With it in front of her, she wrote her report in that day's code, folded it, and slipped it into an almost empty cigarette pack. Replacing the book in her heel and freshening her lipstick, she pushed loose strands of hair from her forehead, and went downstairs. Walking to the nearest public phone, she took a cigarette, crumpled the pack, and let it drop to the floor of the booth. After lighting the cigarette, she dialed the number of the phone and made imaginary conversation until a man across the street struck a match, lit a cigarette, then dropped it and walked towards the booth. She finished her non-conversation quickly, hung up the receiver, and left.

# CHAPTER XI

C ane slammed the door behind him, turned on the light, and knelt beside Peter. He felt his pulse, then pulled him inside the room and closed the door. Peter began to stir and Cane sighed in relief that Peter was all right. The room had been ransacked, the phone ripped from the wall. That takes care of the bug. His new clothes were scattered over the floor. The bed and pillows were torn. An overstuffed chair was upside down, the springs ripped out. The traveling bag he'd bought in Montreal was in shreds. God! Somebody gave this place a going over.

Then he noticed the body. It was partially under the bed. Cane bolted the door. What the devil? Had Peter caught him searching the room and, afraid he had found the skull, killed him? He pulled the body out, rolled it over, then stood—electrified at what he saw. Jesus Christ! After a long moment he released his breath and gazed dumbly at the dead man. He'd been with him less than three hours before at the Marienplatz. It was the Swedish photographer. His hand was frozen to his belt buckle and, as it fell back, released a stiletto. Cane picked it up with his handkerchief and examined it. Its sleek tapered blade, honed to a razor edge, was attached to a finely wrought cast bronze buckle in the shape of a tree. The tooled leather belt was itself the sheath. Blood was caked at the hilt. Peter had had a narrow escape. A guy who uses a knife like that is no ordinary fashion photographer.

The bullet had gone through his trench coat, sweater, and heart. Small caliber, built for close work. He turned back to Peter, who muttered a string of curses, opened his eyes, and tried to focus.

"Are you all right?" Cane asked.

"Stupid question." He tried to sit up, then eased back to the floor. Touching his chin gingerly, his eyes watering, he zeroed in on Cane accusingly.

"God, man, I'm sorry."

Peter didn't answer. He felt his chin again, then closed his eyes.

"A wet cloth—that's what you need," Cane said, more to himself than to Peter, and headed for the bathroom. He stumbled over a second body. "Goddamn son of a gun...." and caught his breath. Crumpled up behind the door was a large man—dead, a pearl-handled Derringer .22 in his hand. This would be the gun that killed the Swede. He'd never known Peter to carry a Saturday Night Special. What the hell had gone on? He pocketed the small gun. Cane didn't need to check his pulse to know the man was dead. There was no blood, and a casual inspection turned up no wound.

But it turned up something else that triggered goose bumps down Cane's spine. He was about the same size as himself, Cane guessed, hair an iron gray, wiry with a little curl, and he had a moustache.

Then Cane swallowed hard. It was like looking in a mirror before he had shaved off his moustache. The dead man was a pure reflection of himself. A dead-ringer.

The wet cloth forgotten, Cane rushed back calling "Peter! Wake up! Peter! Peter!" He cuffed his face, grabbed his shoulders, and shook him. "What have you done?" He pulled Peter to a sitting position and leaned him against the bed. "Come on—Peter, wake up!"

Peter groaned. His eyes opened, glazed and cloudy, then closed again. He touched his neck; he moved it delicately. "Damn! I think my jaw is broken. What did you hit me with?"

"The lapis princess." Cane shook his head. "Peter, I'm sorry...."

"God...."

"Christ, Peter! How was I to know it was you?"

"Hastings was supposed to have told you." Peter answered weakly. "There's a goddamn covey of bodies in here. What did you do before you met Hastings? Line 'em up for kicks?"

"I didn't do it—I thought it was you. Who's the guy in the bathroom?"

"Damn if I know...." Peter shook his head and attempted to rise, then thought better of it and sat back. He looked at the body near him. "The room was just like this when I came in. The light was on, and I thought you'd be waiting with a bottle of Scotch. This is what I found. I decided I'd better get the hell out. And that's what we'd both better do. Help me up!"

Cane half-lifted Peter to his feet. "Are you all right? Can you make it?"

Peter sat down on the bed. "Give me a minute longer. God—my head! My neck! My jaw! Where the hell are my glasses?"

Cane found them and handed them to Peter, whose head was weaving gently from side to side.

"Cane, we've got to leave this place looking like someone got you. Did you get a good look at the guy in the bathroom?"

"Right. Could be me for sure."

"I thought it was at first until I started to help him. Then I knew. But you better believe it is no coincidence. He was here for a purpose. Probably to take your place. Search them both good."

Cane went through Jannasen's pockets, examined his billfold, small identification folder holding credit cards and a couple of large Swiss bills, a light meter, a mother-of-pearl pocket knife, and some small change. He picked up the dagger and its sheath, handed them both to Peter, and said, "Quite a toy he plays with." Searching the body further, he found a thin money belt in the waistband of his boxer shorts, which he deftly removed. "That's about it. He probably has stuff stashed in his shoe heel. Well, hell, let's take his shoes." He pulled them off, adding, "I was with this guy a few hours ago."

Peter looked up, wincing with pain as he did. "You were? Who is he?"

"To tell the truth, I don't know. I'll clue you in later. We've got to check these bastards."

"Yeah. Switch your ID with the guy in the bathroom and let's get out of here." He was twisting the dagger between his fingers. "You know, I think this was used on your double. It wouldn't leave much blood. There's a little caked here, but it's been wiped." He stood up gingerly, then followed Cane to the bathroom. He leaned against the door jamb and watched Cane kneel beside the body. "He looks more like you than you do. When did you shave off the fringe?"

"It was a case of necessity in New York." He looked at the dead man and shook his head. "I'd like to know where they found him." He was dressed in a brown tweed sports jacket, tan slacks and shirt, with a green shadow-striped tie. Cane took a snub-nosed Smith & Wesson .357 Magnum from a shoulder holster.

"I think we need that," he said without looking up. "Be the devil to get the holster, too." Cane pulled the left sleeve of the jacket off the stiffening arm, removed the holster, then examined the jacket. "Loaded for bear, and he uses a Derringer—strange. Out of character for me, by God!" In his pockets were a couple of New York theater stubs, a package of Marlboro cigarettes, a pipe, and a half-filled plastic tobacco pouch. Cane sniffed, then looked at Peter.

"They did a sure-enough job of researching. Even to my favorite blend." Inside the coat Cane found a billfold, a plastic credit card folder, and a U.S. passport, all of which he exchanged with Wilhelm Schwartz's passport and wallet. As he stuck them in the coat, he felt a stiffness in the lining. He fingered the material. There was something there besides cloth.

He took the knife he'd found on Jannasen and ripped a seam. "Look at this!" He ripped other seams. Through the entire coat there was an inner lining sewn with thousand dollar bills.

"My God! The man's a walking bank," Cane exclaimed. "We'd

75

better take it with us."

"You better believe!" Peter quickly came to life and helped Cane pull the sport coat off the dead man. Cane transferred the passport and billfold to his hip pocket.

"Wait a minute—I've got to shave him! They know Wilhelm Schwartz here with no moustache." He stepped over the body, found his razor and, in seconds, discovered the moustache was false. He dropped it in his pocket. "I might need it," he said, then picked up the coat, handed it to Peter and added, "Let's split!" He looked back. "We better take his shoes, too."

"Wait! Where's the skull?"

"Safe. Come on! Let's go down the fire escape—oh hell, wait." He stopped in the middle of the bedroom. "I've got to take these clothes." He picked up the *Lederhosen*, shirt and jacket, slapped the hat on his head. "Look for the socks—the boots--they're here somewhere—and the suspenders—"

"Let's get the hell out of here. Are you crazy, looking for those damn things?"

"No. I've got to have them." He found the socks and suspenders, picked a pillow case off the floor, and stuffed the clothes in it. "You go first. I'll shut the window." Taking a last quick look around and satisfied that there was nothing that could trip up the Tamale operation, he turned out the light and followed Peter through the window, closing it softly.

Peter was waiting in the alley. He slipped carefully past the shaded window on the floor below, and by the frosted window in the men's room off the tavern. Whoever picked his room, Cane reflected, had chosen it well.

Behind some large trash containers, Cane emptied his pockets into the pillow case, dropped in the gun and holster, rolled it as tightly as he could and shoved it under his arm.

"The car is around the corner," he said, leading the way.

As soon as they reached the street, the sound of an oompah band from a beer hall reached them. Cane shook his head.

"I'm so sick of that goddamned music. I hear it in my sleep. But I'm not complaining. Here's the car." The street was dark except for the glow of a street lamp half a block away. He stopped in the act of unlocking the door and turned to Peter.

"Hell, we can't take this car—it's rented to Wilhelm Schwartz! Where are you staying?"

"Across town at the Deutscher Kaiser, but we can't go there. We mustn't be seen together."

"Right. But I've got to get the skull out of the trunk. It's booby-trapped. Damn! I hope I can unhook it in the dark." He unlocked the trunk and lifted the lid, then whispered, "Look, it's got a paralyzer hooked to it. If it goes off, I've had it for at least half an hour. You grab the soccer ball and take off as fast as you can."

"The soccer ball?"

"The skull's in it. Here goes." He lighted a match and in its glow, found the wire. "Easy does it, easy."

He had the canister. Home free! He pulled it out, dropped it in his pocket, and lifted the soccer ball still in its net bag.

"Golf clubs—tennis—archery—? Pretty damn smart, Cane."

"But a shade old for this assignment! Anyway, this was a perfect hiding place until I could get it to Hastings. Pete, get a taxi and head for your hotel. I think I know where I can spend the night, and tomorrow I start life as Josef Cranach. I'm going to do some shuffling and not leave a trail. Get in touch with Hastings. Tell him I'll see him tomorrow at the Cornelius Bridge. Good luck!"

"You too, Chili. You'll need it!" The two men embraced briefly and went in separate directions.

Cane walked a couple of blocks to an all-night Laundromat, carrying his pillow case like a sack of laundry and swinging the soccer ball. He ran the shirt and knickers through the wash and let them spin dry while he looked for a better container. He found it on top of a garbage can. A pasteboard box from Plaschkek. Next best thing to having luggage, Cane decided. He took his pillow case and the box into the restroom, locked the door, and carefully repacked everything including the soccer ball and the net bag. With the short jacket and with the hat stuck on the back of his head, he should look rakish enough to be taken for a true Bavarian. Then he gathered his still-damp shirt and *Lederhosen* and folded them carefully. At least they looked as if they had had their share of wear and tear.

He walked a block, caught a taxi, and went to the Theresienwiese where the festival showed no signs of diminishing. He borrowed some twine at a food tent, where he had a sausage and roll, and tied up his package. Now it looked like an authentic purchase.

From there he went to a phone booth and looked up Haupmann at Birkenstrasse 9. So damn many Haupmanns! Why hadn't he gotten her full name? Ah, he dialed the number, glancing at his watch. A little late. Eleven o'clock. But with just a dram of luck—

He heard the ring—once, twice, three times. Come on, be home!

Then it was answered with a sleepy "Ja?"

"Wilhelm Schwartz here, you remember?"

"Ah, yes. The friend of Heinrich."

"Frau Haupmann, I need help. You are the only person I know. I had confirmed reservations at the Attendorf Hotel. But before I checked in, I came to see you. Afterwards I stopped by the Theresienwiese and you know how time gets away. When I got to my hotel, they had let my room go. I've checked all over Munich, and there's not a room to be had. Would you rent me a room for the night? I'll find something tomorrow—"

"But of course! Of course! You can stay as long as you like. I am pleased you would call me. But, dear Herr Schwartz not as a renter, no, as my guest. Have you had dinner?"

"Yes, thank you. You are very kind. I'll be there soon."

Cane took a taxi and got out two blocks from Birkenstrasse. He lit a cigarette, leaning against an iron fence as he smoked. But no cars passed, no pedestrians. It was a residential street, quite asleep. Satisfied he wasn't followed, he picked up his box and walked quickly and directly to 9 Birkenstrasse.

A porch light was on and before he knocked, Frau Haupmann had the door open. "Wilkommen, Herr Schwartz! What a pleasure this is!"

"The pleasure is mine, I assure you, Frau Haupmann. Always I shall be in your debt." Cane took her hand and bowed politely.

"And now we have a beer," she said, "but first I show you your room." She led the way up the stairs to a front bedroom. "All right?"

"Wonderful. It is very nice." He placed the box on the bed.

"Your luggage?" she asked.

"The airline misplaced it. It's supposed to come in tomorrow. These are some things I bought today."

"Well, come now and we have some beer."

Cane could think of no excuse to stay her hospitality. He followed Frau Haupmann into her parlor, and until past midnight they drank beer and talked. Actually, she talked. Cane would nod or shake his head as the conversation demanded. When the Black Forest cuckoo clock cooed one, Cane rose. "It's been a full day, Frau Haupmann."

"Ja! Here I keep you up all hours, Herr Schwartz. Forgive me. You sleep good, now."

Cane went upstairs slowly, fighting an inclination to hurry. He closed the door softly and put a chair under the knob. He wanted ample warning in case she decided to bring him a nightcap.

Turning his attention to the box, he untied it quickly. First he examined the money belt. It held ten thousand Swiss francs and a card which read Niels Janassen and a box number in Zurich. How about that! The skull was headed there when it had been diverted into his stewardship. That was something to think about. Could Marianne Mason, the self-styled American journalist, the beautiful lady he'd seen in an Oklahoma cemetery, the light-as-a-feather dancer he whirled around the Marienplatz, be mixed up in this? *You better believe!* Suddenly he felt old. His years tumbled about his shoulders. To be racing on this course, he reflected, one needed to be younger and smarter—especially smarter. Quick. Able to anticipate convoluted turns of events and, above all, not to be side-tracked by a pretty face and a sparkling personality. Hell, maybe I'm not so damn ancient after all.

He directed his attention back to the knife belt. It was an intriguing weapon. Cane had never seen anything quite like it. He tried on the belt and pulled out the dagger in a quick defensive movement. Classy, he thought, and pretty damn lethal! He ripped some more seams of the coat. The inner lining held U.S. thousand dollar bills sewn into the front and back. He counted a hundred without tearing up the coat, and guessed there must be close to three or four times that. Something like half a million bucks! He hung the coat in the closet. He'd have to get a needle and thread tomorrow. Better to leave the money there than try to hide it.

Turning to the U.S. passport he got a jolt. It was made out to one Canyon Eliot of Colorado. The picture was him all right. Where in the hell had they gotten it? So this guy was going to take his place on the Nazi team—how about that? The picture looked more like Cane than Cane did right now. He had the same huge mustache he'd had when he left Colorado! Son of a bitch.

The gun. He flipped the release and the barrel dropped. It was loaded with six .357 Magnums. The Derringer, though, was empty. Damn, he should have left the pistol! What was he thinking?

He transferred the money clip and bills to his pocket, then examined the shoes, first Jannasen's.

He twisted, turned, and finally pried off the heels and found what he expected—a hollowed-out space in each of them. In one was a small syringe with an almost invisible needle beside it. Cane guessed it was a fast-acting poison. In the other heel was a small code book in Swedish. So, who the hell are they working for—the Swedes, for God's sake?

The shoes of his double revealed nothing. Cane even took the soles apart. "So much for that. Hastings will have his hands full after we meet tomorrow."

He stripped to his underwear, turned out the light, then walked to the window. The street was quiet. The soft glow of an occasional night light behind closed shutters broke the monotony of dark windows. At the turn of the road, a solitary street lamp cast a small circle of light.

The sky held clustered stars in autumn brilliance. But in the distance, in the upper foothills of the Alps, dark clouds pushed above the charcoal outline of the angled roofs across the way. Cane's shoulders tingled with the unease he felt. What had gone wrong? Everything! He pursed his lips, running his hands across his chin. The woman—*who is she working for?*

He was supposed to meet her at nine. As far as she knew, he was dead. Or did she know? He took a cigarette and lit it, inhaling slowly. He hadn't realized how much he was looking forward to seeing her.

A whirlwind of conflicting thoughts churned his mind. What if Frau Haupmann heard on TV that Wilhelm Schwartz was dead? What if the woman went undercover, and he never saw her again? He pushed that thought from his mind. He knew he would meet her this morning. Unless—she expected him to be dead?

It began to rain. The drops rattled like pebbles on the tile roof. The din dulled the sound of the cuckoo clock that determinedly cheeped the hours. It was far into the morning before he finally fell asleep from exhaustion.

He was awakened when the chair against the door moved. He leaped to his feet. It was Frau Haupmann with coffee and rolls, apologizing for waking him, wondering why he'd placed a chair in front of the door. Cane, in jockey shorts, took the tray through the door, thanked her profusely, and said he'd he down later.

The storm had passed, leaving only a dull monotonous rain dripping from the eaves, running in rivulets down the panes, a low murmur of winter.

# CHAPTER XII

Gusty drafts of rain beat against the bus window. Magen Ben-Yanait reached for the overhead buzzer. When the bus stopped, he picked up his scarred lunch pail and climbed wearily down into the rain, stepping over a rushing gutter. Apparently a working man beginning an interminable week of labor, he entered a small café near the freight terminal. Dressed in a German's railroad worker's uniform of grease-stained coveralls, with a cloth cap pulled over his eyes, he had a day's growth of beard that made his face look sooty. He leaned on the counter and ordered coffee and a Berliner. His eyes roamed the room restlessly while he ate the jelly doughnut. Before he'd finished, Kruppel came in shouting hellos and *Guten Tags*, scattering raindrops like a shaggy dog.

Ben-Yanait dropped some change on the counter, picked up his pail and left, walking toward the yards. Kruppel's truck was parked near a Guterwagen. He stepped into the cab, removed his cap, shook off the rain. *"Verdammt!"*

Kruppel drank his coffee in a gulp and returned to his truck. He nodded briefly to Magen, turned on the ignition, put the truck in gear, and drove off. The Mossad agent offered him a cigarette.

*"Danke."* He lighted it without taking his eyes off the road.

"You were busy last night."

*"Ja."*

"A fiasco...."

"Ja."

"Want to tell me about it?"

"It was an accident."

"Even so, it was bad. The American was a fine fellow. A tragedy to kill him. Now we know less than we did before. No idea where the skull is. Both of them dead—the American and the Russian. God, but you were thorough! Let's hope the police and the KGB will think they killed each other."

"They will, Jasmine. Right now it's pat."

"Damn shame! How did it happen?"

"I just had time to get the bug in the phone before this man showed up. It wasn't Eliot. Eliot came in about half an hour later. I know it was a bad place, but I couldn't work out a better one on such short notice. The recorder was in the bathroom closet next door. I have the tape."

He shifted his body to take a quick glance at Ben-Yanait.

"It's a silly thing about hot tamales sent to Hastings. From the way they talked, I could tell they'd found the bug. I left it going and went to eat—this was about eight o'clock—and ran into Eliot and another man as they came out of Eliot's room. That was unfortunate; but they didn't see my face, and I don't think either of them associated me with the bug."

He turned onto the Autobahn, headed for Peiss. Traffic was beginning to thicken. The day was dawning gray and wet. Ben-Yanait waited and Kruppel returned to his story.

"His companion left, but Eliot stayed behind for ten or fifteen minutes. I was in the tavern when he passed through, and saw him get a beer and go to the Platz. I watched him meet this man—his control, I suppose. It was the perfect time to search his room. I used a pass key then, just as I opened the door, a man attacked me."

"The Russian?"

"I guess. I'd never seen him before."

"Extreme carelessness on your part."

"An understatement, sir."

83

"Then?"

"He had this belt knife and he knew how to use it. I had to shoot him."

"With the Derringer?"

"Right. I shot through my pocket. I think he died instantly."

"And then?"

"I searched it again but found nothing. He had already torn the room apart. The skull definitely is not there. Then Eliot returned while I was going through the closet. I saw his reflection in a mirror as he opened the door. Of course, he was shocked when he saw the dead man. He made a sort of choking sound, then turned him over and pushed him under the bed."

"Why would he do that?"

"I don't know. You'd think he'd get his things and get out. But then he started searching the room through the mess of stuff on the floor...."

"That's strange, certainly for a man who comes in, his room is torn apart and he finds a body, a murdered man, there."

"I thought so. Possibly he decided that whoever had shot the intruder had also taken the skull. But the skull wasn't there, so I don't know. Of course, I knew he'd get to the closet sooner or later, and he did. I had my weight on the door and, as he opened it, I shoved against him and came out hard. I threw my arm around him and struck him with the edge of my hand, at the nape of his neck."

Magen shook his head. "It's a damn shame it killed him."

"I only meant to stun him so I could get away. He must have had an old injury at the cervical vertebrae. Could have, you know. He made a lot of parachute jumps during the war."

"That's probably the reason. So, then you got out—by the door?"

"Yes, but not until I took the Russian's knife and made a stab wound in the back of Eliot's neck. I put my Derringer in the American's hand. It looked like he made a damn lucky shot."

"Of course, you left the room clean?"

"No fingerprints, naturally. But clean, no. The Russian had torn out the telephone, so I didn't get anything more on the tape. I feel bad about the American."

"Fritz, you mustn't blame yourself. These things happen; it's unfortunate. What about the car?"

"A blank. There was nothing there except a bunch of sports equipment in the trunk. It was filled with stuff—skis, golf clubs, tennis racket, a soccer ball—"

"A soccer ball?"

"Yeah, in a net bag."

"Good God, man, that's it!"

"What do you mean?"

"I mean that's where the skull is hidden—in the trunk!"

"No, it wasn't there. I looked good with my flashlight."

"Don't you see? It's in the soccer ball. The other was cover. I'll go back and get it. They won't discover the bodies until the maid cleans up."

"Jasmine, you won't find a thing. That was an ordinary soccer ball."

"Did you pick it up?"

"I didn't have to. I know a soccer ball when I see one." Fritz lowered the cab window and flipped out his cigarette. He followed the road at a steady speed, watching through the metronomic rhythm of the windshield wipers.

The Israeli laughed, jamming his fist into his hand. "Turn around quick! It's the perfect hiding place. Hurry, we need to get there before daylight."

Fritz, plainly exasperated, shook his head muttering as he turned the truck around. "My deliveries are going to be late."

"It's all right, Fritz; I promise. Oh, Jerusalem! This is our day!"

It took less than ten minutes to reach the car. With the expertise of a second-story man, Fritz had the trunk open in seconds.

Everything was there. The skis, the tennis rackets, the golf clubs in the beat-up bag, the archery equipment—everything except the soccer ball.

Fritz was shaken. "It was right there. I swear I saw it. Who could have taken it?" he asked in a stricken voice. "The Russian dead, and the American. Who else knew about the skull?"

Ben-Yanait slammed the lid of the trunk, his face grim. "No one," he muttered, "that's the crux of the whole thing. *No bloody one!* No one but us and the KGB and the CIA!"

# CHAPTER XIII

*Munich*
*Thursday, October 2*

For Anya the dawn broke cold and wet around the drab hotel. She woke with a sense of dread, and pulled the down quilt closer about her shoulders. What was it? Something terrible was about to happen—or had. Then she remembered. Jannasen. The last time she'd called his room was midnight, and he hadn't returned. She sat up in bed, reached for the phone, and called again. There was still no answer. Her feeling of unease grew, until she couldn't stay in bed. She threw back the quilt and dressed hurriedly. Too early, even for coffee. Then she noticed the envelope slipped under her door.

She knew it must be a communiqué from the KGB resident officer. She smiled when she opened it. Clever, the ingenious uses to which they put current American fads. This was a birthday card, risqué and gaudy. It could be examined by anyone, and there was no hint that it held a secret message from her Control. She took the code-guide from the heel of her shoe and broke it down. Long before she finished, the color had drained from her face and her breath was tight.

*Natalya,* she read, *threatened with prosecution because of article in underground magazine. Bad situation. Advise.*

She sat holding the small birthday card with its happy greeting, staring at it, rereading it. Then she shredded it into tiny pieces. Oh God, Natalya, what have you done?

She remembered the night she'd arrived from New York. Was it only Saturday? Sasha had driven her to the apartment after the debriefing; Natalya was there with two friends. They had fallen into each others' arms. Then she'd rushed to the nursery to kiss the warm cheek of Mischa. Hugged him, kissed him again, then returned to Natalya and her friends. Natalya was so lovely. Her small-boned face with its delicate features, her dark blue eyes and black lashes and her sun-bleached hair shoulder-length and tousled, made her appear nearer twelve than twenty-six. More like a big sister to little Mischa than his mother. Who would ever dream she had the strength and intellectual stamina to take on the Soviet Union?

Introducing Anya to her friends that evening, she proudly showed off their new venture. They were finishing the layout of a new magazine for women. It was their second issue. Anya felt chilled. In contrast, they were exhilarated. Their talents, their youth, their dedication to this new project frightened Anya. She tried to caution them, but they laughed and brushed aside her warnings.

They opened a bottle of wine and drank to the success of the new magazine, ignoring Anya's reserve. It was time, they explained to her, time for the Soviet woman to test the power of her influence, time to give the Soviet woman a feeling of collective security and prestige, authority even. The first issue had appeared a month before in a *samizdat* underground edition of several dozen typewritten copies. Translated and reprinted, Natalya had told her proudly, in France! Their goal, she added, was exploring the true state of women's rights in Russia which, she added with raised eyebrows, "is a thoroughly male-dominated society despite the regime's pledge of complete equality!" Oh Natalya! Natalya!

Anya had said no more. Natalya and her friends left for a coffee house to hear a new ballad singer. That was when she found the book of Natalya's poetry. She was ready for bed, when she noticed the drawer to her desk partially open. It wouldn't close, and she pulled it out entirely. There she found the small book stashed behind the drawer. She read the poems with mounting terror. Then she slipped it in the zippered compartment of her purse. She pretended sleep when Natalya returned.

The following morning, she kissed her daughter goodbye. Blinking back tears, she whispered, "Darling, I love you so much. You are all I have! *Do, oh do be careful!*"

"Mama, don't worry. I can take care of myself."

Anya gripped her fist in frustration. *Lovely Natalya, my Donna Quixote,* she thought, *determined to singe her wings. Please God, don't let the fire consume her.*

Anya walked to the chair where she'd thrown her purse the night before, picked it up, and opened it. She took out the small book of poems and carried it to the window. It fell open at a poem Natalya had written when a friend, a lover, was sent to a Norilsk copper refinery in far North Siberia after he'd graduated from the University. He'd wanted Natalya to go with him.

She read it now, whispering it to herself.

*SIBERIA Obiter*
*The Night is there endowed with Beauty*
*The lovely contour of the sky,*
*The flower stars, the Steppes reflect*
*The agony of Death.*

*The voice of Mountain's distant thunder,*
*Blessed Sanctuary, land of sorrow,*
*The unforgiving ice reflects*
*The agony of Earth.*

*The vastness of our dark souled Mother*
*The torment of the troubled sea*
*The echoes of the storm reflect*
*The agony of Man.*

That would be enough to get her a one-way ticket to Siberia, Anya speculated. Tears sprang to her eyes, and she brushed them away angrily. She was a servant of the State, bound by oath to destroy her enemies. What Natalya had done was her own affair. She wouldn't listen. The age-old cry of separate generations! The Agony of Man be damned! She wished she could have seen a copy of the magazine. Had they signed their names? Surely they wouldn't be so foolish. But there's a rising ego in every writer that makes him want to put his name to whatever he writes. Had someone in the Center seen it?

Did she herself have an enemy within the Center? That could be. Very few rise so high that there's not someone on the step below, aching to pull them down. Someone, perhaps, who knew that the quickest way to attack Anya would be through her daughter.

She closed the book of poems. That anguished cry of youth when a love has gone away. Natalya of all people should appreciate the industrial expansion of Siberia. Her young man had probably fallen in love with the vast frozen Steppes, as so many did.

Well, the first thing to do was to get word to Nikolai Ivanovich Pugachev. If anyone could help, he could. The next two hours were spent writing a message and coding it. She was impatient that there was no way to get it to her courier until ten that night.

She replaced the small volume of poetry in the zippered compartment of her purse and brought out an aged, scratched and blackened pipe. Her eyes softened. She rolled it between the palms of her hand. Why had she taken it? She didn't know. It was there when they left, and she'd dropped it in her purse. She didn't know why. Canyon Eliot! She remembered she was supposed to meet him at nine.

The phone rang and she answered it quickly. Surely it was Jannasen. But it was the American, speaking an atrocious German-accented English. "Miss Mason. I thought you would be waiting at the front door. It's well past nine o'clock."

"Oh! Yes—I'm running late. I'll be right down."

"And don't forget your friend, Jannasen."

"Oh. He, well, he has decided not to go with us. Give me ten minutes." And, as she dressed, she was mentally ordering Jannasen to be at the hotel when she returned.

~~~~

It hadn't been an easy morning but at least, Cane speculated waiting for Anya's elevator, the storm had passed and left in its wake the promise of a lovely mother-of-pearl day. So many problems! Not the least of which was wondering if word was out yet about the double killing in his hotel room. Was the Wilhelm Schwartz cover blown? And where could he stash the soccer ball? Poking around in a storage closet off his bedroom, he found an opening to the attic in the ceiling. It was a square trap door that pushed up and, in the light of a match, Cane saw it was full of dust, cobwebs, packing boxes, and an old empty trunk—perfect for his box of clandestine loot.

Dressed in his Bavarian outfit and surveying himself in the full-length mirror, he had to admit that he looked more native than most. He wished he could add the phony moustache. Then he'd really look like the genuine article. Frau Haupmann was delighted with her guest. She clucked over him like a mother hen, pushing more coffee, more eggs, more sausages, more rolls, more compliments. When he finally broke away, he asked to borrow a needle and thread. What color? Any color. Then what started out as a simple request had developed into a major problem. Anything he could do with needle and thread, she could do better. But finally, in the privacy of his bathroom with the shower running full blast, he got the jacket patched together.

Now he had stowed away the soccer ball, the jacket, the money belt, the knife belt and the guns, all in the attic trunk. He folded his suit into the Plaschke box, added the two pair of mutilated shoes, retied the box, and slipped it under the bed. Then, with his Tyrolean hat on the back of his head, and whistling a tune, he went downstairs to tell Frau Haupmann goodbye and that he'd be back that afternoon.

It wasn't easy getting away. Not, that is, until he promised to take her to the Oktoberfest. "You see, Frau Haupmann, I must find my luggage and get my car that broke down. So much to do. So little time." He bowed over her hand.

In fact, looking back on it from the advanced hour of nine forty-five, it had been a hard day. The television, for instance. He couldn't take a chance on Frau Haupmann's hearing that a Wilhelm Schwartz had been killed that night in a small hotel in Schwabing. So, while she was in the kitchen, he lifted the fuse from her television set and dropped it in his pocket.

Now he was waiting for the pseudo-American, Marianne Mason. How was she involved with the dead Swede who had come gunning— no, knifing—for him? The adrenaline flowed a little faster at the thought. What would she have to say about her companion? Did she know he was a Swedish spy? And when, for God's sake, did she know and why did the Swedes get into the picture? Were they working together, or covertly against each other?

When he saw her step out of the elevator, he couldn't have kept the admiration out of his eyes if he tried. She was wearing a copper suede coat with a yellow wool skirt and matching turtleneck sweater. She had on soft brown leather boots that crinkled at the ankles, and a purse hung from her shoulder. She was working her fingers into brown leather gloves as he hurried to meet her.

"Fraülein," he said, bowing slightly from the hips, "I must say you do look charming for so early in the morning!"

She looked him up and down archly, then her smile flashed and her eyes twinkled.

"You sound surprised. But *you* are the one!" Her glance raked him over, from the fluffy white feather in his gray-green hat to his gray Austrian boots. From the embroidered *Loden* jacket, the shirt still wrinkled from its laundering the night before to the *Lederhosen* and knee socks. She shook her head in disbelief.

"My! 'Charming' doesn't really do you justice. Lovely? Well," she made a twisting motion with her hand, then added, "Beautiful? Words defy me!"

"I know," Cane smiled modestly, "don't try. Beauty is its own reward. And lucky the girl who has the eye to appreciate it!" He held the door for her, then said, "Please forgive my English—it's very rusty. I use it so seldom."

She raised her brows and looked at Cane sideways as he hailed a cab.

The day passed quickly. Nymphenburg Palace was impressive, the gardens lovely, the fountains spectacular. They spent an hour disagreeing about the relative assets of the Most Beautiful Women in Munich whose portraits, hanging in two rooms of the castle, had been commissioned by Maximilian. Cane insisted that the golden-haired one wasn't worth the kingdom she had cost the King.

"Then you've never been in love."

"You're an authority?" He glanced at her through the corner of his eyes.

They walked through the carriage house and, afterward, took a taxi to the fair. Wandering through the beer halls and down the midway, eating grilled chicken, drinking beer, nibbling giant pretzels, buying souvenirs, they laughed at everything and nothing. They watched sideshows, rode the Ferris Wheel and, in a small tavern, danced a polka to a three-piece band. When the music stopped, Cane lifted Anya off her feet in a quick whirl, holding her close enough that he felt her heart beat—or maybe it was his own.

Walking back, Anya put her arm through his. As they slowly walked in step, he felt the rise of her breast. Easy, old man. This is no female—this is a spy! At the top of the hill near the taxi stand, he stopped and gave her a long appraising look.

"Fraülein," he said, "I like your eyes. Your mouth is a little off-center where the dimple is. Your eyebrows don't quite match, and your widow's peak is a little crooked. A scientist would tell you that's caused by mixed-up genes. But, all in all, your face isn't bad.

For an American, that is. A little uneven, I would say. But then, it's a mongrel race, you know."

"Well, hoo-boy!" She stepped back with her hands on her hips and a frosty look in her eyes. "You're a little uneven yourself—for a chauvinistic, opinionated, truncated, taliped German!"

"Taliped?"

"Well," she answered, looking him in the eye, "I'm trying to be as insulting as you—and I find it difficult!" She turned and walked rapidly towards the taxi stand.

Cane caught up with her and took her arm. Pulling her around, he raised her hand almost to his lips, his eyes holding hers. "When can I see you again? Tonight?"

"Tomorrow. Same time, same place."

"You never did interview me for my ideas about pushy women."

She waved. "Tomorrow."

"Tomorrow at nine." He closed the door of the taxi and, as it drove away, waved. He stood watching until it turned the corner, then smiled. By damn! She's some woman!

Cane, looking at his watch, whistled. In an hour he was to meet Hastings. He'd almost forgotten. Forgotten Hastings, forgotten the skull. Forgotten that this woman's companion was murdered in his hotel room. No question, he was too old for this sort of thing. But the mysterious Marianne Mason had grabbed his attention and held it. And he still didn't know if she was working for the Russians or Swedes. But one thing he knew for sure, she could raise his temperature a notch or so.

# CHAPTER XIV

*Munich*
*Friday, October 3*

C ane took a taxi to the Gartnerplatz Theater and walked
two blocks to the Cornelius Bridge. To the south, gray low-
lying cumulus clouds dropped a thin fog over the river
and brought a metallic obscurity along its banks, a one-
dimensional free form that muted everything it touched. It drained the
color and shape from the buildings along the Erhardstrasse, from the
bulk of the Reichsbank and Wittelsbacher Bridge to the smoke stacks
beyond. A splendid stream of light touched the trees near the Deutschen
Museum with gold and turned the sluggish Isar into a simmering green,
as vibrant and varied as a slab of malachite.

A carpet of wet leaden leaves dulled the sound of his steps. At the
corner he paused, waiting for the pedestrian light. Seeing Hastings
near the bridge abutment, he had a sudden feeling of unease, of tension
rising from his belly. He tried to shrug it off, but no amount of self-
control could gloss over the events of the night before. He was left
with no legend, no cover, no car, and with an interesting bunch of arms
hardware, and a fortune in currency.

Hastings crossed the bridge diagonally to the steps that led to the
garden. Cane allowed a dozen or so commuters to hurry across the
Erhardstrasse ahead of him, before he turned to follow. At the foot of
the steps he paused, surprised to find a charming half-circle garden
hidden below the stream of traffic. The flower bed, ringed with a stone
parapet, was filled with rose bushes and centered with a pink marble

pedestal supporting a handsome bronze bust of Mad King Ludwig. An irreverent pigeon perched on his head, and a host of his kin were lined along the stone railing.

Most of the roses were gone, but the bushes were still thick with leaves and heavy with hips as large and red as sand plums. The view down the Isar was fuzzy through the growing fog. Immediately below, a skinny-prowed sandbar was arbitrarily appropriated by gulls, migrating ducks, and wading birds. The late afternoon traffic had begun in earnest along the Erhardstrasse, but the noise from the boulevard failed to filter through the shield of trees and bushes along the opposite bank above the garden.

It was a totally peaceful spot Hastings had chosen, and it seemed they were the only two in all Munich familiar with this postage-stamp retreat. Cane joined Hastings on a wooden bench backed against the stone buttress of the bridge, ignoring his raised eyebrows and quizzical expression. Hastings shook his head.

"Damn, Chili, but you're something to see!"

Cane pulled out his pipe, muttering, "Lay off." He lit the pipe with cupped hands, then said, "I guess you've been in touch with Peter."

"Yes, last night. All hell has broken loose at the Ministry." His face was stony. Then, with a thin-lipped smile, he added, "Peter said to tell you that, when I have the dubious pleasure of seeing you, he'll sue for damages, assault and battery when you get back to the States. Also that his jaw, no thanks to you, is *not* broken."

"Christ! I feel bad about that. I clipped him before I even saw him. The last person I expected was Peter."

Hastings grunted. "You surprised him as well. Internal Security, that is the *Geheimpolizei*, has taken over the affair, and right now it's under wraps. I don't know how long they can keep it quiet."

"What did you find out about the picture?"

"Everything. No problem. I should have recognized him right off. Standartenführer Otto Thyssen. His face is almost as familiar as Hitler's. He's either beside him or behind in nearly every photo taken of Der Führer before the war."

"He was that important?"

Hastings nodded. "We don't know much about his early background, except Hitler was very fond of him. Almost like a son. One picture we have shows them together in Hitler's old touring car going to Thyssen's wedding. Hitler was his best man."

"That still doesn't explain the KGB interest in his skull."

"Right. But you can depend on it—if the Russians really want it, then so do the Israelis. The Mossad could have been in on the massacre in your room."

"So, what's your theory?"

"The skull could have something—or everything—to do with the treasure confiscated from the Jews. And, God knows, a hell of a lot was taken. Some of it found after the war was used for reparations, but there are millions in gold and precious stones unaccounted for. Thyssen's name was emblazoned right on top of the whole bit."

"The hell you say! How?"

"The loot was brought from concentration camps all over Europe by the truckloads. It amounted to billions in gold and foreign currencies, diamonds, jewelry, and precious metals. We have official lists from the Nüremberg trials. The Germans are a very methodical people. They kept records of everything. Crates of treasure were taken directly to the Reichsbank in Berlin, where they were placed under a special account of the SS Economic Administration headed by General Oswald Pohl and guess who his first assistant was?"

"Our friend, Otto Thyssen."

Hastings stood up, pushed his hands deep in his pockets.

"You are right. So, as the war progressed from bad to worse for the Germans, top Nazis began leaving the country in droves and they needed money. It was probably Thyssen who expedited its transfer from Germany to Argentina. But that was only a small part of the vast accumulation of Jewish loot. After the war the treasure had disappeared as had Thyssen. There was speculation that Hitler had hidden it near

Berchtesgarten, and that set off one of the greatest treasure hunts in history. For years, caves and lakes in the Alpine Redoubt have been combed with little result. Of course, the salt mines turned up the museum treasures, and divers brought up a fortune in counterfeit English pounds from Lake Toplitz."

Cane nodded. "I remember that. They also brought up the body of a German diver who tried to salvage it. I can understand the interest in Thyssen—but his skull?"

"Hell, I don't know either. But I called Ludwigsburg Center this morning."

"Ludwigsberg Center?"

"I forget you've been out of this for some time. That is the German Government agency set up in the fifties for the investigation of Nazi war crimes. It's not too effective now, but they have more than 100,000 dossiers on German Nationals and Volksdeutsche who were directly involved in murder—the camps, hospital exterminations, Gestapo, the like. And I don't know how many others there are, such as Thyssen, who have a dossier there but, because of the statute of limitations, cannot be arrested. They were cooperative to a point. However, I can go through political channels to collect his file. Perhaps we won't need it. He's presumed dead. I have his SS dossier, Nazi party number, dates of his officer's commission, and his promotions, all recommended by Hitler. I also have some information on his wife.

"They've kept tabs on her and their two sons. She left Berlin toward the end of the war and went to a small Bavarian town near the Austrian border called Alpendorf, and she still lives there. When Thyssen disappeared after the war, she got a divorce and later married a man named Karl Müller. They have a son. Müller has a souvenir shop in Alpendorf, sells wood carvings, postcards, and trinkets. The boys are Alpine guides and are reputed to be the best in the area for hunting, fishing, and skiing. The middle son was killed in a hunting accident two years ago. The oldest is Stefan, the younger Hans. Stefan is married."

"Nothing about how Thyssen happened to be in an Oklahoma POW camp under another name?"

"No, he just seemed to have disappeared after the war. His wife certainly didn't know where he was."

"He switched identities in Italy, so what was he doing there?"

"We have no idea. He spoke Italian and was a sort of personal emissary from Hitler to Mussolini at his Lake Garda headquarters. That's all I have for now."

~~~~

Fritz Kruppel had spent this day much as any other, delivering his sausages, joking with customers, taking orders for the following week. But when he passed a certain tavern, he parked his truck and went in. He ordered a beer and asked for a match. The waiter handed him a folded book of matches. He lit the cigarette, dropped the matches in his pocket, finished his beer, commented briefly on the weather with another customer, and returned to his truck.

He read the message written inside the folder—10/3/4, and knew exactly what it meant—an emergency. He must meet Jasmine at the bench by the river at four o'clock. He'd have to hurry. Half an hour later, leaving his truck parked on a side street, he met Magen at the bench under the Linden trees.

The news the Israeli agent had was unreal. Fritz shook his head. Who was the man he'd killed in the American's hotel room?

"We won't know until they can check fingerprints. The police think it is Schwartz, but they'll know differently tomorrow. In the meantime, we've got Schwartz located at 9 Birkenstrasse."

"How did you find him?"

"Pure luck. Out of curiosity, we sent an agent to question von Stober's widow. We knew that was Eliot's only lead. It had to be the first place he'd go. Sure enough, he'd been there. Our man pretended to be a former member of von Stober's Para Division and invited her to a reunion they were going to have. She was excited and told him all about Schwartz's being here, and—get this—that he was staying with her. That he had been in the Division, too, and should be invited."

"Luck is right."

"Our man knew Schwartz was dead, and he argued with her, but not for long. She described him perfectly, and told about his coming in late last night with no room, no car."

*"Gott im Himmel!"*

"Now, to business. You go pay her a visit. She's Frau Haupmann. Tell her Schwartz sent you for his things. You were old buddies, and you're going to meet him. Offer to pay for the room—insist, as a matter of fact. I'm sure he asked to rent the room."

"Where is he now?"

"With Hastings, his friend at the Consulate, at the Cornelius Bridge. We'll keep our eye on him. Meet me at the apartment when you've got his luggage. I'll go there now and wait."

~~~~

Cane's pipe was clamped between his teeth as he stared across the rose bushes. The sun had given up and dropped behind a cloud bank. The fog was heavier over the river. A beacon revolved mistily atop the smokestack past the Wittelsbacher Bridge. That bastard Thyssen! What secret did the bloody skull hold? He took a final pull from the pipe, emptied it against the bench, and dropped it in his pocket. "What do you think we should do?"

Hastings stood up, walked to the parapet, and leaned against it. The fog was thicker. The birds had deserted the sandbank for the night shade protection of the trees and shrubbery. He turned, walked back to the bench, and sat down.

"It's a goddamn new ball game," he said. "A whole new ball game, a whole new set of rules, and we've a war criminal on the mound." He dropped his cigarette on the gravel path and ground it out viciously.

"In the mound, I should say. Minus his skull," Cane commented dryly.

Hastings rubbed his chin thoughtfully.

"By God," he said, "toss in a hook and you never know what you're going to catch. But Otto Thyssen—wow! So we go to work. A little hunting trip down in the mountains might do you some good. A nice vacation—exercise, fresh air."

"Near Alpendorf." Cane nodded with a faint smile. "And use the Müller boys for guides?"

"My thought exactly. You can get acquainted with the Müllers, maybe even let them know the bastard is sure enough dead. It would be a relief, I think, to everyone concerned. Certainly to his wife."

"I'll carry the good news. Now, back to last night. Who found the bodies in Room 35?"

"The maid. And all pandemonium broke loose. They can't figure out where the shoes and gun went. Where's the skull?"

"Safe. It's in a trunk in Frau Haupmann's attic. Also the jacket, guns, money belt, and knife. I guess Peter told you we relieved them of a heavy set of artillery and currency. Also my double's passport. I'll check it all with you as soon as possible."

Hastings nodded and rubbed his chin.

"Peter was worried about you, until we let him know you were safe at Frau von Stober's. That is, Frau Haupmann."

Cane stiffened. "You had me covered?"

"Oh, yes." The corner of his mouth twitched in a very small smile, and he gave Cane a sidelong glance. "You know, you're a clever bastard." He leaned back against the stone buttress and, from behind his hooded eyes, said with a sardonic grin, "I must say, I never dreamed you'd go whole root hog and die."

Cane raised his eyebrows and nodded. "I thought I looked pretty good, too. But with the Schwartz cover blown, I've got to fall back on Josef Cranach or Carl Becker. Somehow I can't imagine Becker in *Lederhosen*."

Hastings shrugged.

"We'll see. However, we'll change your appearance before you get to Alpendorf. The police think Schwartz killed the KGB agent, and he killed Schwartz. Tit for tat, so to speak."

Cane's expression changed. "What do you mean, KGB? I thought he was Swedish."

"Didn't you know? You were with him yesterday." Hastings stood up, shoved his hands deep in his pockets, and leaned against the parapet.

Cane stared at him blankly, then joined him at the stone railing. "What the hell do you mean?"

"He was a top KGB agent, code name Sable, stationed in Stockholm. We thought you knew. Peter said you did. His legend is a fashion photographer, and his name and rank are Lieutenant Niels Jannasen. He's an East German, but we don't know his real name."

The muscles in Cane's jaw tensed. "And the woman? I suppose she's KGB, too?"

"We supposed you knew." Hastings appraised him carefully. "They tell me you were on the way to getting pretty well acquainted this morning."

Cane spun around angrily to face Hastings. "What the hell! Have you had a tail on me all the goddamn time?"

Hastings faced him coolly and nodded. "We have. And, whether you like it or not, we'll continue to keep you under surveillance as long as you have the skull in your possession."

Cane didn't answer. He studied the distant horizon with narrowed eyes, then took a deep breath and returned to sit on the bench.

"I understand," he said in a low voice. "Go on."

"Well, you should know that this woman you were so cozy with is a senior agent with the First Directorate, which is responsible for gathering foreign intelligence for the KGB. She has been, among other things, a Cultural Attaché at the embassy in Washington and a member of their UN staff. She's traveled widely across the U.S. with various touring groups, and lived in Paris where she worked for Aeroflot. Her code name is Regina. She's a smart cookie. Don't underestimate her for a second."

"I knew there was a connection, but couldn't put my finger on it. The code book in Swedish threw me off. I couldn't decide if they were working together or against each other. But I did know she was no American journalist. She introduced me to Jannasen as just that—Niels Jannasen, Swedish photographer. When I saw him in my room last night, I recognized him immediately."

"How did you meet them?"

"My doing. I saw her first in the cemetery at Fort Reno. Yesterday I could hardly believe it when I saw her at the Marienplatz. It was simply too much of a coincidence. I introduced myself as Schwartz, and we carried on from there. I made a date to pick them both up at nine this morning to go to the Oktoberfest. Naturally he didn't show, but the lovely agent and I had a super time." He sighed. "But I didn't learn anything, and neither did she. She knew I was a phony German, and I knew she was a phony American."

Hastings laughed. "Well, she's a pro from way, way back. And you'd better believe she was startled to hear from you. It's conceivable that Jannasen was supposed to have come back with the skull, and you were supposed to be dead. She didn't seem worried about Jannasen's disappearance?"

"No. If she had a care in the world, she hid it very well."

"The most important thing now is to get you out of Munich as soon as possible. The car's down the street. Let's go."

As they climbed into the tan Volkswagen, Cane said, "I made a date for tomorrow morning. Should I contact her again?"

"No. Hell no! Let her wonder. She'll have heard by now that you killed her partner." Hastings put the car in gear, pulled away from the curb, gave Cane a quick glance, and said, "A little more action than you expected, huh?"

"To agree is the understatement of all time. Who was the other guy—my double?"

"They've taken fingerprints. We'll know tomorrow. After we get your stuff, we'll go to our place and color you up a bit."

"Fine." Cane nodded, then added, "Now, tell me everything about the woman. You know she speaks really good regular American English...."

"She would. Her name is Anya Vasilievna Petrovna. She's been an agent for Moscow Center for at least fifteen years, possibly more. She spent ten years as a child in America. Her father was an agricultural expert who defected in 1955. Anya was seventeen then. We don't know what happened or why. He called the State Department one morning, and they took charge."

Cane whistled through his teeth. Then he asked, "Did she ever try to contact him?"

"No. He died shortly after his defection."

"How did that happen?"

"It was an accident. He fell down a wheat elevator shaft near Chicago."

"Hmm. Were the Russians responsible?"

"It looked like an accident. That's what it was called."

"Why would she do that—spy against the U.S.? Because of her father, you think?"

"God knows. Oh hell," he said, looking into the rear view mirror. "We've got a tail." He straightened, then settled back, relaxed. "It doesn't make any difference now. We'll lose them after we get your stuff."

Their shadow stayed with them until Hastings turned into Birkenstrasse, then passed on. But both knew he would be watching where they went, and when they left. He stopped the car at number 9, and Cane said, "Come in with me. You can keep the friendly Frau busy while I climb up in her attic."

Frau Haupmann opened the door in unconcealed surprise.

"Why, Herr Schwartz! Your friend said you wouldn't be back. He even insisted on paying for the room...."

Cane pushed by her. "What do you mean, 'friend'?"

"The one, the large man, you sent to get your things."

"Oh, God! You don't mean—you didn't—" He tore past her, and took the steps two at a time. She looked helplessly at Hastings.

"I didn't want to take the money. I told him Herr Schwartz was my guest...."

Cane heard her voice fade as he flung open the door and looked under the bed. The box was gone. Holding his breath, he hoisted himself from a chair into the attic, and then released a long sigh of relief. The trunk hadn't been disturbed. Everything was there.

Minutes later, the jacket over his arm hiding the belts and guns, swinging the soccer ball in its net bag, Cane ambled casually down the stairs. When he saw Frau Haupmann, he broke into a broad smile.

"Dear, dear friend, have you a box or sack to drop this jacket in? I don't know why that stupid fellow didn't get everything while he was here. I'll meet him shortly, but it's a nuisance carrying this."

"Ja, ja! Of course." She brought a plastic bag large enough to hold everything, at the same time talking about the Division Reunion. She was so glad he'd be there, too. And all his other friends. Cane smiled and nodded as she talked, then kissed her on both cheeks and on her hand before they got away.

"You don't think you overdid it?" Hastings asked with a certain irony.

"No," he grinned. "You can't overdo a good thing! I wonder what she was talking about—a Division Reunion?" He dropped the bag on the back seat, then climbed in beside Hastings. "You know, that bastard took the only clothes I have. And of course, the two pair of ripped-up shoes. That will give him something to think about. Who do you suppose it was?"

"I'd guess the Mossad. We'll come back tomorrow and get his description." He pulled out into the street and, shortly after he turned off Birkenstrasse, headlights appeared in the rear view mirror. "Well, here's our friend. Now listen. We'll give him a run for his money, then we'll hit the Marienplatz—there's always a crowd there. I'll leave the car in a 'no parking' zone. Take any subway, all the evasive action you know, but end up at 17 Kaulbachstrasse. Make sure you're not followed there. That's at University Station—U-Bahn Universitat at the English Gardens. Got that?"

"Right."

"And don't lose the soccer ball."

"Don't worry. I just wish I was wearing something else."

"There are enough Bavarians around you won't be noticed. But lose that bastard behind us."

Hastings slipped in and out of traffic. Once he turned quickly into an available parking space, and the car following had to pass with the traffic. They saw two men, both in dark clothes. The car was a black Opel.

~~~~

"Not much to identify them except the license number, and it's probably fake. We'll check it out." In minutes, their tail was on them again. Hastings whipped into and out of narrow streets, and finally lost them going the wrong way in a one-way alley. They slipped into the Marienplatz, left the car, and took separate subway entrances.

Cane got on and off the Olympic Stadium train until he was satisfied there was no one following, then went to University Station and soon found 17 Kaulbachstrasse. Hastings opened the door before he could ring the bell, then led him up steep uncarpeted stairs to a third floor landing, and unlocked a heavy oak door. The room was strictly business. It certainly wasn't furnished for comfort. A chrome-framed mirror hung over a chipped lavatory. Army cots were at right angles, with a square table in the corner that held oversized ashtrays and a metal goose-necked lamp. Mottled worn-out linoleum covered the floor. Two chipped blue-painted chests stood at the foot of each bed. A wardrobe with peeling paint and a full-length mirror was against the wall. The furnishings spoke strictly of utility décor. Wrought iron grills were permanently affixed outside the windows.

"To keep the 'ins' in and the 'outs' out?"

"Both. We use the whole building. It's as electronically secure as any in Germany."

Cane looked around, then nodded. "Well, when you need it, it's good to have."

"Like now," Hastings answered.

Two hours later a young man, an expert in his field, had transformed Cane. He'd been outfitted with a well-worn brown tweed suit, soft wool hat, a couple of turtleneck sweaters, chamois hunting pants and jacket, and ammunition vest. He had a good well-scarred portable typewriter, hair the color of bleached driftwood with eyebrows to match, and a rifle.

"World War Two—what?" he asked Hastings, balancing the nine-pound rifle with a telescopic sight in the palm of his right hand.

"A Gewehr 43. It was used almost exclusively on the Eastern front. Part of your cover. You fought in Hitler's Barbarossa campaign, ended up in Vienna, your home. You left the gun with a sister to rush north and surrender to Patton's army." He smiled. "You weren't the only one."

Cane shifted the rifle to his shoulder. "I know," he said. "They had good reason." He swung it toward the window and sighted down the barrel. "Excellent, even at night. Is that infrared?"

"Right. We put that on. It's a six-power, wide-lens scope."

Cane stood at the window sighting through the grill past the courtyard. "Bloody hell! It's like being there. I hope she shoots as good as she sights."

"You can depend on it." He pulled a couple of envelopes from an inside pocket. "Here is all the information we have on the Müllers. It's not much." He handed them to Cane and added, "This is your hunting license and non-resident permit. They'll be expecting you at the hotel.

*The English Sportsman* magazine has made reservations for you and asked for the best guides available, which means the Müller boys. They explained you were doing a story for them and that you'd be arriving tomorrow from Vienna." He paused, jingling some coins in his pocket, then continued. "Your car is a vintage Mercedes, Austrian tags. Nothing to brag about so far as looks go, it has all the dents and bumps and scratches that several previous owners put on, but it has a modified super-turbo engine that will get you out of anywhere fast. There is also a secret compartment under the front seat activated by a small bolt you pull to the front that has the extra passport you brought. Carl Becker, American tourist in the chicken export business, I don't know how you'll ever use that. There are the car papers, and a new license plate if you should need it. A shortwave radio is in the hub of the spare; in case you need to leave Alpendorf in a hurry, let us know. But now you're Josef Cranach, Austrian freelance writer doing an article on hunting in the Bavarian Alps for the English magazine. Do you have it all? Let's go over it again."

By the time he left, Cane knew his cover as intimately as he knew himself. He looked different; he felt different; he *was* different. There must be nothing, Hastings had said, that might cause the Müller boys to associate him with the American Canyon Eliot.

"Someone wanted to impersonate you. Whoever hired the double knows he's washed up and the money in the jacket along with him. So they are going to be gunning for Cane Eliot, alias Schwartz. No slip-ups, friend."

"Roger," Cane said with a confidence he didn't feel. He swung the rifle to his shoulder and wheeled in a simulated ambush.

"The Müller boys," Hastings added, "from what we've found out, are the real thing. Fine guides, really know the country. You should get your deer and everything else you need. Buddy-buddy up to them, but not too fast. Take your time. These people are naturally suspicious of strangers, but their business is hunting. When they know you have news of Thyssen, they—well, you'll have to play that by ear. As a journalist, you would have had the opportunity to learn about Thyssen—then, oh hell, they might already know about it. Anyway, good hunting! And, if you see Peter, don't be surprised."

"Peter?"

"He needs some recreation and relaxation after his little accident," Hastings said. "He's interested in bird hunting. They have the best rock partridges in the country. He is also checking out a rumor that bits of the Jewish treasure are beginning to surface through fences. Interpol just alerted Scotland Yard."

"And the connection could be the Müller shop?"

"It could be simply an educated guess, but it bears looking in to."

The agent rose and they shook hands.

"Your car will be parked in front. Here are the keys. Chili, good luck." He picked up the sack with the dead man's coat, then swung the soccer ball in its net bag over his shoulder. "You'll be glad to get rid of this as well as the other stuff."

"Yes, but I'd like to keep the .357 Magnum. Insurance, so to speak. You know that will shoot through a car."

"Well, see that it doesn't! All we need is an international incident over this and we'll all be put out to pasture, if we're not ground into hamburger first. Goodbye, Chili. Luck!" They shook hands again. Cane waved him down the stairs, heard his steps echoing in the stairwell.

Undressing slowly, he poured half a glass of whisky, punched the pillow at the head of the bed and, half sitting, half lying, stretched out balancing his drink on his belly. A hell of a day! A KGB spy. Good God!

He drained the glass, swung his legs to the floor, and picked up the rifle. He played with it, loading and unloading. He swung it to his shoulder in a quick motion following an imaginary target. He went through the almost-forgotten manual of arms. By the time he went to bed, he was as familiar with the German rifle as if he'd used it himself on the Eastern Front.

# CHAPTER XV

The room closed in on Anya. No one in the hotel had seen Jannasen. She'd questioned the doorman and the desk clerk and the maid. She'd checked his room, and the bed hadn't been slept in. She ruffled her hair angrily. How dare he do this to her! It would be the last job he'd have with the Center.

How could she have forgotten him while she was at the Oktoberfest? Of course it was because she knew he would be waiting when she returned. She folded her arms and crossed to the window. It had been fun, this day at the Fair. When was the last time she had fun for its own sake? Life is real and life is earnest, some American poet said whom she'd memorized at Miss Katherine's Academy, but neither he nor anyone knew the truth of it like a Russian. She had even pushed Natalya to the back of her mind.

Anya threw her coat over her shoulders, picked up her bag, went downstairs to walk around the block. The air was crisp and cool. The afternoon sun wavered weakly through distant thunderheads. But the turmoil in her mind was real. Jannasen was a proper worry. And certainly Natalya and her friends. Then there was Eliot—cover name Wilhelm Schwartz. She knew who and what he was. They were after the same thing. She had the secret and he had the skull. Nothing, absolutely nothing must stand in the way of her original and final objective. She had to have the skull. And today she hadn't even tried.

She had been too busy having fun. *Fun!* Such a silly word. She felt like a traitor. Why, at least, hadn't she made an effort to find out where he was staying?

There was an answer to that, she rationalized. A Freudian psychoanalyst would say it was because she hadn't wanted to know. When Jannasen left her at the hotel, she had a strong feeling that he was going after the American and she had been afraid for him. Jannasen was a particularly vicious kind of hit man. A killer who loved the bloody gore of knives. So when Eliot called she'd been relieved. But that didn't answer the pressing question *where had Jannasen gone and where is he now?*

She took a deep breath, frowned, and pulled her coat close. The problem of Natalya—what to do? Tonight she'd get word to Major General Pugachev. He could help more than anyone. Who had warned her? She rubbed her shoulder; the tension was almost unbearable, and she had accomplished nothing with Eliot.

"Tomorrow," she said, "tomorrow I'll find where Eliot is staying. There'll be time enough then to get the skull."

Her mind slipped back to Jannasen. It's unheard of for an agent on the job to disappear for twenty-four hours. Karuski, of course, would know. She glanced at her watch, decided it was time to return to the hotel. Crossing the lobby to the bar, she picked a booth that faced the door, ordered a glass of Riesling, and sat back to wait for Colonel Karuski.

Sipping her wine, Anya watched the candles flicker as waitresses in bright-colored *dirndls* swished by. She couldn't channel her thoughts. They leap-frogged from Jannasen to Eliot to the skull to Natalya All links in the same chain. She gave a sigh of relief when Karuski came in. She watched as he stopped at the bar and ordered a vodka. He drained the shot glass in a swallow, then ordered another. She caught his eye, and he joined her. Immediately she realized something was wrong.

His face was grim; dark circles cushioned his eyes. He leaned across the table.

"Anya," he whispered, "Sable is dead. I just heard."

She caught her breath, then answered slowly.

"I think I knew when he didn't return last night. What happened?"

"It was in the American's hotel room. The CIA agent shot him and Sable killed Eliot. They killed each other—"

"Oh, no!" Anya interrupted, shaking her head. "That's impossible!"

Karuski placed his hands over Anya's. "It's true. They eliminated each other. Unbelievable!"

Anya's face was a mask. Shaking her head, she insisted, "No, Comrade Colonel. That's not right—"

"Regina, will you hear me out?" The Russian stopped her impatiently.

She watched in silence as he pulled out a package of Stuyvesant Filters, methodically selected one, and lighted it from the candle on the table. A waitress stopped, but he waved her away.

"I heard the whole story from one of our men at the police headquarters." He held up his hand as Anya tried to interrupt. "No. Let me finish. They killed each other. It's very strange. Sable's knife is gone, and also his money belt. No weapons were found and their shoes were missing. Someone was in the room after the killings. It was ransacked, and the door bolted from the inside."

He was watching Anya closely and stopped talking to ask, "Anya, what's wrong? Are you all right?"

She nodded. She felt icy. Her fingers were clenched in her lap. Then the words tumbled out and panic frayed the edge of her voice. She struggled to keep it calm.

"I know you're wrong about one thing, Sergei Stepanovich, because I was with the American from ten-thirty this morning until the middle of the afternoon. I left him at the Theresienweise barely an hour ago." The silence between them was tense—electric.

Karuski stared at her. Finally, in a dry voice he said, "Regina, that's impossible. The dead man has been identified as Wilhelm Schwartz whom we know is Canyon Eliot, CIA."

Her voice was knotted an octave lower in her throat.

"Then he was meant to be his replacement by someone who knows about the skull. Believe me, Comrade Colonel, I know Canyon Eliot and he knows me."

Karuski filled his lungs and released a long stream of smoke that drifted towards the door. He finished his vodka in a gulp, and a slow smile worked its way across his features. Then he broke into a loud and booming laugh.

"That puts the whole picture in a different frame!" He was in a great good humor when he called the waitress for a bottle of wine. Then he lifted his glass. "To our success." He ran his tongue across his lips, savoring the taste, and failed to notice the tense expression on Anya's face. He had forgotten Jannasen. All that mattered was the American, and Anya was the bait. His eyes were bright when he looked at her. "Does he know you're an agent?" he asked.

"I would imagine so." She felt drained. Her voice faded. "He is a smart man, Comrade." Then she added softly, "No one knows better than I."

Karuski was immediately bouncing with energy. "Everyone thinks the body is Schwartz," he said. "The Germans are quite upset. They are keeping a tight lid on it for as long as they can. The way I see it, Eliot or Schwartz killed Sable, then killed his double who was sent to erase him and take over. You can't help but admire efficiency like that." He paused, took a sip of wine, and wiped his mouth. "When will you meet him again?"

"Tomorrow. In the morning at nine." Her voice was hardly more than a whisper. She moved her glass in nervous concentric circles on the table. "I'm sure he knew that I didn't know about Jannasen. Eliot asked where he was."

"What did you tell him?"

"Just that he'd decided not to go." Her voice was without expression. Chill bumps pricked her back and arms. "I didn't find out where he was staying—where he has the skull." She shivered involuntarily and rubbed her arms. It was hard to keep her voice steady. "You say he took Sable's shoes? That means he has the code and the syringe."

"That's right. But use the code tonight. I'll be in touch with Center through the Resident. Don't worry, we have them running. He stayed somewhere last night. Probably at a CIA burrow. And you're to meet him tomorrow?"

"Yes, at nine."

"Well, if he shows up, we'll be waiting. But I have a feeling that this is one time you will be—how do they say in English—stand up?"

"Stood up. You think so?" Her voice was strong and bitter, her eyes dark and cold.

"He'd be stupid to see you tomorrow. And I don't think for one minute he's that."

"No, Comrade Colonel, he's not that."

The silence grew between them.

"I have a thought, Anya, that might help," Karuski said. "It's just possible he'll go see Thyssen's wife. That would be the logical thing to do—hoping that she knows something. And you know," he looked up smiling, "she just might."

"Where does she live?"

"In a small town about sixty miles east of here. Alpendorf. She's married to a fellow named Müller who owns a souvenir shop."

"If it's all right with Center, I'd like to go there. Perhaps I can make friends with Frau Müller." She drained her glass and sighed. "We can't let the American get away with this."

"I agree. He seems to have won the first round. But we're closer to having possession of the skull than we were."

~~~~

Magen Ben-Yanait, in his railroad worker's outfit and carrying a lunch pail, hoisted himself into Fritz Kruppel's truck as the Peiss butcher serviced the café near the freight yards. He didn't have long to wait until Kruppel returned.

With no preliminary greeting, the Israeli said, "The man you killed has been identified. He's Helmut Acton, a hit man for the Spider organization, just recently arrived from Argentina. Probably for this job."

Kruppel put the truck in gear and drove slowly toward the town center.

"Well, well," he said, "so now we hear from the *Spinne*. The Spider. A bloody efficient outfit. Damn them all to hell. The whole bunch—all organized for one reason—to bring the Fourth Reich back to power."

Magen nodded.

"To help dyed-in-the-wool Nazis make a comeback. It'll never die out. And of them all, only the Spider has substantial funds and resources to be an underground political power."

"God help us! Where does it come from?"

"One source, Fritz. They have access to Otto Thyssen's stolen funds."

"How did the *Spinne* get on to Eliot so quickly?"

"No telling. Having a German officer's skull dug up in Oklahoma, then carried on Associated Press all over the world would interest them considerably."

"You think they know the secret of the skull?" Kruppel looked at Magen

"Absolutely. And because they know it, they want it destroyed. That will take the KGB, the CIA, and us off their backs. Acton was supposed to have gotten rid of Eliot and taken his place to dispose of the skull. Then the Moscow Center man interrupted and upset his plans, and you finished him. The Spider, of course, thinks Eliot did it all and, while that would make them have a healthy respect for him, they are determined to wipe him out." Ben-Yanait stubbed out his cigarette and laughed. "This is a hell of a business we're in."

"Where is Eliot now?"

"I should think on his way to Alpendorf to find out if the good widow of Thyssen will let drop a clue or two."

"And her husband?"

"Ah, Müller the tradesman. There is the key. I'm convinced the control center of The Spider is there and Müller is a part of it. Jewels as well as cash could be washed cleanly enough through his store."

"Which means Thyssen told his wife about Hitler's little treasure cache, and she's passed it on."

"Right."

"Well, the Spider is a good name. Its web reaches around the world."

"At least to Argentina and back. I'm afraid for Eliot. It's a dicey business. He'll go into Alpendorf in some kind of silly disguise, probably as a journalist, and be a sitting duck for the Spider."

"Come into my parlor, said the spider—" The Blocker braked for a sharp turn.

"Yes. So I'm going to Alpendorf and do a Boy Scout turn. I'm going to save a CIA agent from the enemy. I want you to notify Tel Aviv where I am and what I'm doing. From there, I'm going to Rimini, Italy."

"Rimini?" The Blocker looked at Magen in surprise.

"Sometime, sooner or later, the Americans will wake up to the fact that the secret of the skull is in its teeth. That's when they'll take the skull to Rimini, where Thyssen was last seen, and start checking with dentists. And that's when I get the skull."

"I'll call Tel Aviv in about an hour."

"Good. Tell Control that from Alpendorf I'll go directly to Rimini. I'll be in touch." He motioned to a bus stop. "You can let me out here; I'll take a bus to my car."

"Good luck, Jasmine."

"I think we need some. The fickle lady has been thumbing her nose at us lately. *Shalom*, Isaac. *Shalom a le khem*."

Kruppel slid the truck into gear and drove off slowly. There goes a *mensch*. For a short time, they'd been comrades-in-arms. He didn't know his name, only a code word, Jasmine. But with the affection he had said *Shalom, Isaac*, it was clear he didn't expect to see him again. Kruppel touched his hand to his temple in a quick salute and said softly under his breath, *"Mazel-tov*, Jasmine."

# CHAPTER XVI

*Alpendorf, Austria*
*Sunday, October 5*

T he morning, already half-spent before Cane left Munich, was fog-filled and cheerless, saturated with ragged twisting fingers of gray chiffon mist. He had deliberately postponed his departure. It wouldn't do to drive into Alpendorf too early. Had he come from Salzburg, the logical stop from Vienna, it would be a three-hour drive against an hour or so from Munich. Cane packed his gear on the back seat, settled behind the wheel, felt for the bolt that opened the secret compartment with additional passports. He nodded grimly. The implication of the extra passport wasn't encouraging.

Moisture condensed and slid into snaky rivulets down the windows. Methodically the wipers cleared two fans across the windshield while Cane studied the map. The route fixed in his mind, he refolded it and stuck it behind the sun visor.

Following Kalbachstrasse to Vetinerianstrasse, then turning left on Ludwig-Leopold, he cut through the center of town, passing within a block of the Theresienwiese. He remembered the Oktoberfest. The beautiful Soviet spy. Was she waiting still? Then he headed southwest on the autobahn. His foot was heavy on the accelerator and the needle curved around the dial. No question about the power of this car. He came to the lake, Starnbergersee, then cut off on Highway Two. With little traffic, he flew past Weilheim Oberbayer and crossed the highway to Oberammergau.

In the open country, the fog began to burn off. The sun, lazy at first and anemic, rose faster until the razor-edged hills beyond sharpened into a rich and vivid purple. Then he was in their midst. The hills were bright with gemstone colors—garnet and agate, coral and topaz and jasper bonded into a dark green bevel of fir and pine. Cane saw none of this. One sobering thought controlled his mind: KGB women were as ruthless as their men. Like bird dogs, they had a single objective drilled into them with their training, and nothing—nothing would deter them.

Would he see her again? Ah, yes. No doubt about that. If Moscow Center had ordered her to get the skull, he'd see her again.

As the road narrowed and twisted higher, he eased up on the speed, watching for the sign to turn off into the dragon's teeth of the Alps. In something over an hour and a half since he left the Schwabing, Cane saw the sign—Alpendorf, 15 km.

He turned right on a loose shale road and a quick climb into the mountains began. The road twisted back and forth, leaving hairpin turns like a ribbon of Zs below. There was no way, Cane decided, that one could stumble into Alpendorf accidentally. Occasionally he passed logging trails turning into hillside scars where timber was being harvested.

The road dropped to a series of small meadows. The stream, which had been so turbulent and frothing as he ascended, now spread into a smooth stretch of mill pond with a small community of farm houses and brown Alpine cattle grazing along its banks on the last of the summer grass. Soon they'd be driven down the mountain to their winter quarters wreathed with flowers and bells for the annual fall ritual.

He passed an old monastery with crumbling walls built into the side of a craggy bluff, then a thirteenth-century castle that had guarded the valley since knighthood flowered and the small fiefdom of Alpendorf had flourished in its shadow. Now the medieval town stretched ahead in the lee of a broad precipice that had eroded into the frozen folds of a sculpted waterfall. Above, twisting along the mountain heights, were ski trails and the skeletal braces of lifts that rimmed them.

Soft plumes of smoke rose from neatly fenced, smoothly plastered and extravagantly decorated houses tiered in carefully layered terraces above the Platz. A small white church, its bell tower capped with a black onion-shaped peak, stood apart on the rising shoulder of a hillock. The village, cupped in the folds of the foothills, brooded peacefully, framed in yellow birches and red sumac. The steep gabled three-storied hotel, with a balcony above the ground floor, stood on one side of the Platz.

A gilded falcon hung from an iron bracket above carved swinging doors and fanciful yellow-painted scallops decorated the eaves.

Cane pulled up to the front walk of the Falconhof in a whisking flurry of gravel, killed the motor, and rolled down the window. The Platz, encircled by scattered rundown shops, the hotel, and the Rathaus, was paved with cobblestones. Its hub, a fountain of graduated basins, hosted a cloud of mottled-colored pigeons. Several iron benches were scattered haphazardly among a few cars, a motorcycle, and a pickup. Gaudy tattered remnants of last year's circus posters hung in the window of a vacant store. There was little activity.

The Rathaus, gabled with corbiesteps like every other city hall in Germany, was to the right of the hotel. Its windows were diamond-paned and braced with boxes of cascading flowers. Its tower clock chimed the hour eleven with a dull low-pitched sound that had no echo.

He saw the sign between a woodcarver's and a sporting goods shop—*Müller's Mountain Souvenirs.* From the apartment window above, a down duvet lay across the sill. A revolving clock hung over the door and, lettered on the plate glass windows in peeling gold leaf, were the words *Watches, Cameras, Alpine Souvenirs, Mineral Stones.*

Stepping out of the car, he pulled down the front seat and gathered his gear. Pushing his hat to the back of his head, he looked up at the cramped half-timbered hotel. To the left, a flagstone terrace hemmed with flower box balustrades held wooden tables with attached benches. On the opposite side, a winter's supply of chopped logs was stacked in neat honeycombs. A tiger-striped cat with an extraordinary tail and a predatory crouch, stalked unseen prey in the logs. He pushed his paw tentatively into a crack, his tail twitching nervously. One iridescent-green pigeon railed stridently, strutting on the roof, his feathers ruffling in the wind.

Cane hoisted the portable typewriter under his arm, picked up his bag, gun case and satchel, and walked up the petunia-bordered path to the shaded veranda. He shoved open the heavy door with his shoulder, then waited for his eyes to adjust to the semi-dark lobby. Placing the gun and typewriter carefully beside his suitcase near the door, he swept the room with a quick glance.

From the back came the heavy sweet smell of beer. Trophy heads of boar and chamois and moufflon hung on rough paneled walls. Black hand-hewn beams supported a ceiling dark with age. Near the cubicle called *Reception* was a blue meter-square tile stove, and snuggled hard against its base an old white and liver-spotted German Shorthair hunting dog slept and wheezed in measured breaths.

The soot-stained fireplace, large enough to roast an ox, took up a good part of the west wall. A half burned tree trunk smoldered among dying embers. In the back, a small café boasted an elegant bar in an arched alcove with cushioned stools and a brass rail. Booths lined one side, on the other stood a mammoth sideboard loaded with dozens of heavy beer steins. In the center were a few round, rough-hewn tables with Formica tops and peg-legged chairs.

Around one of the tables, a half-dozen men were drinking coffee when Cane entered. Their conversation stopped and they watched as he crossed to the desk, spun the register around to sign it. They watched, to a man, as he glanced up at the trophy head of a Royal Stag with seven-point racks that dominated the office. They observed him shaking his head in admiration as his eyes kept returning to it.

A short broad-shouldered paunchy man with a full beard, balding head, and a professional smile separated himself from the group at the table and walked to the desk. He picked up a thin-rimmed pair of glasses, peeped over the bifocal curve, and said, *"Guten Morgen,* Herr

Cranach. We were expecting you. I am Josef Krantz, your host." His voice was as plump and comfortable as his appearance.

"*Guten Tag,* Herr Krantz. I'm glad to meet you. You know why I'm here." He motioned to the trophy behind the desk. "I'll be perfectly happy to take home such a rack and to write a story that will blow the minds of my readers."

The proprietor laughed. "You do not think, my friend, to capture such a specimen?"

"If I have the Müller boys to guide me—"

"But it is near the end of the season. However, as you say, with the Müller boys nothing is impossible. They are superior guides. Stefan is over there." He raised his arm and called, "I say, Müller, will you come here?"

Cane turned to see the tall guide shove back his chair with a grating rasp. He looked to be in his late thirties. As he came toward Cane, he pushed a shock of thick blonde hair from his forehead. A great pack of muscles bulged through his red cotton shirt, and pale blue eyes looked out from under a bleached fringe of thick brows. He was as tall as Cane, more powerfully built.

"This is Herr Cranach, Stefan, from Vienna. The one I told you about who writes for the *English Sportsman Magazine.* He needs a guide to stalk the *Rothirsche.* I told him you were the best."

"Ja. Herr Cranach, I want to say that Josef Krantz has never been known to lie." His smile failed to reach his eyes, but his handclasp was strong. "Come and have some coffee, or beer if you wish, and we'll talk about what you have in mind."

Herr Krantz handed Cane his key, saying, "It's 3-A, right on the front overlooking the Platz."

A group of men left as Cane and Müller approached the table. Stefan introduced Cane to the man who remained. Moustached, weathered, a fringe of gray hair showing beneath a green Tyrolean hat, he was near Cane's age.

"Herr Cranach, this is Max Reiser, the finest shot in Alpendorf. He will hunt with us."

His handshake was solid, his eyes a sharp blue, disconcertingly direct. Cane held them with a level gaze until Reiser turned away. Now why did I do that? Cane wondered. There's a conflict working here already. What is it about me that you don't like....?

Stefan indicated a chair and Cane sat down.

"Ah, good. Here is Hans, my brother." Cane was astonished to see a cloned duplicate of Stefan Müller come through the swinging door. The younger man was as tall, as muscular, as tanned and blue-eyed as his brother. He wore grubby *lederhosen*, mountain boots, and a faded green flannel shirt. His handshake was firm, his eyes friendly.

"We were expecting you," he said. "I'm sorry I won't be hunting with you, but Max will stand in for me. A beer, Elsa," he called to the waitress, "for me and our client."

Cane pulled out his new pipe and filled it from a plastic pouch. Elsa brought the beer, two liter steins in each hand, and giggled when Hans slapped her ample rump.

"Hans Müller," she threatened, wiping her hands on her apron, "one of these days I'm going to spill yours on your head." The men laughed.

Then the talk turned to hunting and Cane passed a pleasant hour. He made a date for the following day to finalize their plans, then gathered his luggage and walked up the creaking stairs to his room. They seemed nice fellows, he thought. Hard to believe Stefan had such a father as Otto Thyssen.

In his room, he flung open the casement windows and looked down on the Platz. The pigeons still held possession of the fountain, some ruffling their feathers in the sun, others bathing lustily. Past the Platz, he noticed both Müller boys entering the souvenir shop. Well, he'd made a good beginning. It was pure luck he'd met them so soon and straight off passed muster. Or had he?

He wondered idly how they'd react when they found out that Otto Thyssen was dead, and buried over thirty years in an Oklahoma cemetery. Standing in the window, running it through his mind, he decided the boys might know nothing of their natural father. It would be better to talk to Müller before approaching his wife.

Tossing his suitcase on the luggage rack, he opened it and dropped the lapis princess and Derringer in his pocket. Taking out the fifth of Chivas Regal he'd packed as an afterthought, he sat it on the table by the window. Closing the case, he flipped one fastener, then pulling a hair from his head, he twisted it around the latch. There was nothing in his bag now that would interest anyone, but he had a genuine curiosity in knowing if anyone in Alpendorf was concerned enough about him to search his luggage. He lifted the typewriter to the table beside the bottle of Scotch, opened it, sat down, and inserted a sheet of paper.

*The Bavarian Alps in October,* he wrote, *are floodlit with color. The air has a special fragrance, a tingling excitement. It's the time for making plans to stalk game, to pack far back into the hills, a time to listen to streams making their last free run before winter.* He continued for half a page, then left the sheet in the typewriter. Just a small clue that showed, by God, he was who he said he was!

Downstairs he spoke to Herr Krantz, reached down to pet the dog, noticed the filled alcoves and café tables, and remembered it had been some time since breakfast. Herr Krantz guided him to a table, introduced him to the men already eating, and explained he'd come from Austria to hunt the Red Stag, the *Rothirsche.* That brought forth a series of hunting tales, a great deal of laughter, and much skepticism as to the luck he'd have. After a hearty lunch of *Rehrucken,* saddle of venison prepared hunter-style with mushrooms and potatoes in wine gravy, he complimented Herr Krantz on his chef, drained the last of his beer, and expressed his desire to have a further drink with the gentlemen later during his stay in Alpendorf.

Cane lit his pipe and casually sauntered forth from the hotel. He caught a glimpse of himself reflected in a plate glass store front. If he didn't know better, he'd swear he was Tyrolean born and bred.

# CHAPTER XVII

Abell tinkled somewhere in the back when Cane pushed open the door to Herr Müller's store. Around the walls framed blown-up posters of spectacular ski jumps and mountain scenes advertising film shared space with mounted heads of game. A glass counter held enameled bracelets, Eidelweiss pins, and gold-plated jewelry on one shelf with cameras and photographic equipment on the bottom shelves. To the side was a wide assortment of wood carvings from a three-foot tall Bavarian maiden with thick braids holding a basket full of flowers to wooden bears, dogs, birds, and crucifixes. Across the store was another showcase filled with watches, more expensive jewelry, and mineral stones.

"Well, Herr Cranach, looking for souvernirs?"

Cane turned quickly, surprised to see Hans Müller. He laughed.

"I guess not. I was just hoping to see your father. I'd like to meet him and perhaps interview him for my article. He's been around here for so long, he'd know interesting stories of the legendary red deer."

"He would that. And great stories they are. But unfortunately he is in Italy on business. Whether he'll be back before you leave, well, I don't know."

Cane nodded, smiled, looked down at the glass, and pointed to an enameled Edelweiss pin. "I'm sorry to miss him. I think I'll take the pin—our Austrian good luck charm. Is your shop pretty busy this time of year?"

125

"Not with hunters. They aren't all that interested in picking up sculptures of Bavarian children or jewelry. But the tourists who come to see the autumn colors in the mountains, and the campers—they like to buy small souvenirs to remember vacations. My mother takes care of the store, but she's involved right now, so I said I'd take over. That's a pretty pin, and a good Austrian symbol. Since you're our client, let me give it to you."

"That's certainly generous, and I'll accept with pleasure! Thank you, Hans. Nice to see you again. I'm sorry you won't be hunting with us. But I expect to have a great time with your brother. *Tschuss.*" He waved a casual goodbye and turned to go.

As he opened the door and heard the tinkle of the bell, he paused—now would be a good time to get a camera and some film. Anya would show up sooner or later and he would like to get a picture of her. Make that plural. Purely professional reasons, of course. He closed the door, turned, and saw Hans had already disappeared. Cane shrugged, then resolutely walked back to the counter and was just ready to call Hans when he heard a woman's voice.

"You're an idiot if you think he's an honest hunter. And you gave him an Edelweiss pin! Stupid! Stupid! He's a hunter, all right—a Nazi hunter. And of course he'll trace the skull to Rimini. You fool!"

"I couldn't throw him out, Mamma, you know that. Someone should have alerted me that he was coming."

Cane froze. He slipped out as quickly as he'd entered, knowing the bell would tinkle its warning again. He went into the sporting goods store next door and, from behind a rack of sheepskin coats, watched Hans step outside, look around, then disappear into the store. Cane killed the better part of an hour trying on caps, coats, and jackets before he bought a scarf and took the long way back to the hotel.

The alcoves in the lobby and the small café were still filled with diners, tourists back from a walking tour of the old monastery, campers whose backpacks lay in a heap by the door. He spotted Peter with a two day's growth of beard sitting at a table with a stein of beer and a plate of Wienerschnitzel. They ignored each other, but Cane felt a certain security in seeing him there.

In his room, he checked the bag. Not only was the hair gone, but both latches were fastened. Ah! That was careless. The intruder forgot he'd opened only one and when he'd closed the lid, he'd snapped both fasteners automatically. Well, Cane, it looks like someone besides Hans and his mother is suspicious.

He began a systematic search for bugs. There were two. One in the overhead light fixture, the other on the telephone. Not very imaginative. Yes, he was suspect, all right. It had been done after he left to see Müller.

At any rate, they had plenty of time to search his room while he was hiding out. Rimini, the woman had said. Rimini. Cane remembered Rimini very well. That's where Thyssen-von Stober was taken prisoner. It was also the Eastern bracket of the Gothic Line held by Kesselring against the U.S. Fifth and the British Eighth Armies. In the autumn of 1944, Rimini had fallen to the Allied armies.

So what was Otto Thyssen doing there?

Well, for one thing, the 1st Paratroop Division was there, and so was Major Heinrich von Stober.

What was it that Frau Müller was so afraid he would find in Rimini?

This clearly was a development of which Peter should be informed. He wrote a quick note, sealed it, and dropped it in his pocket. He found the café partially cleared and Peter alone at a table finishing his lunch. Cane nodded casually, ordered a beer, and sat down across from him.

"You are here for the hunting also?"

"Yes," Peter nodded, pointing with his fork. "But only for the birds. Not for the big deer which I hear you will be stalking."

"Birds?"

"The Rock Partridge."

Cane whistled. "That's quite a hunt. You'll be above the timber line."

"Yes. Into the scrub thicket about 3,000 meters up."

"That'll be a rugged climb."

"And a rugged hunt. They are scarce. But there is no better eating. I had hoped to get the Müller boys as guides, but I heard you beat me to them. Good luck on your expedition."

"Thank you. I'll need it." Cane stood up and smiled. "And luck to you also, my friend." He drained his beer and left. The waitress picking up his stein found his lighter. "Oh, the Herr left this—"

Peter on cue picked it up. "I'll see that he gets it."

Sometime later, when he knocked on the door, Cane met him with a finger to his lips forming the word *bugged*. Peter nodded.

"Herr Cranach, you left your lighter in the lobby. I'm returning it."

"*Danke schön.* I'd hate to lose it. Damn careless. Come in, won't you?"

"Sorry, but I'm spending the afternoon in the woods. I'll see you around, I'm sure."

"Yes, I'll be here several days." At the same time, he handed Peter an envelope and received one in return. After Peter left, Cane closed the door then carefully opened the letter so there was no crackling noise for the hidden microphones to pick up, and read: *Chili, the man in your room, your double, has been identified. He is Helmut Acton, former SS officer and Nazi war criminal known as Antonio Perez from Argentina. He is a member of The Spider, one of the post-Nazi organizations formed after the war to aid SS survivors who want to return to Germany and go into business. Spider has access to the Thyssen treasure and will go to any length to protect it. His hair was dyed. It's pure white, and his skin was made up to look tanned. He didn't look that much like you in daylight. Petrovna the Russian is here. But more than that, the Mossad is also here. Business is booming. Be careful.*

Cane used his lighter to burn the note, then flushed the ashes down the toilet. So another party heard from. The Mossad! And Anya—Christ! She didn't waste any time waiting for him to show at the hotel. Had she followed him from Munich?

A key rattling in his door lock interrupted his speculation. He froze, then took the lapis princess from his pocket and tiptoed to the door.

Whoever was trying to get in was pretty damn noisy. He flung open the door, and Anya stumbled in, one hand on the key and the other on the door knob. They stared at each other for an incredible minute. An overnight case was on the floor beside her with a maroon wool coat draped over it.

"I—I'm sorry. I seem to have the wrong room—" Then recognition flooded her face. "Ah—h—"

Cane muffled her mouth with his hand as he pulled her into the room.

"Shhh—" he whispered, "the room is bugged. Be careful what you say." She nodded and he released her arm. Hell of a note! It had taken her exactly half a second to recognize him. He picked up her bag and coat, set them inside the door, closed it softly, and turned the bolt. With his finger in front of his lips, he turned on the old-fashioned radio that was built into the wall beside the bed full volume. An oom-pa band blasted the room with sound, and nothing they would say could carry over that.

He returned with a wide grin, enjoying the shocked look on her face. "You sure move fast. Who did you expect to see here?"

"Well," she smiled in an effort to recover her composure, and shrugged, "not you. Certainly not so soon."

Cane looked down at her. She was wearing a turtleneck sweater, a rosy sort of color, and a skirt to match with a wide dark red leather belt that matched her coat.

Anya answered his look with a pressed-lip smile, and shook her head.

"You see, it's not all that easy to stand me up!"

"Extenuating circumstances. Will you forgive me? I promise not to make it a habit."

"You did startle me. I guess my room is across the hall...." She stared at him, then added, "I must say you change your hair color oftener than a hairdresser's model."

"That, my charming Anya Vasilievna Petrovna—lately Marianne

Mason, American journalist—is to keep you guessing."

"Well, Canyon Eliot, the late Wilhelm Schwartz and God knows who else, you're wanted for murder in Munich. That should come as no surprise."

He shook his head and answered coolly, "Your friend, Niels Jannasen, KGB agent from Stockholm, code name Sable, was dead when I returned to the room. Also one Helmut Acton, who bore a marked resemblance to me. I searched them both, found a Center code book, the needle, his knife and money belt. They're now in the consulate, safely locked up."

"I don't believe you."

Cane walked to the window, then turned.

"It doesn't matter whether you do or not. It's true."

She followed him to the window and touched his arm. "Then where's the skull?"

"That, my lovely Soviet, is a closely guarded secret. I must say this calls for a celebration of sorts. Will you join me in a toast to the business we're in and especially to an ugly, dirt-stained, porcelain-toothed skull?"

"I will. But I'd really like to see that ugly, dirt-stained, porcelain-toothed skull." She followed him to the dresser and watched as he poured Scotch in each glass. He handed one to her, caught her eye in the mirror. "Prosit!" he said.

"Neat?" she asked.

"Too much of a good thing?"

"Well, it's rather an uncivilized drink compared to vodka. But here's mud in your eye!" She took a stiff swallow and coughed.

"That dates you," Cane grinned. "Rather lace it with branch water, since I've no civilized soda?"

"No, my American friend. This is fine." She shuddered and sipped the whisky.

"There is only one chair. Or would you prefer the bed?"

She laughed and said, "The bed is fine, thank you." Sitting on the edge, she crossed her legs and flashed an impudent smile in his direction.

God, she's lovely. The rise of her breasts beneath the cashmere sweater, their soft division accented with a gold chain and jade pendant. The curve of her hips and the long line of her legs. The soft kid boots that crimped at the ankle.

"How did you get here?" he asked.

"By car, of course."

"Alone?"

"Naturally, why?"

"Well, sometimes pretty agents like you have guardian angels who watch over them. Knife-carrying ones."

Anya's smile broadened. "Do you think I need one?"

"Christ, no! You're a pretty formidable opponent on your own. If Jannasen had been half as smart, he'd still be alive."

"Let's not talk about him. What did you say your name was?"

"Actually, I didn't say. That's the sort of thing you're supposed to find out for yourself but, since you ask, I'll tell you. Josef Cranach, Austrian journalist."

"Not very original."

"Oh, but it is. I'm doing a story on the *Rothirsche*, that's the famous Bavarian Red Deer, for the *English Sportsman Magazine*. Strictly legit."

"But *why* are you here?"

"That's it. No secret. Drink up, a toast to friends under cover."

Anya met his eyes, raised her brows, and nodded. They touched glasses.

Cane stood up and walked to the open window. "Anya," he said softly over his shoulder, "I enjoyed yesterday."

She held her glass with both hands and sipped without answering.

"Didn't you?" he insisted, turning to look at her.

Their eyes held for several seconds before she nodded and glanced away.

Thin rays from the late afternoon sun broke through the window in prismed shafts, making her dark hair glisten and her skin and hands glow, and brought exciting shadows to her face.

Cane laughed, severing the tension that had risen between them. "You should know," he said, "that for a middle-aged Russian woman, you are very beautiful."

"Well, bloody damn," she answered, joining him at the window, "that's a cross-eyed compliment if ever I heard one." They stood together at the window looking over the Square in silence. The pigeons were gone. And the cars and truck. The pickup was still there. A few pedestrians were about, bundled up with caps and scarves against the autumn evening. Lights flickered on in the shops. Cane saw that the *duvet* was gone from the window sill, and lights showed both in the Müller apartment and in the souvenir shop below.

Anya shivered and Cane pulled the casements to and turned on the lamp by the bed. "Let's put your things in your room and take a walk around. No telling what excitement we can discover in this busy place."

# CHAPTER XVIII

Magen Ben-Yanait drove the World War II Jeep to the bend in the road past the monastary and the meadow before he slowed to a stop, got out of the car and looked down on Alpendorf. From the height he could see the whole town, tiny as a toy in the distance—a picture postcard village—settled in the burnished foothills.

He returned to the Jeep, drove it slowly back the winding shale road until he came to a stretch of hillside where the timber had been cleared. Turning off the road, he bumped over an almost inaccessible logging track and left the Jeep hidden in a stand of fir trees a mile from the shaley track. He cut enough underbrush to camouflage it, took a backpack from the front seat and set off up the nearest rise overlooking the town. By early evening he had made a comfortable camp. The sun's last rays highlighted the opposite peaks. From a flat boulder he studied Alpendorf with binoculars. Panning over the church above the village, he saw the hotel to the left of the Platz and the houses rising one above the other around the rimmed bowl of the town. There were the short streets that framed the Platz and there was Müller's Souvenir Shop. Holding the glasses there for some time, he watched the lights come on in the shop and then in the apartment above. In the gathering dusk he noticed pedestrians crossing the Platz.

Panning to the hotel he stiffened. Twisting the control on the infra-red binoculars, he brought Cane's face so close he could see the scar on his jaw. Cane was seated facing him on the terrace of the hotel drinking from a steaming mug with a woman whose back was to the Israeli. She was smartly dressed, slender and youthful. Certainly she did not look local. Well, he shrugged. The American has good taste in women. I wonder where he picked her up?

Then the woman turned and pointed across the Square toward the Müller's Souvenir Shop. Ben-Yanait had a full close-up of her and a puzzled frown crossed his face. Where had he seen her before? She seemed unaccountably familiar.

Was she a movie star? An actress? He tuned the binoculars even sharper, bringing her in so close he could see the dimple near her mouth. And as quickly as that he knew. That was Anya Petrovna, super top-flight KGB agent! He had seen her in Paris when she worked for Aeroflot and in New York as recently as a year ago at the United Nations. There was nothing about Petrovna he didn't know. That her father had defected when she was a teenager and shortly afterward had died. That she had a daughter. That Petrovna was a grandmother. And he knew as surely as spring follows winter that she was after the Thyssen skull.

They were talking, their heads close, occasionally sipping from the mugs in front of them. He saw Cane reach across the table and take her hand, but only for a moment.

Anya withdrew it quickly. He saw the by-play when a stocky, sandy haired man approached and was waved off by the almost imperceptible shake of Cane's head. The stranger paused at the door of the Inn to give both Cane and the woman a long look. So who was *he?* Dusk was closing in, but Magen could see clearly enough through the infra-red lenses. Cane rose, extended his hand to Petrovna and together they walked across the Square. They didn't seem to be talking. Cane's hands were pushed deep into his pockets as if they were lead weights and Anya had hers pushed up each coat sleeve like a muff. They strolled slowly across the cobbled Platz in step. Soon they were out of sight.

Ben-Yanait took a long breath and stood up. Replacing the

binoculars in their case, he began the careful descent to his camp. He shook his head, his expression grim. That poor bastard, not only had the American walked into a Spider's web, but the Russian Bear had him by the throat.

~~~~

Wrapped in silence, Cane and Anya crossed the Platz. The pickup was gone. The fountain trickled from its saucers, the sound exaggerated into a waterfall by the stillness of the evening. The night moved down from the mountains and grew heavy around them. The shapes of trees and houses dissolved into the foothills and became a part of the sky. Street lights were blurry yellow globes that did nothing more than mark the corners of the Platz. Bright rectangles of light flickered from invisible houses. Stars appearing suddenly seemed close enough to touch. Cane's thoughts revolved like a spinning beacon around the conversation they'd had as they sat on the terrace drinking mulled wine. He had asked, expecting no plausible answer, "Why are you here?"

Anya had replied, seriously enough, "Would you believe I'm writing a cookbook for *The Woman's Eye*?"

"From roving reporter to cookbook author? Well, no." Cane laughed.

"It's no laughing matter. Cookbooks are the all-time rage now. There are cookbooks on everything but Bavarian game and that's what I'm doing. My editor contacted Herr Krantz and his chef is my advisor." She looked at him sideways then and added softly, "Frau Müller has some family recipes she's sharing with me tomorrow."

"Frau Müller!"

"Yes. That's their place, the souvenir shop." She had turned and pointed across the Platz. "Herr Krantz took me over when I arrived this afternoon and introduced us. She's the typical German Hausfrau, flattered, I think that a New York magazine wants her recipes for cooking venison and Rock Pheasant. That's a special game bird in the Bavarian Alps."

"Yes, I know."

"I have an appointment with her tomorrow morning."

Cane wanted to say, "Anya, be careful. She's dangerous." Instead he said, "A cookbook author! I'll be damned."

So they walked around the Platz looking in windows, making trivial conversation, until Cane said, "All this talk about cookbooks and venison and pheasant has whetted my appetite...."

"Mine too. Let's eat."

Cane wondered about the propriety of two spies, Russian and American, chummily dining together. What would Peter say? He wasn't sure his friend knew Anya by sight. When he'd almost joined them on the terrace Cane had waved him off. Perhaps he should get together with Peter and plan their strategy.

They walked up the path to the door and Cane held it open. Peter was eating with a full bearded man, obviously his guide, at a front table. Behind them Max Reisner and Stefan Müller were drinking beer and snacking from a platter of hard-boiled eggs and smoked eel. They motioned for Cane to join them He nodded to Peter as he passed, ignoring the questioning look in his eyes.

The two men stood, acknowledged Cane's introduction of Fräulein Mason from New York. Stefan, seating her, said, "My mother was pleased that you want to include some of her special recipes in your book, Fräulein Mason."

Anya rewarded him with a warm smile and said, "I enjoyed meeting her and I'm looking forward to tomorrow." She charmed the men and Cane had little occasion to enter the conversation, which ranged from cooking venison to skiing. They ordered a hearty dinner of sauerkraut and pork chops and finished it off an hour later with apple strudel and coffee.

Afterwards, Stefan pushed back his chair, leisurely filled his pipe, lit it with a long draw that pulled the match flame far into the bowl.

"So," he said, "we're going to hunt the Red Deer?"

"I hope so," Cane replied, his own pipe held firmly between his teeth.

"We will need luck and a great deal of it." Stefan suggested.

"Whether we have luck or not, " Cane answered, "it's the hunt that matters."

"I'll drink to that," Max said with a metallic chuckle. He stood up, looked at Stefan. "We'd better go. It's getting late."

Stefan bowed to Anya.

"Fräulein, will you excuse us? We've enjoyed this evening and perhaps I'll see you tomorrow at my mother's."

Anya's smile was radiant as she replied, "It's been delightful. Goodnight." She looked at Cane and added, "It's time I went up too. It's been a long day."

Cane gave her a cynical glance before following her up the stairs. At her door he said, "Goodnight, Fräulein Mason. Good luck with your cookbook."

"There's no call to be facetious, Herr Cranach," she answered loftily. Then looking at her watch, she added, "It's not that late. Why don't you come in for a nightcap? I have a fireplace and a half full bottle of wine I brought from Munich."

"You've twisted my arm sufficiently," Cane promptly answered, taking her key and opening the door. "A fireplace, that puts you in the privileged guest category." Inside he checked quickly and unsuccessfully for bugging devices. Then he turned on the wall radio. "Just in case," he explained, turning his attention to the fireplace. He laid the fire carefully from twisted newspapers and kindling to the three logs he placed on the grate, then touched his lighter to the newspapers.

Anya divided the bottle of wine equally between two drinking glasses from the bathroom and handed one to Cane. "Prosit! As you Austrians say."

Cane clicked his heels, bowed from the waist and answered seriously, "Down the hatch, as you Americans say." He pulled a pillow off the bed, dropped it on the floor and sat down in front of the fire, leaning against the footboard of the bed. The flames licked tentatively at the bark of the logs, sputtered, popped and with a crackling roar the logs seemed to catch fire simultaneously.

"Did you know," Cane asked, "that it's a scientific fact a fire should only be built with three or five logs—always an odd number?"

"Is that a fact?" Anya stood watching the play of shadows across his face, then dropped to the floor beside him. "And upon what remarkable scientific calculation do you base this conclusion?"

"It's called the Cranach theory of fire building. I must say this is cozy. Almost as nice as a Colorado ranchhouse...."

"Or as cozy as a dacha on the Moscow River. In the winter it's lovely. But then it is also in the spring and in the fall and in the summer. I wish you could see it."

"How long have you had it?"

"It was my grandfather's. Now it's mine."

"Then it doesn't belong to the State?"

"No. It's mine. It's where I'll retire when I'm old."

Cane looked at her, unable to imagine Anya ever being old. "It'll be lonely," he said. "Or do you have a husband hidden somewhere?"

Anya laughed softly. "Oh, no. No husband. Only a daughter and a little three-year-old grandson, Mischa, the light of my life."

"A daughter! Somehow I'd never thought of...."

"Of me with a family. Ah, yes. And with family problems."

"You mean serious problems besides things like dug-up skulls and such?"

She stared into the crackling flames and their glow reflected in her eyes and danced across her face. "My daughter, Natalya," she said softly, "is beautiful, talented, extraordinary. And she's in trouble."

Startled, Cane looked at her in surprise. "She is? How?"

"She—she's independent. She wants to change the world. Our world. And she isn't afraid of anything."

"What does she have to be afraid of?"

Anya looked at him and her eyes narrowed. "You are naïve. Russians don't go around like your Carrie Nation chopping things up with a hatchet."

"And that's what your Natalya wants to do—chop things up with a hatchet?"

"Not literally. She's using her pen. She's worked for the Writer's Union weekly *Literatura* since she graduated from the university. But for the last year or so she's been a quasi dissident. It bothered me, but I figured she was just trying her wings. But now....," she paused, sipped her wine, rolled the glass between her hands. "Well, it's out of control. Just recently," she dropped her voice to a whisper, "Natalya was published in an unauthorized magazine, a *samizdat*—that is an underground edition that has been picked up, translated and reprinted in France and West Germany."

"What does she write about?"

"The abuse of women in prisons, unhealthy conditions in maternity hospitals, the lot of the Soviet woman."

Cane whistled. "Christ! That does take courage."

"It's not courage. It's madness! It's suicide."

"For you too?"

"No, there's no danger for me. There's a certain embarrassment, of course. But one can't really be held responsible for the actions of one's child. I discussed it with my superior at the Center yesterday. Right now she's under a sort of house arrest until I get back. She's in no danger personally."

Cane sighed and poked at the fire. "I'll admit you've a hell of a problem. Do you think she might be exiled?"

"God forbid! That's the worst thing that can happen to a Russian."

He looked puzzled. "I don't understand. That's not better than being re-indoctrinated?"

She jerked her head impatiently. "You don't understand. You couldn't. There's a bond between the Russian and his earth that is unexplainable. We all feel it. Nobel prize winners have refused to accept their honor in person for fear they can't return."

Cane shrugged. "Oh, that's a nationalism and it feeds on itself in every country in the world."

"I disagree. What the Russian feels isn't just nationalism. It's something that has been bred in us for centuries." She hesitated a long second and added, "Russians want their dissidents and they want the Politburo."

"Then what your daughter writes is something they want to hear?"

"Oh, no! Well, perhaps. But she exaggerates. Her poetry is satirical. It has been read in circles where it's thought smart to stick out your tongue at the establishment."

"Well, she has guts!" Cane drained his glass, stared at it as though surprised it was empty. "Why don't I send down for some more wine?"

Anya shook her head. "No. Of course I shouldn't have mentioned this to you. I don't know what got into me. It must have been the wine. So no more. You'd better go. Or do you want to tell me the story of your life?"

Cane grinned, shaking his head. "Dull compared to yours." He stood up, extended his hand and pulled Anya to her feet. "Goodnight." At the door he turned. "Anya, seriously, if I can help, in any way at all, will you let me?"

She shrugged. "Enough has been said, too much really. Goodnight. I'll see you tomorrow."

When Cane opened the door to his room he found Peter sitting on the bed, a drink in his hand. The radio was turned up loud. Peter waved his glass generously. "Sit down and have a drink."

"Thanks. But do enjoy my liquor and make yourself at home." He sat down in the chair, stretched his legs and crossed his ankles. "Where's your room?"

"Directly beneath the Russian Sparrow's."

"Ah, then you have a fireplace too."

Peter laughed and raised his eyebrows. "The better to seduce you with, my dear."

"No, Pete. Nothing like that. Would you believe she's been telling me her problems. We haven't even mentioned the skull."

"That's how they all begin. Win your confidence and your sympathy. In no time at all you're hooked."

Cane laughed. "Thanks for the warning. What do you hear from our friend?"

"Just for you to keep on your toes. There's a connection between Müller and the Spider, but of course he told you that."

"Why did you come?"

"Sort of a body guard to see that nothing happens to you. Like for instance getting too chummy with the opposition."

Cane's smile faded, and his eyes grew icy.

"I resent that." He crossed to the dresser and poured a half tumbler of Scotch into a glass.

Peter put his arm around the older man's shoulder.

"Cane, you're doing fine. I just don't want you to be swept away by the Russian Chick. She's a pro. We haven't anyone that's close to her in looks, intelligence and just plain charisma. She snows everyone she meets. And she's cost more than one man his career—and life."

Cane shook off his arm.

"That's enough. Goodnight, Pete. I'll see you around." He opened the door.

Peter placed his glass on the dresser. "Okay. Tomorrow, then." He left without looking back. Cane closed the door behind him.

Cane stared at the door, his expression grim. Then he quickly drained his glass and rinsed it in the bathroom sink. He undressed slowly, conscious suddenly of the cold. He turned out the light, crawled under the down *duvet*. Sleep was a long time coming.

# CHAPTER XIX

*Alpendorf*
*Monday, October 6*

Anya awoke restless and disturbed. All night her fragmented sleep had been raked by vague, disembodied figures with the faces of Natalya and Cane, Pugachev and Cane, Mischa and Cane, and Cane and Cane and Cane. Cane in bewildering sequences—floating through the birch forest along the Moscow River near the dacha. Cane and Niels Janassen dueling with great sabers that bent like rubber. Cane in a cowboy hat wavering mistily about her Moscow apartment with little Mischa in tow. Shaking her head and curled in a knot she pulled the comforter over her shoulders. Dear God, whatever possessed me to tell Cane about Natalya? How stupid! Her eyes opened wide. *How dangerous!* What could he do with the information? She leaped out of bed wide awake.

What could he do with it? He could ruin her. That's what. All he had to do was drop a hint to his control. Let the word get back to Langley and the bits and pieces would fly. In no time it would be on the re-run to Center and she'd be considered a double agent. It could ruin Pugachev, too. And Siberia would be a holiday for what would lay in store for both her and Natalya. And Mischa! What would happen to him? Her throat tightened. She tried to swallow and choked. *What had she been thinking of?*

Anya shivered. It was still dark and the room was cold. Turning on the light she quickly pulled on slacks and a sweater. She wondered if the hotel would be stirring yet. Coffee would help. Combing her hair, braiding it, she pushed it under a wool cap, pulled on a windbreaker and ran down the stairs. No one was about. A pale night-light shone in the office. The great porcelain stove—the *Gotischer Studenoften*—was cold. A half-burned log in the fireplace glowed faintly and gave out a bit of warmth. The dog was near the hearth asleep. He growled softly without opening his eyes as Anya passed.

In the kitchen a bent, wrinkled old woman mopped the flagstone floor.

"Guten Morgan, Grossmutter," Anya said with more enthusiasm than she felt. "Is there any coffee?"

The old woman twisted her head with its thin gray topknot and looked around without moving her body or her mop.

"Ja, Enkelin, I made for myself on the stove."

The coffee was in a huge granite pot, water and grounds boiled together. Anya found the mugs, poured a full steaming cup and sat on the edge of a table, lifting her feet as the old woman pushed the mop toward her. The coffee was black and strong.

"When will breakfast be served, Grandmother?"

The old woman shook her head, shrugged and continued mopping.

"Do you live near here?" Anya persisted.

The old lady nodded. She dipped her mop in the bucket of suds, twisted the rags and kept on with her work.

"May I pour you a cup of coffee? It's awfully good."

For the first time the old woman smiled. Her face was leathery and lined, creased into a thousand wrinkles. Her eyes were the bluest Anya had ever seen.

"Ja," she answered with a sudden warmth. "Fräulein, you are kind to an old woman." Her smile showed missing teeth and red gums.

"I like for you to call me Enkelin—granddaughter—Grossmutter." She poured the coffee. "Do you know the Müllers?" she asked as she handed her the cup.

A shadow crossed the old woman's face, her eyes dulled perceptibly and she seemed to shrink. She put down the coffee without tasting it and picked up her mop, refusing to look at Anya again. After two or three more attempts to rekindle the aborted conversation, Anya murmered, "Danke Schön, Grossmutter," and left. She met the breakfast help coming in, but she had forgotten about eating.

Outside she took a deep breath and rubbed her arms nervously. What was it about the Müllers that frightened the old Grandmother? Was she walking into a trap? And Cane, would he use what he knew against her? She sat down at the same table where she and Cane had been the evening before. The night was wearing thin. Shapes were forming out of nothing. The stores across the Square were lighter than the hills and the hills were faintly etched against the sky. Anya heard the door open and was surprised to see Cane.

Holding two cups of coffee he was obviously looking for her. "Good morning. The old lady told me you'd gone out. I knew you couldn't be far. Coffee?"

"No, thanks. I've just had some."

"You're up early," he set the cups on the table.

"Yes," she answered shortly.

"Couldn't sleep?" He sat down beside her, struck by her desolate appearance, her vulnerability. "Anya, what's wrong? Is it Natalya? Have you heard something?"

She stood up quickly, pushed the coffee cup away so that it sloshed over and glared at him.

"Will you go away? Just go away and leave me alone." She rushed into the hotel.

Cane looked after her, frowning. Something was wrong.

Something had happened since she talked to him last night, but clearly she intended to handle it herself. He needed to make peace with Peter. Certainly he had been uncooperative to say the least with not only his superior officer, but the best friend he had in the world. It was up to him to make amends. He finished his coffee, then walked up to the next floor and knocked on Peter's door. There was no answer. He knocked again.

A maid passed, her arms piled high with linens. "Oh, Herr Cranach, the American left early this morning to go hunting. He should be back by lunch."

"Very well. I'll see him then." Cane returned to the café and ordered a full German breakfast. It's going to be a long day. Four hours yet before he was to meet the Müller boys and Max Reisner for lunch. The thought of Reisner made the hairs on the back of his neck stiffen and itch. He rubbed his neck. It didn't take much imagination to realize that the Spider organization had him spotted. He wondered if Peter knew.

Breakfast finished, he drove slowly around the Square and then out of town the same way he'd arrived the day before. Across the meadow, he turned onto a logging trail, bumped over rutted tracks until he came to a clearing. He left the car, checked back over the trail to see if he'd been followed, then began to explore the area.

Beyond the clearing, the logging track started again and led to a dead end marked by a cross-tie rail fence. Immediately behind the fence was a precipitous drop into a boulder strewn canyon. Holding on to the railing, Cane leaned far over trying to see the bottom. He could hear the roar of the white water rapids boiling from the belly of the mountain, but couldn't see them. The opposite side of the ravine had a more gently layered slope thick with scrub pine and ferns.

He walked back to the clearing. It had been used in the past for picnics. Overgrown firepits, edged with half-buried stones, still held packed ashes and debris. It didn't look as if a truck or car had been this way for months. Brush had grown over the tracks and small trees between the ruts. After he felt well acquainted with this section of the mountain, he drove back to the shale road and continued exploring other logging tracks. He felt sure that this would be where the hunt for Red Deer would start and to know the general terrain would of course be a help. And it was inevitable that he would find the Jeep belonging to Magen Ben-Yanait. Pine branches and underbrush camouflaged the Jeep, which Cane examined carefully. Who did it belong to? There was a Munich license number, but that didn't mean it couldn't belong to someone in Alpendorf. Why would someone in Alpendorf hide an old Jeep. Was it stolen?

Magen watched him, carefully staying out of his way, hoping fervently that the American wouldn't find his makeshift camp.

Cane was forced to leave before he was ready in order to keep his luncheon date with the guides. He returned to Alpendorf needled with a prickling curiosity. Why the devil would anyone hide a Jeep halfway up a mountain? It hadn't been there long. The brush covering it hadn't wilted. The tracks were fresh. Certainly it was there for a reason and Peter must be told about it.

Stefan and Max were waiting when Cane joined them, apologizing for being late. Lunch was a pleasant affair. It lasted well into the middle of the afternoon. Beer, meatballs in a caper sauce, mixed vegetables topped off with a chocolate tort and black coffee. Then more beer and filling of pipes. Cane was in a mellow mood. Max made a point of being agreeable and if Stefan knew about the scene between his mother and Hans the day before he gave no sign.

"The weather is due to change this evening," Stefan advised. "There is a possibility of rain tomorrow. If it's pouring we'll postpone, otherwise dress for it and we'll take our chance."

"I'll be ready."

"We'll meet in the lobby about six. I'll have lunches, coffee, everything we need."

"Which direction will we take?" Cane asked.

"North. We circle the high tor, known as the Witch's Crown, until we reach the ski slope. There we are above the precipice. That's where the old boy hangs out with his harem. The worse the weather the better our chances are to find him."

Cane was quiet for a minute, then he looked up and asked, "We don't go out toward the monastery?"

"Oh, no. We circle from the Platz, go back of the Rathaus, then take the trail toward the peak. It isn't as far as it sounds." Stefan pushed back his chair. "We'd better get our gear ready. So until tomorrow morning. Auf Wiedersehen, Herr Cranach."

"I'm looking forward to it."

Max lingered a moment. "I suppose you have plenty of ammunition. It isn't as if it's the first time you've hunted big game?"

Cane took his pipe from his mouth and shook his head. "No," he replied quite seriously, "It isn't the first time. And I do have plenty of ammunition. I appreciate your concern." Their eyes locked briefly.

~~~~

Cane sat for some time smoking and wondering if there had been a by-play of words that he might have missed. They seemed just what they were supposed to be. Guides. But there was something missing —something wrong. His thoughts trailed off in another direction. He didn't know about the road behind the Rathaus. So what had he found in the opposite direction? What about the hidden Jeep? Did the Müller boys have something to do with it? He emptied his pipe in the ashtray and went upstairs. Perhaps Peter was in.

He knocked on Peter's door, but there was no answer. It must have been a full day's hunt. At the top of the stairs he glanced briefly at Anya's closed door. She had made it clear enough that she didn't want anything more to do with him. He wondered if she knew about the Spider organization. He had to presume that the KGB knew everything and more than he did. At least they knew *why* they wanted the skull.

Anya seemed entirely too alone to be pitted against the Müllers and against the Spider. He hoped the Center would send a sitter to look after her. One that had more sense than the Swede knife slinger.

He pushed open his door. Opening the casements he welcomed the rush of fresh cold air, fragrant from the mass of flowers in his window box. In the Platz the pigeons preened and fluttered and played leapfrog around the fountain. Someone had scattered grain and it was hunt and peck around the cobblestones where a host were gorging themselves.

147

The wind ruffled their feathers and the sun glinted off them like silk. The same cars were parked as haphazardly as they had been the day before.

Below, in the yard, the cat was creeping through the petunias, one paw at a time, pressed flat, toward a flock of sophisticated sparrows who eyed him warily.

In the path regarding the drama with raised head, ears alert was the old dog. Beyond the stores, beyond the razor-edged peaks, scraps of ragged clouds caught the last rays of the sun and reflected them in a kaleidoscope of primary colors.

Then he saw Anya coming across the Platz, where she stopped at the fountain to watch the pigeons. Evidently she had just come from the Müllers. Dressed in a swirl of pleated skirt that swung as she walked and billowed in the wind when she paused, a brown jacket and an orange scarf tied at her throat, she looked great. Her head was bare and her hair caught highlights from the setting sun. The wind tangled strands about her face and she brushed them from her forehead impatiently. She'd discarded her boots, Cane noticed, wearing flats across the cobblestones. He smiled down at her as she crossed the street carrying a briefcase, her leather purse swinging from her shoulder. Carefully stepping across the dog, she was out of sight.

Cane leaned against the casement frame, no longer smiling. He filled his pipe, lit it. Was Peter right? Was he hooked as Peter thought he might be? Was she playing him like a game fish—plenty of line, then reel in quickly—more line out, then reeling in a bit more each time until a spent and weary fish is netted. No. Not that. He shook his head decisively. She wasn't like that. And he damn sure wasn't a game fish!

He watched the shadows lengthen then disappear as the sun dropped behind the western slopes. The clouds thickened and curled menacingly below a gray and solemn sky. His mind returned to Anya. His thoughts slipped back to that day in Oklahoma when he first noticed her. He remembered how she got out of her car and shooed away the Angus yearlings at the cemetery gate. How gracefully she came over the stile from the POW section. How surprised he had been when he saw that she was older than he'd thought. A mature and gracious stranger. He recalled the astonishing interlude at the Marienplatz when she appeared with the KGB agent and he had his first doubts about her. The great time they had at the Oktoberfest. Then yesterday. Somehow he'd broken through her reserve and found a worried mother. That worry was for real. No, she wasn't playing a game with him.

Why, then had she been so abrupt this morning? That hadn't been a game either. Cane closed the casements and fastened the shutters. He turned on the lamp and refilled his pipe methodically. The thing for him to do, he admonished himself, was to stay as far away from Anya Petrovna as he could. He stared at his reflection in the mirror over the dresser and nodded as he held a match to his pipe. Because, old boy, in spite of everything, what Peter said could happen *has*. You're hooked. You're hooked like no poor fish has ever been. You'd better talk to Peter right away.

A light knock on the door startled him. He opened it and was surprised to find Anya there. A disturbed and troubled Anya.

# CHAPTER XX

I t was late afternoon when Peter pushed open the hotel door, his guide behind him, each of them carrying two braces of Rock Pheasants.

Josef Krantz came from behind the office counter. "What beautiful birds, Herr Landis! Where did you find them, Schmidt?" "On the far shoulder of the Witch. The weather was perfect. We couldn't have asked for a better day." He took Peter's birds, then added, "And let me tell you this Yankee is a crack shot. He never missed." He slapped Peter on the shoulder with a thumping whack. "Come, Krantz, have a drink with us. The Yankee is buying!"

Peter's mind was on Cane. It had been a wearing day and he wanted to return long before Schmidt was ready. He wondered how Cane's luncheon went. And about Cane and the Russian woman. It was an annoying situation and he needed to talk to Cane about that right away. It was impossible to get away from Schmidt and Krantz and the crowd of men who gathered around them admiring the birds.

They had one drink, then another, before Peter could gracefully leave. He stopped briefly in his room to leave his gun and jacket, then went up the flight of stairs to Cane's room. He heard the jarring sound of the radio blaring through the door. Someone was there with Cane. He listened at the door, but could only hear the shaking rhythm of the oom-pah band. He crossed to Anya's room and knocked. It was locked that posed no problem. In a short time he'd made an effective entry and search, but found nothing of interest. Not even a loose heel on the boots in the closet. He checked for a false bottom on the bag. Her briefcase held a mock-up of a cookbook, a notebook with several recipes listed alphabetically and regionally, a letter from the editor of *The Woman's Eye*. Peter read it quickly. That magazine is as Russian as *The Soviet Woman*. However there was nothing in the letter to hint that Anya was anything other than a culinary writer. Of course, it's probably in code. Convinced that there was nothing more to find, he left. He listened again at Cane's door, then returned to the café and ordered dinner.

~~~~

When Cane opened the door and saw Anya he quickly flicked on the radio. Then he faced Anya who had closed and bolted the door and was leaning against it. Her face was white.

"Cane, you are in terrible danger. You must leave immediately!" Her voice held a strident urgency.

Cane was puzzled. "What is it?" He was conscious of her hand on his arm, of her brittle nervousness, of the genuine distress in her eyes. What had happened since this morning when she'd wanted nothing to do with him? "Have a drink and tell me about it."

"Yes. Yes, I need a drink. And you must listen carefully. A terrible thing is going to happen tomorrow."

Cane moved slowly toward the dresser where the Scotch bottle stood on a tray. He didn't want to break Anya's hold on his arm.

There was a pleasant sensation of warmth where he felt her fingers and he wanted to keep them there as long as possible. He poured the whisky into the glasses and handed her one. He waved to the chair and she sat down. "Now," he said, "tell me what this is all about."

"You remember the old woman in the kitchen this morning?"

Cane nodded.

"Well, I don't think people treat her very well here, and she took a liking to me. This evening when I returned to the hotel, she was cleaning my bathroom. She's been watching for me all afternoon, she said. She has worked for the Müllers and here at the hotel for years. They are so used to her they don't pay any attention to what they say in front of her." She paused to get her breath and sip the Scotch. Cane didn't interrupt. "Do you know about an organization called the Spider?"

"Yes," Cane answered. "What do you know about it?"

"This is their headquarters—their German base. The other one is in Argentina. The Müllers are important members. Do you know their purpose?"

"Yes. They have a fund to help ex-SS officers go into legitimate businesses here in Germany. Why are you telling me all this?"

Anya took a deep breath. "The man you are supposed to have killed in Munich was one of their leaders. He had a lot of money with him and they think you have it. They know you are with the CIA and they know about your associate." She frowned, then added, "Do you have a partner working with you here?"

Cane didn't answer. "Go on," he said.

"They are planning to kill you both tomorrow."

"And that's it?"

"Well for Heaven's sake, isn't that enough!" She stared at him for a moment with flashing eyes, then jumped to her feet. "I should have known better! I break my own security to warn you and what do you say—'And that's it?' Well bloody damn!"

Cane caught her arm. "Wait a minute. Anya, I do appreciate your coming to me with this. I know about the Spider and while we didn't have conclusive proof that the Müllers were involved we were operating on the assumption that they were. And yes, Anya, I do have a partner here. I've been trying to reach him all day. He went bird hunting early this morning. I hope he's all right."

"When you get in touch with him, will you leave?"

"Anya, we can't do that any more than you would leave an assignment."

"But when you know you're going to be killed, you can certainly take some action." She was on the edge of the chair leaning toward him.

"When the time comes we'll take action." His jaw tightened.

"But you insist on going tomorrow?"

Cane nodded.

"But there will be the two of them against you. The old woman said there will be a hunting accident. She didn't hear what they planned for your partner."

Cane backed against the dresser, his arms folded, regarding her seriously. Why had she come to warn him? Was she that interested in his health and well being? Or was it simply that she needed him alive to lead her to Thyssen's skull? There was a lopsided grin on his face when he answered. "And I'm the accident that's about to happen?"

She shook her head in annoyance. "How can you joke about something like this?"

He sat on the edge of the bed and leaned forward, his elbows on his knees, his hands clasped.

"We were expecting something like this, Anya."

"How can you protect yourself?"

He shrugged. "It's a little to do with keeping your rear covered, your powder dry and everything to do with luck."

"You're making fun of me."

"Never that."

She stood, sighed, placed her glass on the dresser and said, "I need to go...."

"A heavy date?"

Cane reached for her hand and pulled her beside him: "Before you go, tell me your impression of Frau Müller and the sons."

"I didn't meet her husband, he's out of town, but Frau Müller couldn't have been nicer. I had lunch with her and we spent a pleasant afternoon." She turned to face him. "Did you know she had a son killed in a hunting accident?"

"Yes. Did she tell you about it?"

Anya nodded. "I felt sorry for her. She showed me his picture. He was a loving son, she said."

"A loving family. Have you forgotten they are planning a family killing tomorrow?"

Anya's eyes widened. "Oh, no. She's not involved. Just the older son and the other guide—Max something."

"Don't kid yourself. She knows all about it."

"You're cynical like all Americans. You've never had a family relationship. You wouldn't understand how one feels about a child."

He interrupted softly. "You're right. I don't have a family. My only son was killed in Vietnam."

Anya caught her breath and touched his arm. "Oh, Cane! I didn't know. Forgive me. Cane, how dreadful for you." She shook her head and murmured, "I'm so sorry...."

Cane pulled a package of cigarettes from his pocket and offered her one, then took one himself and lighted them. They smoked in silence for a long minute, then Cane said, "My wife died during the war when the baby was six months old. My grandfather, who raised me, had a heart attack before I came home. Well—hell, I've never been able to talk about it."

"Tell me please. Did he look like you?"

Then Cane was talking about Canyon Jr. How he helped brand and rope cattle before he was a teenager. His school years, his college. His girls. His practical jokes, their camping trips and river rafting. His Navy training. His months in Vietnam. His death. His funeral. The years moved lean and hungry in his memory and when he finished he felt a remarkable sense of ease. As if a great load had slipped from his shoulders.

He stopped talking as suddenly as he had begun, like a dam breaks and then runs dry. He was conscious of Anya's nearness, the warmth of her body beside him. When he glanced at her he saw tears in her eyes. "Well," he said, taking her hand, "thanks for letting an old man rattle. Things came to mind I hadn't thought of for twenty years and more."

The two cigarettes had burned out long before in the tray.

"Thank you for telling me."

Cane leaned down impulsively and kissed her cheek. The electric shock they felt surprised them both. They stared at each other startled, unable to break the magnetism that held them.

Then Anya jumped up and said, "I—I must go." But she didn't move.

"I know," Cane answered. He touched her face tentatively with his finger tips and felt her tense. She took a deep breath and touched his face, moving her finger gently down the scar on his cheek.

Cane put his arms around her and kissed her softly. His tongue touched her lips. Gently he explored the corner of her mouth, found the dimple there. He drew back and looked at Anya, at her moist eyes, her lips barely open. She was truly beautiful, exquisitely grave. He felt her tremble.

He picked her up, kissed her soundly and carried her to the door, then turned back laughing.

"I've just carried you over my threshold, love. And now you're mine!" He placed her carefully on the bed, slipped off her flats, then cupped her face in both hands. Her lips were soft and quivered against his. He brushed her face with his lips, exploring her eyes and throat with his tongue. He unbuttoned her blouse, buried his face between her breasts, covered them with his lips. "Anya, oh God!"

Cane undressed her slowly while her hands caressed his face and chest and tangled his hair. Her body responded to his touch with a vibrant, exhilarating ecstasy. He took her hungrily. Her body arched to his and the feel and taste and smell of her was on his lips and nostrils and body.

Afterward they lay intertwined, touching, exploring, pressed together, feeling a wonderful intimacy, emotionally drained, their pounding hearts slowing, their breathing returning to normal.

And then they were conscious of music. The oom-pah band was deafening and they hadn't heard it at all. Anya sat up and laughed. Her hair was falling and she reached to take out the pins that held it. She shook her head and her hair fell across her breast. Cane buried his face in its waves.

This time their lovemaking was slow and warm, stretching to the limit their enjoyment of each other. Lying in his arms, Anya whispered, "I never expected to have a—a wonderful thing like this happen, ever."

Cane leaned on an elbow over her. "Anya, I lo—"

She put her fingers across his lips. "Don't say it, darling. Never, never say it. This is a bonus we should never have had. So don't say it. Never think it!"

For a time they slept, braided together.

When Cane dressed for his hunt, Anya pulled his comforter around her and watched. She watched as he pulled on his heavy hunting pants and boots, his turtleneck undershirt and plaid flannel top shirt. She watched as he checked his gun, and filled his vest with cartridges, and she shivered involuntarily.

Cane stooped to kiss her. "For two cents I'd chuck the whole thing and come back to bed!" He kissed her again. "But duty calls and I must answer." He gave a mock salute. He dropped the lapis knife into his pocket with the Derringer, picked up his gun case. He kissed Anya again. "Be here when I get back!"

"Cane," she whispered, "Oh, my darling, be careful—be careful!"

# CHAPTER XXI

The night dissolved into a bone chilling, fog-dimmed form of daylight when Cane, Stefan Müller and Max Reisner drove away from the hotel. The men were silent, the atmosphere was strained. No one seemed to have any interest in making conversation.

Cane's mind was on Peter, whom he had just left. The visit had been entirely unsatisfactory. The fact was he regretted the impulse that had made him stop on his way downstairs. He was delighted to find Peter safe and told him so. He informed him about the camouflaged Jeep, wondering if he knew something about it. No, Peter had answered, but he'd look into it. He had related the news from Anya that they were both on the Spider executioner's hit list for the day. Peter's attitude had been irrational. He credited her warning on the Soviet practice of distributing dis-information and implied that Cane was not only a fool to believe her, but that he was bordering on becoming a KGB stooge. He hinted that his usefulness to the Company might be over. He added, moreover, that when Cane returned, he expected a full accounting of everything Cane had or had not done and with a possible disciplinary action. The tension between them was brittle and electric.

"What the hell, Peter, this is for your safety. You've been marked and today is the day. For God's sake be careful."

Peter had laughed mirthlessly. "If you hadn't had the Russian

Sparrow in your bed all night, I could hear you better." He had closed the door in his face.

What a goddamn mix-up. Anya, beautiful Anya, who loved him and wanted to help them. And Peter, brave resourceful Peter whom he loved like a son, bitter now and unreasonable. Then the first glimmer of a singular thought crept into his mind. Defect. Her father had, perhaps Anya would also. He took a long breath and tried to push it all to the back of his mind. God knows I'll have my hands full just staying alive today. Cane rubbed the back of his neck, but the itch that was there would not go away.

The murky headlights of the truck picked up the narrow macadam paving, wet and glistening as they circled the Rathaus. Then almost immediately they were on the rising shaly road toward the mountains.

Half a mile from the village Max turned the Ranger pickup off the road onto an almost invisible track. Climbing over boulders and ruts it heaved from side to side on an incredibly steep incline that hairpinned through a heavy stand of fir and pine. The fog changed into a steady drizzle and the windshield wipers fanned back and forth in a hypnotizing metronome.

"Perfect for hunting," Stefan broke the silence. "The rain will deaden the sound as we walk and will kill our scent. Makes stalking easier."

Cane nodded without replying. How were they planning this "accident" he was to have? Early on or near the end of the hunt? He had a feeling there would be no chance to stalk the Red Deer today. *He* was the quarry, and he'd have to put it all together to stay alive.

One thing in his favor, he reflected, no—two things. First, he'd hunted in the Colorado Rockies all his life. Stalking game was nothing new, but these Alpine guides didn't know that. Second, he knew he was in danger, but they didn't know he knew. He fingered the small Derringer. He'd left the S&W in the secret compartment of the car. A shoulder holster holding a .357 Magnum wouldn't look cricket on a deer hunt. He had two shots, if things warmed up, and in a tight situation there was always the Chinese princess.

Müller was talking. The *Rothirsche*, Stefan said, are almost impossible to track this late in the season. They are wary and smart as hell. There was one old Monarch they were going to try for, a fourteen point Royal Stag who weighed close to twenty stone and whose territory was in an almost inaccessible area of forest bracketed by a swampy meadow and the precipice that hung over the village.

At the end of the hacked-out trail they left the pickup. "It's still an hour hike," Max said, pulling gear from the covered bed of the pickup. "And a rough one."

The men twisted into their light backpacks, which held lunches, coffee and whisky. They checked out their guns, filled the ammunition packet that hung from their belts, then started their silent climb up the mountain in the wet gray dawn.

It reminded Cane of the war years when he'd tracked through mountains like this as silently as they moved now. But there was a difference. Then Cane trusted the man behind him carrying a weapon. Now he had a prickly feeling that made him rub the back of his neck and forced him to use all the control he could muster to keep from glancing back at the man behind him with a deer rifle slung over his shoulder. He shifted his own gun so the stock was just behind his armpit and the safety and trigger close at hand. The time he'd spent getting acquainted with the Gewehr 43 was time well spent.

His rifle had created a mild sensation as he unzipped its case.

"My God," Max Reisner said in awe, making a move to take the gun, but withdrawing his hand when Cane stiffened. "I didn't know any of those came back from the Eastern Front."

"Mine did," Cane answered quietly in an offhand manner, daring them to dispute him. "I left it in Vienna when I decided I'd rather surrender to the American Third Army than the Russians."

Max nodded. "Ja," he said, "I also. I chose the Americans...."

"And a good thing," Stefan Müller added, taking his own gun from its case. "Few of the Wehrmacht on the Eastern Front came back, even fewer with their guns." He cast a sidelong look at Cane. "We may be today and tomorrow—even the next with no promise of luck." Müller pulled the bolt on his rifle, checked the barrel, loaded it, snapped on the safety. He slipped it under his arm and asked, "Are you ready?"

"I'm ready," Cane answered, sighting down the barrel of the Gewehr at a distant peak, pleased at the power of the scope. The men walked in single file, Müller leading, Cane and Reisner following, climbing constantly, along game trails. They worked their way across a ravine, and came at last to a wooded point bordered by a graveled scree formed by an avalanche sometime in the past and a narrow swampy meadow. Above and to the right a long stretch of rugged upside-down terrain stitched together with a few windswept conifers and craggy bits of mountain shrubs, advanced to a cliff edged with a fringe of forest silhouetted against a gunmetal sky.

"And that," said Stefan pointing up, "is where we go."

"Just how the hell do we get there?"

"We separate here," Stefan said answering Cane's question, "and work our way through the woods to the other side of the swamp, then over the rocks. There is a game path above that is rough to follow, but it goes up to the cliff. It's possible the old fellow will be in the woods, but I doubt it. He stays as high as he can until the heavy snows force him down. He knows he's safe there. He's a smart bastard. Had to be to stay alive this long."

Then Max spoke to Cane. "It's a tricky territory, Cranach. The brush is thick and it's rugged. Since you've never hunted the *Rothirsche*, I'm going to give you some pointers." He shrugged. "Sometimes they work."

"And they are....," prompted Cane.

"When you're stalking anything it's a stop and go thing. Be as irregular as hell. No rhythm, understand? You stop and stay absolutely still, listening, then—a few steps and listen again. But never the same number of steps. Break up the rhythm."

"I understand."

"Nine out of ten hunters will move forward a certain number of paces between pauses. That's bad and animals catch on quick. They move either at a steady clip or at an ambling gait with frequent pauses and random steps. The hunter with a quiet irregular pace is often mistaken for another animal and it allows him to move into close range before being detected. Another thing," he shifted his shoulders to make his pack more comfortable, "I hope your hearing is good. Listen to the birds; watch the squirrels. A change in their pattern of chirping or movement can tell you a lot."

Cane nodded again. Max hadn't told him a thing he didn't know.

Stefan reached into his pack and pulled out a plastic tube.

"One more thing. We're in the Old Man's territory. With rutting season in full swing you might get a lead on him through bellering." He held up the tube. "This is a little invention of mine." He held the plastic pipe to his mouth and the unmistakable guttural resonance of a stag's bugle came forth, gliding upward until it hit a high clear note, then dropping to a squealing grunt and ending with a series of squeal-like yaps.

"Amazing!" Cane said, impressed. "Let me try it."

"It's done by sucking in rather than blowing out. And if a bull is anywhere near he can't resist the challenge," Stefan instructed, handing Cane the tube.

Cane took the limber piece of plastic and held it with one hand at his mouth making it air-tight and holding the other end up slightly. In minutes he had mastered it. "Great invention. You should patent it." He offered it back to Stefan who shook his head.

"Keep it. I have another." He laughed. "We just don't want to call each other in. It's been known to happen."

Cane remembered his grandfather's admonition when he was just a kid. "Never trust a man who laughs only with his mouth." That was Stefan. His eyes were inscrutable in the early morning light. "Oh, one other thing, Cranach. Sometimes he'll send the girls on ahead to see if it's safe. Keep an eye open for the hines. Look for fresh scrapes and rubs on saplings where he has worn the bark honing his rack."

"*Ich verstehe*. I understand"

"Now, Cranach, we'll separate here and meet at the edge of the cliff above the scree at noon. There are some ski runs up there that will help you locate it. You will follow the same trail toward the precipice above the village. That's to your left. There's a stream you'll run into and you can follow it up the mountain. It's the one that makes the waterfall. I'll go through the center and Max will work his way on the other side of the swamp. We'll try to herd him toward you."

"Good," Cane answered.

"It's rough going, Cranach, watch your footing. And use your bugler frequently."

"Right." Cane shifted his pack tucking the stock of his rifle under his arm and moved out. There was something about the whole morning's expedition that didn't ring true. The voluminous instructions. Surely not to ease a conscience. But Müller was right. It was damned rugged. Under other circumstances he would have enjoyed it. He grinned. That "grunt-tube." A great idea to use in Colorado elk hunting. But here? Not on your life! It was the perfect way to let Müller and Reisner know his whereabouts whenever they chose to move against him.

The cold drizzle was no bother. Bad weather made for good hunting. The Germans knew how to do it right. Warm waterproof wool, wonderful Loden cloth. Easy to move in and not the slightest sound when he brushed against an overhanging tree limb. He glanced back. Max and Stefan were out of sight. The forest was quiet, closing around him like a blanket. In the short space of time it had taken to move away from the others he was engulfed in a silence so acute that every sound fell on the ear with an exaggerated clarity. A flutter of wings, the chirp of an unseen bird, the crack of a twig was magnified tenfold in the woods. He could hear a drop of water splash on the stock. A heavy, intense feeling was in the air.

Half an hour later he came to the edge of the cliff. The village was below, veiled by mist. Following the trail around a house-sized boulder he saw the stream. Flecks of foam whitened its jade green color when it ran shallow over pebbles and rocks toward the precipice. He followed the stream for half a mile, watching the darting shadows of trout, crossing game trails that had no sign of fresh spoor. Neither did he find scrapes or rubs on any tree.

Abruptly he stopped. The hairs at the nape of his neck stiffened. He took cover in the woods and froze. If he continued to follow the stream toward its source as Stefan had instructed they would know exactly where he was at any given moment, even without the bugler. They could move in on him at any time. He decided to make his own way to the cliff rendezvous by crossing the ski run the best he could and continue through the woods on the opposite side.

He was conscious then of an awesome stillness. A chattering bird hushed. A squirrel stopped motionless on a branch in front of him. The steam from his breath drifted like smoke into the trees. A hine stepped daintily out of the woods. A half-grown fawn followed. Cane grinned. The tension eased. With his family here, was the Old King far away? He realized then that as far as he was concerned, the Monarch was perfectly safe. He had all he could do to protect himself. After the two had finished drinking and moved on, he crossed the stream at its narrowest point with the help of a protruding rock and a log. On the opposite bank he lost no time taking cover in the woods.

He wondered where Müller and Reisner were. He hadn't heard a sound since they separated. He had the idea that he was the only one sent off by himself. They were probably waiting for him to round a bend in the stream to take a pot-shot. Then they would carry back the report of a terrible hunting accident. Thought it was Big Red and by God it was the Austrian!

The drizzle stopped. A wind blew up and low clouds drifted toward the cliff. He kept the wind in his face, but only from force of hunting habit. The Red Deer was safe, but how he'd love to come face to face with him and salute the old guy. Cane grinned. He'd never felt such a comradeship with a stag before.

Climbing steadily, he crisscrossed back and forth to make the going easier. No point in reaching the cliff too exhausted to defend himself. The roar of white-water intensified and he discovered the confluence of two fast moving, mountain rapids. Where in the hell was he? Müller hadn't said anything about another stream.

He glanced at his watch—ten o'clock. It had been a long morning and he was famished. He and Anya hadn't thought of food last night. He grinned and shook his head. It was yesterday noon since he'd eaten, now he couldn't wait to get into his pack. Slipping it off his back, he placed his gun carefully beside it and sat down on a fallen log. Pulling out his flask he took a long swallow of Scotch that warmed him to his toes. He ate the Bockwurst, rolls and apple and didn't think to wonder if the Müllers had poisoned the highly seasoned sausage until he'd finished. He shrugged as he pitched crumbs to the jays that chattered at him. Too late now. He had a feeling that he'd better take advantage of this peaceful hour. He poured coffee into the thermos lid and lighted a cigarette. A climax was building.

Sometime later he stood up, ground out his cigarette in the wet carpet of pine needles, then stretched. He felt good.

Cane looked around for the proper kind of tree, then jumped for a stout branch and pulled himself up into a fifty-foot fir. He climbed until he had a clear view of the mountain, the rocky scree above the swamp and the cliff. The feel of winter was even more pronounced above ground. There was a low wailing as the trees gave back the sound of the wind. Above, etched against the colorless sky were two moving Vs of geese deploying in battle order toward a warmer country.

He scanned the area with his glasses, then gave an involuntary start and cursed softly.

# CHAPTER XXII

**M**üller and Reisner sat in the shadow of a boulder almost invisible above the scree, their guns across their knees. Max held binoculars and was studying the forest. He ranged them in a wide arc and Cane instinctively ducked behind the tree trunk. So that was it. There would be the regrettable hunting accident as he came out of the forest for the luncheon rendezvous.

Dropping out of the tree, he sat down on the log and lit another cigarette. They had open season on him and not a damn thing he could do about it. He couldn't take care of them accidentally. However, he might circle behind them to the pickup and drive it back to Alpendorf. Easy enough to explain he'd lost his companions and had come back for help. Let Hans go get them. He would feel a damn sight safer in the village than in the Bavarian Alps with two experienced Alpine mountaineers gunning for him.

He twisted into his pack, picked up his gun. He would continue working his way up, he reasoned, until he crossed the cliff then would come down on the far side of the scree near the pickup. In his pocket he felt the reassuring bulk of the small gun and the princess nestled together. There wouldn't be a chance to use the rifle if they came at him. But he could sure as hell shoot from his pocket and explain later. It took two hours of hard climbing to work his way over the rough crags and granite boulders to reach the cliff. Keeping within the border of the trees, he panned around the valley with his binoculars. The scree was immediately below him, the cliff probably forty feet high. He couldn't find Müller or Reisner, but his skin tingled and Cane turned slowly knowing he was in trouble. He felt himself in the cross hairs of a gun sight, and he had no idea where it was.

A branch cracked. He swung around, his gun at this shoulder, but Max Reisner shoved it up as Müller tripped him. The gun exploded harmlessly as he dropped to his knees losing the gun. He dived toward Max, but Müller gave a loud whoop and pushed him toward the cliff. Reisner kicked as he went down and Cane grabbed his leg. The German fell, but kicked again and Cane rolled over the ledge.

It was a bare, autumn-naked tree growing out of a crevice that saved his life. He had hugged the cliff edge so desperately that instead of being flung out as the guides had planned, he slipped underneath out of sight into the branches of a scrub oak. The Germans had no way of knowing if he'd fallen to the floor of the valley or if his body was wedged somewhere below between rocks. Easing himself out of the tangle of branches he shinnied down the trunk and listened. Rocks he had dislodged in his fall were still clattering far below, their rattle gradually diminishing.

He heard Stefan shout, "*Verdammt!* I can't tell how far he fell. Work your way down. Be sure he's dead. I'll go to the village to tell them we've had an accident and bring help."

Cane heard Max edging his way off the ledge. He came into view briefly. Cane felt in his pocket reassuring himself the lapis knife and Derringer were safe, then started down the bleak almost perpendicular mountainside, paralleling the Bavarian guide, keeping boulders between them. Halfway down he took cover in a sparse clump of fir, then stopped to listen. A jay's strident call warned him that Max was close by. A half dozen or so Alpine Cloughs were gliding easily on air currents above the valley. A pair of marmots sitting upright on their haunches in the lee of a small granite boulder eyed him warily. He moved a step forward hoping they'd not whistle a warning and alert

Reisner. He didn't hear Max until he spoke.

"Herr Cranach, you will put up your hands and turn around slowly."

Cane turned, slowly as directed. He raised his left arm and motioned with his head to his right. "I think it's broken." Max Reisner was three feet away with a pistol leveled from his hip. There was a grim smile on the German's face. "Well, you might say we botched that."

Cane nodded. "You might." He didn't look at the gun. He kept his eyes directly on Reisner. You can always tell what a man's going to do from his eyes. His grandfather had taught him that as a kid and it had served him more than once.

There is a standard way to disarm a man holding a gun if he's foolish enough to be in reaching distance. Sometimes it works, sometimes it doesn't. With practice and practical experience it's worth a gamble. Cane shrugged his shoulders, winced as if from pain, and moved toward Reisner slowly, talking.

"You're right. Something was botched. Is this the way you made your reputation as the best guides in Alpendorf? By robbing your clients? Do you stock a sporting goods store with used gear? My gun should bring a bundle." As he spoke he edged closer.

"Don't act stupid, Eliot. We know who you are and we know what you're after. And we've a score to settle for a friend."

"Helmut Acton, better known in the Argentine as Antonio Perez? A real genuine, dyed-in-the-wool son-of-a-bitch."

"That's your epitaph! Eliot, keep your distance, man!" He spoke too late. Cane grabbed Max's wrist. The gun exploded into a rock and ricocheted down the valley as Cane stooped and gave a quick twisting pull. Reisner tumbled over his shoulder with a fractured wrist leaving the gun in Cane's hand. Landing on his shoulder he jack-knifed into a razor-edged rock that broke his neck.

Cane watched the German make one curling, tortuous effort to rise, then lay still, his face frozen into an agonizing grimace. He searched him quickly but found nothing of importance, then replaced the

Browning automatic in Max's shoulder holster. He straightened and looked around. It was a long drop to the valley. The wind whined across the corrugated surface of the scree. A kestrel hovering in the sky shot downward toward his prey. He breathed deeply. The cold air burned his chest. He rolled Reisner to the edge of the graveled slip then booted him on it. Reisner tumbled end over end and finally rolled out of sight.

Cane worked his way down the slope carefully, and at the bottom found Reisner's body wedged between a boulder and a tree near the bank of the stream

He pulled the German loose and laid him on the bank. Nothing to do now until Müller returns. He missed his rifle. The Company would take a dim view of his losing the Gewehr. They weren't that easy to come by. He was tired, wet, cold. A raven floated close and came to rest on a nearby branch, railing at him. A squirrel scurried up a weathered pine. It was clearing in the east where the wind, with a steady consistency, pushed the clouds to the west. They hung low over the peaks. He sat down on a flat rock and leaned back against a fir tree.

He was sitting there when he saw the *Rothirsche*. He caught his breath sharply. What an animal! The stag stood fully five feet at the shoulder and looked nine feet long. Cane knew he couldn't be that large. His antlers must have been four feet high, a double rack with more snags than he could count. Unaware of Cane, of the dead man, the Red Deer sniffed into the wind and continued to the stream. When he'd finished drinking he listened again and with a dignity worthy of any monarch, turned slowly and followed the stream into the forest. Cane sighed. All in all it hadn't been such a bad day.

An hour later he heard the pickup returning. He walked to meet them, his hand in his pocket, his finger on the trigger of the Derringer. Hans Müller was driving with Herr Krantz and his brother beside him. Stefan Müller climbed from the pickup staring in disbelief. Then, finding his voice, he said, "Herr Cranach! Thank God you are safe!"

"Yes," Cane answered, "I'm all right but Max slipped and had a bad accident. I reached him as soon as I could, but it was too late. He's over there."

Cane expected Stefan to look for the gun, which he did, then to see if it had been fired. But he didn't check the cartridges. Turning to Stefan, Cane said, "I thought you said it was impossible to get here by car!"

Müller answered quickly, "Oh, no, Mien Herr. You misunderstood. You said you wanted a good mountain trek to write about, the backpacking, you know." A sullen line settled around his mouth.

Cane's eyes narrowed to slits, but he nodded agreement. "So, I did." He stood aside as they wrapped the body of Max Reisner in the tarp that covered the bed of the pickup and lifted him into it. Then the three had a quick consultation out of Cane's hearing. Krantz looked at Cane and said quietly, "I'll ride with Max."

I'm not home free yet, Cane thought. I should have kept the gun and let them think he lost it in his fall. They'd know I was lying, but they wouldn't be so quick to start something. The hell with hindsight. He let the Müller brothers climb in the pickup first, then followed. Not a word was said during the trip down the mountain. They stopped at the hotel and Krantz climbed down from the bed of the pickup as Cane stepped from the cab. They walked up the brick path together.

"Sad business." the hotel owner said shaking his head. "I've known Max since we soldiered together. It's hard to believe he could have such an accident in these mountains. He was raised in them." Cane didn't answer and after a minute Krantz stopped and looked at him "It was you Stefan said had fallen and was badly injured."

"I was lucky." Cane shook his head. "Max must have been coming to help me. Too bad." They entered the hotel together. "I think I need a drink, would you join me?"

Krantz shook his head without speaking and turned into his office. Cane stopped a waitress, ordered a whisky, a Weinerschnitzel and coffee on the terrace. "I'll be there in five minutes," he told her.

Right now he wanted to see Anya. Anya first, then Peter. He took the stairs two at a time, first to his room then to Anya's. Both were freshly cleaned and empty. Where could she be?

Back on the terrace, sipping his drink, he marveled at the change in the weather. The early morning fog was gone, the clouds had scattered leaving an azure sky fringed with remnants of cotton puff cumulus clouds. He was starting on the Weinerschnitzel when Peter crossed the Plaza and joined him.

"I've heard there was an accident this morning on the mountain, Herr Cranach."

"Ja. Very bad. My guide lost his footing and fell." He didn't look at Peter who had taken off his glasses and was polishing them absently. Cane shook his head and concentrated on his food. Peter replaced his glasses, adjusted them carefully, then said in a whisper, "Well, it appears they made a play for you. You're sure they're on to us?"

Cane nodded, his mouth full of food.

"Why would she warn you?"

"I don't know, but I'm grateful. At least I was prepared. Have you been approached in any way?"

"No. But the town is upset. I think it's time we left."

"I agree. But where, Munich?"

Peter shook his head. "I've been in radio contact with Hastings. I told him about the scene between the Müllers mentioning Rimini. Since that was the place of Thyssen's voluntary capture, he thinks it would be a good idea for you to check it out. Follow any lead you can think of. Doctors, lawyers, bankers, dentists, hotel proprietors who were around then. Anyone who might have had some business, social, professional or accidental contact with Thyssen. Do you still have his picture?"

"Oh, yes. It sounds like a good idea when you are clutching at straws. So I go on vacation. The Grand Hotel used to be one of the top ten." Cane stretched his feet out straight, crossed his ankles and his eyes searched across the Platz.

"It still is a lovely old hotel." Peter frowned down at him. "You wouldn't be looking for someone, now would you? A Russian, perhaps?"

Cane tipped his head slightly and gave him an oblique look. "Yes," he answered defiantly, "I am."

"Oh, God!" Peter dropped his cigarette and ground it out with his foot. Between tight lips he asked, "Can't you stay the hell away from her?"

"Peter," Cane pulled his feet back under him and looked up at the younger man. "I think I can get her to defect."

Peter's voice was brittle. "You're pipe-dreaming."

"Well, her father did."

"And she hated him for it. Don't blow it, Chili. News travels fast. I'd hate for Langley to hear you've shacked up with a Red Sparrow. If you can't leave her alone, I'm taking you off. You can go back to Colorado and play with your Longhorns."

"Now just one damned minute," Cane interrupted, his voice a terse whisper. "I killed one Spider today. I have taken care of our business here very well and I'm going to finish the job you hired me for."

"She'll never defect. For one thing, look what happened to her father immediately afterward. Then there's her daughter and grandson. She's working you over and the sooner you realize it the better off we all will be."

Cane stood up. "Damn it all, Pete. I wish you'd make an effort to understand. Believe me, I can bring Anya around."

Peter's eyes turned icy, his voice was bitter. "This is an order, Chili. Leave her alone." The two men faced each other making no attempt to hide their anger. "Face it or be relieved as of right now!" He looked at Cane a full minute then turned abruptly and went into the hotel.

The muscles in Cane's jaw tightened as he stared after Peter. Finally he lit a cigarette, inhaled deeply and watched the stream of smoke dissolve. He kicked a pebble off the flagstone, slowly entered the hotel and returned to his room. The phone was ringing when he opened the door.

*Tuesday, October 8*

Cane picked up the receiver. "Ja?" he answered. "Cranach here."

"Herr Cranach, I am in the next room and I have something of interest for you."

"Who is this?"

"A friend, sir. A good friend. I'm in room 3-B next to yours. You may bring a gun if you wish. I'm unarmed. But you will be interested in what I have to show you." There was a click as the connection was broken.

"What the hell now—" He checked the Derringer and the lapis, both in his hunting jacket pocket. He walked down the hall and knocked on 3-B. The door opened and a middle-aged man motioned him inside. Cane looked him over carefully, positive that he'd never seen the man before. Round faced, pot bellied, he had bright friendly eyes and thin gray hair that grew over his collar. A complete stranger. Cane stood in the doorway, his hand on the Derringer and looked around the room, then back to the man. "I'm Joseph Cranach," he said.

"And I'm Horst Rudhart." Neither man offered to shake hands. "Would you like a drink? Scotch, Schnapps?"

"No." Cane answered shortly. "What is it?"

"First we close and lock the door. We don't want unexpected visitors, you understand. Then we pull the blinds." He bowed and indicated a chair. "Now, we sit down and watch a movie."

Cane had a hard bottomless feeling in the pit of his stomach. Jesus Christ! There'd been a camera going the whole goddamned time! He felt sick.

But he didn't show it. He relaxed in his chair, crossed his legs, pulled out his pipe, filled and lighted it.

The first clip showed Cane and Anya sitting side by side on the bed. Then it showed when he picked her up and carried her directly into the camera for a close-up so distinct he could read his lips. It showed when he put her down on the bed and when he undressed her. Christ, she'd set him up! So there they were for all the world to see. After an interminable time the film rolled to a stop. Maybe the film ran out. Or more likely, she'd probably edited it herself. And she'd told him she hadn't brought a sitter! His mistake. He should have asked if she'd brought a photographer.

Rudhart opened the blinds. "A touching affair." Then he laughed and said, "You Americans do like puns, I believe."

"I'm no American. I'm an Austrian journalist and I don't know what your game is. I'm a writer with no boss to carry tales to. I can't believe the *English Sportsman Magazine* would be the least interested."

"I agree. But the CIA would certainly be interested in this charming little affair with a KGB agent."

Cane laughed. "You're crazy, man."

"Not so crazy. We'll trade you the film for a certain skull." Cane stood up.

"I don't know what you're talking about. A *skull*? They'd better lock you up, Rudhart. You might be dangerous. Going around making films like this you'll run into trouble. I have no skull but my own and I don't give a damn what you do with this film. Sell it to a porno broker!" He threw back the bolt, flung open the door and walked to his room. When he was inside, he slammed the door and a deep red flush climbed up his neck and into his face and forehead until his head was hot and perspiration broke out on his temples.

So there was a two-way mirror on the wall across from the bed.

He hadn't even checked it. He should have known because it was permanently attached to the wall above the dresser. They had disarmed him effectively by loading the room with electronic bugs and he hadn't even thought of the mirror. God, he was rusty!

He felt nauseated. So she wasn't a hot shot spy. Just an enemy sister after all. It's *swallow* in the Center jargon—*mazhno*—a girl trained in the fine art of seduction. That was her job, setting up guys. Well, she was damn good at it. What a laugh Peter would get out of it. All ready to defect—what a joke!

He packed slowly and jerked the sheet of paper from his typewriter and closed the case. He felt jaded. Wrung out.

Walking to the window, he threw the casements open and noticed Anya crossing the Platz. She looked like a fashion plate. A bright yellowish tweed coat belted and full skirted was swinging as she walked with a sure quick stride by the fountain. Her shoulders square and straight, her neck slender with a scarf twisted and blowing in the wind, her head held high. Her soft black leather boots wrinkled at the ankle. She looked so Russian! And so lovely. Well, by God, the spider doesn't show his spot until he has the fly in the web. Cane whirled around, flung open the door and took the stairs two at a time. He met her by the terrace.

"Herr Cranach." She greeted him as innocently as if she'd never tumbled around on his bed with a camera rolling practically on top of them. "I hear you had some excitement this morning. Such a shame about poor Herr Reisner."

Cane tried to act noncommittal, but it was impossible. How could she be so casual! "Yes," he answered coldly.

She misinterpreted his expression. "I'm sorry. It must have been terrible for you."

"Get in the car," he said.

She looked at him in surprise. "Why?"

His voice had the sting of a double-edged razor. "Just get in the goddamned car." He led the way.

She settled herself beside him as he put the car in gear with a roar. He drove out of town the way he had come in, past the monastery, then took the first turn into the mountains, driving fast, unheeding. The car splashed through a deep rut of mud and splattered the windows. Circling up one hairpin curve after another, he found the picnic area, drove across it. He stopped in front of the split-rail fence grinding the brake so hard the car swerved to a quivering stop. Cane flung open his door, went around the car, opened Anya's door and jerked her out. He pulled her to him, pushed back her coat and ripped open her blouse. He covered her mouth with savage strength, bruised her breasts. She made no sound. Grabbing her hair with one hand, he pulled her head back and looked at her. "And there are no cameras here." He held her like that, immobile, for a minute longer, then pushed her away with a snarl. She stumbled and fell. He walked to the car, got in, started the engine. "Get back to town the best way you can, and I think you know how. Just find a man."

She got to her feet as he backed the car and ran after him. "What is the matter with you? Canyon, what is it I've done?"

Cane stopped the car. "I was going to take you just like you took me, but I can't do it. You're damn good at your job, so go back to Number 2 Dzerzhinsky Street and tell them you made the pitch, but you didn't get the skull. But give your photographer high marks."

"Cane, I don't know what you're talking about. You must believe me!"

"The hell you don't." Cane turned off the ignition, got out of the car and walked to her. Towering over her, he backed her into a tree. "That charming little movie—in exchange for the skull. I told your friend to go to hell and sell it to a porno producer. You looked fetching in the buff in my bed!"

Her eyes grew wide as she understood what he was saying. The blood drained from her face. She took a quick breath, pushed her hair back from her forehead.

"You can believe what you want to," she said slowly. "It doesn't make a bit of difference. I'm not a child and I've been in this business a long time. If I had done what you think, I've never make apologies. It's a dirty business we're in. I had nothing to do with that so-called movie and I don't know who authorized it. But it doesn't matter whether you believe me or not. That's just for the record. And I won't be walking back." She smiled then there was almost a twinkle in her eyes as she flipped open her bag and pulled out a small caliber pistol.

"I'm taking your car, old friend, and you get back the best way you can. Find a woman!" She backed toward the car holding the pistol level. And still smiling.

"You wouldn't shoot." Cane stepped toward her.

"Try me."

Cane stopped. Damn she was cool. "Hell, take the car!" he said. "I've already walked ten miles today. Just what I need is another hike."

Perhaps he could play on her sympathy. Yet he wasn't really surprised when she backed to the car, got in, started the motor and roared away flinging gravel and pine-needles in his face.

He started walking back to the highway. Minutes later he heard a series of gun shots and broke into a run. Then he heard another shot. Around the curve at the foot of the hairpin bend he saw the roadblock. A man was lying near the car and another behind the car was holding an automatic. Cane heard him shout, "Come out Eliot, with your hands up or I'll blow you out of there!"

Cane took cover behind the screen of firs and hurried down the slope to the road. He couldn't see the face of the man beside the car, but the man with the gun was Hans Müller.

Coming up behind him, Cane said calmly.

"Ah, Herr Müller, I have you covered. Drop your gun before you turn around and please raise your hands." Cane walked to the car, picked up the gun, then took one from the dead man.

Anya was already crawling out of the car. "I must say I'm glad to see you," she said.

Cane ignored her and turned to Hans.

"A little trick I learned from the Red Deer. Your brother told me how the *Rothirsche* sends his ladies ahead to scout out danger." He bowed to Anya. "Thank you, my dear. I'm glad you survived." He turned to Müller.

"Who the hell is this bastard?"

Hans sullenly replied, "He's Max's brother."

"Let's get this road cleared. Where's your car?"

"We walked up. The truck is below." Hans answered slowly, his eyes angry. Then he added, "Eliot, you don't have a chance. The whole town is after you. They know you killed Max. They are taking care of your partner right now."

"You Nazi worm. Nothing better happen to him. Now get that junk off the road. Miss Mason, you'll help him."

"I'll do no such thing. I'll hold the gun and you get it off. Besides," she said loftily, "that's not woman's work."

"So who's a chauvinist?" Taking her gun he stooped and kissed her quickly. "Now, get the hell busy! I don't trust you with a gun."

When the road was cleared, Cane ordered Hans to double the dead man into the trunk. Anya stood to one side watching. Cane motioned for her to drive with Hans beside her.

"Just remember I have the gun aimed straight at your head, Müller. I'd hate to splatter this pretty American cookbook writer with a lot of German blood, or even my car, but if it's necessary...."

At the foot of the road they found the pickup. Following Cane's orders, Hans transferred the body from the Mercedes to the passenger seat of the pickup. Cane fastened the seat belt around the dead man.

"Now," he instructed, "drive straight up to the picnic grounds. I'll be right behind you."

"What the devil are you doing?" Hans held back.

"You'll see." He held the gun on Hans while Anya turned the Mercedes around. Then he ordered, "Move over and fasten your seat belt. I'll drive."

Hans started the pickup slowly. Cane followed, tailgating the bumper of the pickup as it twisted and turned along the shoulder of the road, soaring above the mist-filled valley far below to the right. Hans braked at a sharp left turn, but Cane didn't.

He shoved the accelerator to the floor board and the turbojet engine took off with a leap and a deep throated roar. To Anya it felt like it all happened in slow motion—the car turned to the left ramming the pickup as it turned, ripping the fender half off and leaving it folded into scarred, ruffled rows, discharging a piercing shriek. The pickup bounced once, then took to the air in a slow arc, off the road, through the rail fence and into the canyon.

"My God!" Anya breathed. The force of the collision flung her forward against the belt. Cane twisted the wheel and jammed the brakes until the car was half off the road up the inclined side. The Mercedes was shaking. Steam escaped from under the broken fender and the rattle wouldn't stop. Cane got out of the car and walked to the edge of the ravine. The pickup was in flames.

# CHAPTER XXIV

*Tuesday, October 8*

rom some distance beyond the picnic grounds, Magen Ben-Yanait watched Anya and Cane through binoculars. He wondered why Cane was tailgaiting the pickup to the picnic area and what he saw impressed him considerably. Cane's car looked a wreck—right fender corrugated and smashed—half torn off, steam rising from the car and dissolving in the air. *My God—the man's unbelievable!* He had spied shamelessly on the pseudo-Austrian journalist and the Russian agent wondering who was conning whom.

The CIA agent would never know that the Israeli had trailed Müller and Reisner into the forest and when Max Reisner aimed his pistol at Cane, Ben-Yanait stood on a cliff above, the sight of his rifle leveled on the German's head. Magen didn't need to shoot because the American handled the situation very well.

Now again the American had turned matters around in an extraordinary way. However, his job wasn't finished. It was necessary to keep Canyon Eliot and all his aliases alive. At least until the Mossad had possession of the skull.

# CHAPTER XXVI

Anya looked in the rearview mirror at her reflection, surprised that there was little visible proof on her face of the harrowing hour she'd just been through. Of course, there were the bruises Canyon himself had given her. Pine needles speckled her coat and her blouse was ripped to the waist. Damn him. She pulled the pins from her hair and twisted it into another knot, brushing the loose strands back. Considering everything, she seemed as serene as if she'd been for an evening drive to see a mountain sunset. Proof enough, she decided, that because of her training she was thoroughly indoctrinated to react automatically in any emergency. A robot, she thought, that's what I am. And Canyon Eliot, too. Like those lizards that absorb the color of their surroundings.

She remembered Cane in the cemetery in Oklahoma, a Western rancher. In Munich, the courtly Bavarian gentleman, then an Austrian journalist and now a competent spy disposing of an adversary. That was the true Eliot. Taking on any identity and making it real. But then, no more than I. Two chameleons absorbing the foliage around them.

So now they both had killed. Killing was an important part of their job. For once they had a common enemy. She glanced sideways at Cane. His face was a mask, but meeting her eyes it softened. "I—I'm sorry, Anya...."

She didn't look at him. "I understand," she answered. "Altogether, not a pleasant afternoon."

181

"Do you want to tell me what happened?"

"I ran into the roadblock and ambush that was obviously meant for you. At the first shot I dropped to the floor. When he opened the door, I—I shot him."

They drove in silence for awhile then Anya asked, "Was it bad up on the mountain this morning?"

"Not too. It helped knowing their plans. So I do thank you." When she didn't answer, he asked, "What did you do today?"

"I went back to see Frau Müller. Hans was there and asked how well I knew you."

"I suppose you told him we were old friends."

"No. I told him I'd never seen you before we met at the hotel."

"He could have seen the movie."

She groaned audibly.

"Could they know you're KGB?"

"I hope not!"

"Be careful, Anya."

"You, too."

The silence was an uneasy one. At the back of Cane's mind was the thought of the threat Müller had made about Peter. He drove as fast as the car would let him.

She pushed back strands of hairs with nervous fingers. Without taking his eyes from the road Cane asked, "You're still determined to get the skull?"

"Of course," she answered. "Absolutely."

"How do you plan on retrieving it when it's in the consulate safe in Munich?"

"You don't really expect me to tell you?"

Cane shrugged. "Well, you do owe me something for saving your life."

"I repaid that when I cleaned off the roadblock." She held up her hands, scratched and dirty. Then before Cane could answer she turned on him furiously. "How can you be like that!" Her voice rose with a rasping strangled sound.

Cane glanced at her quickly, surprised at the scathing fervor in her tone. "Like what? I don't know what you're talking about."

"Like—like this. Being so casual. Pushing those men over the ravine—doesn't it affect you at all?"

No more than killing a rabid dog. It was either us or them. I have a peculiar prejudice there." For a long time they were quiet, until Cane asked, "Why should it affect you?"

She hesitated before answering and when she did her voice was low. "I've never—I've never killed anyone before."

His eyes on the hairpin turn he took on two wheels, his face grim, Cane said, "I guess I should say it gets easier, but it doesn't."

"Did you know that the boy in the pickup, Hans, is Müller's boy. The older one, Stefan is Thyssen's son."

"Yes."

"You could be in even more trouble now."

"It will look like an accident. Do you want out at the hotel?"

"Where are you going?"

Cane threw his head back and laughed. "Damned if I'll tell you." They passed the monastery and wondered at the glow in the western sky. They both spoke at once. "A forest fire!"

Then Cane said, "No, it's the village. The whole town must be burning!"

"Oh, God!"

It wasn't the village. It was the hotel. Cane skidded to a stop at the Platz, flung open the door and ran by the fountain elbowing a path through the shocked villagers. Then he stopped across the street stunned. Black smoke swirled in angry billows from the roof and curled into the sky. The mountains, the waterfall, all were hidden behind black churning clouds of smoke. Through the smoke, tongues of flame snaked from windows and eaves. A fire truck poured a pitiful stream of water into its center. Balconies crumbled, a few window boxes still held flowers.

Automatically he glanced up to find his room, but instead he found Peter's. *Peter was frantically trying to break open the window.* Why couldn't he open it? Peter! *Peter!* He saw him desperately working to break the window with a chair. *Peter, oh God, Peter!*

The flames leaped through the balcony and the roof collapsed. The window seemed to fold in slow motion and Peter dropped from sight. Cane couldn't take his eyes away from where the room had been. He watched the window box spilling bright colored flowers as it fell. Peter's funeral pyre. Was it supposed to have been his also? Was this what Müller meant? The Spider organization wouldn't hesitate to burn a hotel or a village or a country to achieve its aims. Did they think they had destroyed the skull too? A furious anger knotted his stomach.

He turned and trudged slowly back to the car. Anya was gone.

For several minutes, Cane sat stunned. The hotel caved in leaving only red, glowing skeletal beams. His face was drawn and severe, his eyes dull, his mouth parched and acrid. The charred smell was in his car, his nostrils, his clothes, his skin. He dropped his head on his arms across the wheel and shivered involuntarily. Peter, Peter, forgive me.

He raised his head, stared at the dying flames for interminable minutes, then started the motor. He turned the car around and drove away from Alpendorf.

# CHAPTER XXVII

*Tuesday, October 8*

The Israeli parked his Jeep a reasonable distance from Cane's Mercedes in the reflection of the hotel fire and sat for a minute watching Anya. The KGB Wonder Girl has the American reeling on the ropes. I might be able to save him from assassination at the hands of the Nazi's but I can't follow him into the bedroom. He moved toward the fire, careful to stay out of her sight.

Then he saw the figure at the window. Poor bastard. He didn't have a chance. There was no doubt in Magen's mind why the fire had been set. Someone wanted the skull destroyed and the two Americans along with it. Very likely Canyon Eliot's life had been saved because of a lovers' tryst on a mountain trail with Anya. But burning the hotel? The people we are up against are desperate.

He watched as Cane stayed in his car waiting until the fire burned itself out, shaking his head at the wreck of Cane's car.. When there was nothing but rubble he followed Cane until he reached the Autobahn and turned toward the Austrian border. Fairly certain he knew where the American was headed he wondered again where the skull was hidden. Had it burned in the fire? Ah, no. Cane is too smart to carry it with him.

~~~~

The newsroom at the consulate received word of the hotel fire from an AP West German news dispatch. Hastings found the copy when he returned from dinner. Damn. He had been worried when he failed to hear from either Peter or Cane. Was it possible the fire covered up a murder? Two?

He carried the teletyped copy to the window, creasing it in accordion folds with his thumb nail, unmindful of the long stream of one-way traffic that left trails of bright red drift down Von der Tenn-Strasse. The President's Palace opposite was dark except for caretaker lights. The park behind was a world of shadows. That was where rubble had been piled after the war. Bulldozed into a hill and landscaped with trees and shrubbery and flowers and paths so that all the scars were gone. Plastic surgery for a city.

But the Nazis were still around. Burrowing like termites into the woodwork. Had they picked off two of his best men? Hastings rubbed his eyes, then his forehead. Or was it the Russians? The matter of the skull demanded answers. The skull in the consulate safe was no nearer a solution now than when it had been switched in a New York post office. He would spend the night in his office.

The message came through at midnight from Innsbruck. It was deciphered by a weary code clerk and brought to him. *Peter is dead. The Spider Organization is not. There are three less than when I arrived. KGB active. Disappeared after the fire. Leaving for Rimini as per instructions from Peter. Becker Grand Hotel.*

Hastings leaned back in his chair and reread the note. So it was Peter. Peter—so special to Cane. He could imagine how desolate Cane felt. Carl Becker would be his new cover. How could he fit a chicken vendor into his search for Thyssen's Rimini background? Eliot would have to be canny to work around that.

# CHAPTER XXVI

R imini was a rather indifferent Adriatic seaport a hundred miles south of Venice firmly rooted on the banks of the Marecchia River beneath a protective bluff of the Coriano ridge.

Cane sat on the terrace overlooking the gardens of the Grand Hotel with a half-emptied bottle of Chianti before him, checking notes he had made from the facts he had. There was something wrong, something he couldn't put his finger on. Why had Thyssen left Berlin for Italy? Easy. Thyssen was one of Hitler's trusted henchmen and it would be natural for the Führer to send him as a liaison between the two partners. But why Rimini? Why come to Rimini just as it was about to fall to the English Eighth Army? Was it because he needed to be captured by them or the Americans so his future—and the future of the Nazi party would be secure?

If he had spent much time here someone would remember him. Who would be the most likely candidates to meet a prominent Nazi socially? Men too old to be in military service. Bankers, doctors, dentists, lawyers.

For three days he checked with those still living. It was a dentist who made the trip to Rimini pay off.

A Dr. Parlotti had an X-ray of Otto Thyssen's teeth! Why had Thyssen come to a dentist in Rimini during the war when the German Army had excellent medical services, and as an SS officer, he would be entitled to the best? Dr. Parlotti told Cane his father had the X-ray in his files, but there was nothing in his records mentioning an appointment or why the X-ray was taken.

So now the skull was here in Rimini. Hastings had insisted on sending it to the bank for safe keeping until it could be checked with the X-ray and perhaps the secret of the skull would be found. Cane had a date with the chief executive officer of the Banco Internazionale di Italie and Dr. Parlotti at four o'clock.

He glanced impatiently at this watch. Two hours to wait. What would they find?

He fingered his glass of wine, twisting the stem first one direction, then rolling it back along his thumb absently as he watched the gray topped breakers rolling into the deserted beach beyond the garden. He was completely startled when he heard a sunny voice.

"I'm afraid to call you by name. It might not be the right one!"

"Oh, God!" Cane looked up at Anya with eyes as chilly as the shadow of a cloud. "I'd think you were following me, if I didn't know better." He made no effort to rise.

"Of course, darling. You know I am." She sat down opposite him. "There's something about you that I can't resist. It's smaller than a bread box and larger than an egg. Can't you guess?"

Cane didn't answer. He pulled out his pipe and filled it from a wrinkled plastic bag, lighted it and looked resolutely out into the garden where a bronze Neptune surrounded with seahorses and water nymphs sprayed fountain jets into a sunken basin. He was determined to keep on top of the situation with Anya. She was too damn smart. Where had she disappeared after the fire? He stared at the fountain with studied interest as a waiter brought an extra glass and filled it. Thanking him in perfect Italian with a pronounced American accent, she turned her full attention to Cane.

With elbows on the table, her chin cupped in her hands, she smiled at him. "Quit sulking. I know you have the skull. The Spider thinks it was destroyed in the blaze. That's why the hotel was set afire."

Cane eyed her coolly. "How do you know that?"

"Many reasons. They figured you were dead on the mountain and the skull was in the hotel. And of course your partner. The Spider thought they would take care of the whole thing."

"You think it was planned to coincide with the ambush?"

"Why, I know it."

"Then how do you account for their knowing I'd be on the mountain when I didn't know it myself?"

"Easy. Hans followed you—us." Anya picked up her wine class and gazed intensely at Cane. "They were watching you every minute. They wanted to be rid of both CIA agents and the skull. They don't need the skull, they know its secret."

"Do you?"

Her smile was mocking. "If I did do you think I'd tell?"

Cane laughed and shook his head.

"Anya, Anya! Why of all people would it have to be you that Peter and I crossed?"

"Peter, your partner? Were you close to this agent?"

"Yes." Cane didn't look at her. "He was my son's best friend."

"Cane, how terrible."

"Someday I'll find the man who set fire to the hotel and I'll kill him." Cane's voice had a slow measured cadence that chilled Anya.

She placed her hand over his, but he didn't move and after a second or two she took it away. If he would only look at her. Show her by some means that he remembered their night in Alpendorf. "Cane," she said, her eyes fixed on him, "Do you know why I'm here?"

"I should think so! It's because I'm here."

"And since you're here, it stands to reason that the skull is here, too. Right?"

"Right." Cane felt the tension ease and his eyes softened. He looked at Anya in her tweedy brown suit with the frou-frou blouse spilling over with lace at the neck and cuffs, at the gold hoops swinging from her ears, at her hair softly coifed in a low chignon.

"Damn, if you weren't so all-fired beautiful!"

She blew him a kiss across the table and answered, "I think you're pretty too. Let's talk about the skull. *If* you'll let me have it I think we can work out a partnership arrangement."

"Drink your wine and stop dreaming."

"You know it's ours. Your friends stole it from us."

"Moot point. Shall we debate the question? The poor Major was lying there peacefully in his grave these thirty-five years until your friends disinterred him. Who stole who is the question."

Her eyes twinkled. "I'll not argue," she answered, "but to satisfy my curiosity, who are you here as?"

Cane shook his head. "Allow me to introduce myself. Carl Becker from Little Rock, Arkansas. Yup. That's in the US of A. And the biggest chicken growing state. I'm just an ordinary merchant looking for Eye-talian chicken markets. And you?"

"Nothing phony about me. Anya Petrovna, Cultural Attaché from Russia to the United Nations on a well-earned vacation."

"All out in the open and above-board. Just like that. Staying at the Grand Hotel, I presume?"

"Where else? There's not a big choice."

"Well, I must say that is great. We'll vacation together. That is, if you don't mind calling on restaurants, the kind that buy chickens."

"I'll love it. But you know where I want to go?"

"Your mind is impossible to read."

"I want to picnic on the River Uso."

"On the far bank, of course, so you can say you've crossed the Rubicon."

She smiled brightly. "Yes, I never dreamed I'd be so close to Caesar's river."

"We'll do it tomorrow. But we already have, you know."

"We've already what?" Anya looked puzzled.

"Crossed our Rubicon. In a hotel room in Alpendorf with a movie camera rolling like crazy. That, my dear Soviet, was the point from which there is no return."

She nodded, her eyes clouding. "Yes, we crossed it. And what a crossing it was! Did you find out who made the movie?"

"It had to be someone in the Spider organization. I hope to God it burned."

"Cane, you must know, please believe me, that night was very special to me."

"It was to me also. And now it's the real Rubicon?"

"Yes." Her expression was serious, her eyes soft and moist.

"All right. Tomorrow. You arrange the lunch. I'll be in charge of transportation and after we picnic on the Rubicon we'll go to Venice and spend the night at the Gritti Palace and cross it again."

Anya frowned. "I'm not sure Moscow will approve, but I'll tell them I'm getting closer to the skull. That's the truth, isn't it?"

"Absolutely. And this time I'll guarantee there'll be no photographers at the Gritti! Now tell me, what has the opposition been doing since the fire?"

"The opposition has been to Moscow."

"Again? You commute to Moscow like we do to Denver."

"This was serious. I told you about Natalya. She's been under a sort of house arrest, and that's like caging a robin. My superior called me home to talk to the magistrate. They want to help me and her. But she doesn't want their help. She wants to be a martyr."

"What will happen, Anya? Exile? Siberia?"

Anya sighed and looked past him toward the sea where parallel waves of gray autumn surf droned monotonously.

"It's hard to say. She can't be sent abroad as long as I'm out of the country. Prison would kill her and exile would be almost as bad. She isn't going to change. It's a case of tilting at windmills and it can destroy her."

Cane reached for her hand. "I wish there was something I could do."

Anya smiled bleakly.

"Oh, for now she's promised not to make waves. At least until I get

back with the skull. If I'm unsuccessful we'll both need to buy furs."
She looked at Cane, laughed, then changed the subject.

"There was the first snow and it was beautiful. Russia is glorious in the winter. We love the cold and the snow is our special benediction, our blessing and our manna. It's saved us from Napoleon and Hitler and it gives every Russian a feeling of renewal."

"It's in your eyes. I think you feel for Russia what a woman should feel for a lover." Her hand felt warm in his and Anya made no move to free it.

"That's close," Anya agreed. "But Natalya wasn't the only reason I returned. There was a great deal to report."

"What did they say about Niels?"

"Hazards of the profession." She straightened up and added, "Oh, by the way, a sitter came back with me. He's replacing Niels."

"He's here now?" Cane dropped her hand like a hot coal.

"He's watching us. His name is Yuri, but he can't read lips in English. He thinks I'm seducing you."

Cane grinned. "The hazards of the profession don't really bother him, then. What does he look like?"

"You know I can't tell you that. You have to understand, Mr. Becker, there are certain rules that apply to our profession. You must play by the rules." She smiled her sweetest. "I really need the skull. Will you tell me where it is?"

"Certainly. I thought you'd never ask. It's in a pasteboard box in a bank vault."

"Oh." Her voice was small. "That's silly, now isn't it? What's it doing there?"

She had hardly spoken when a shocked look crossed her face, her hand flew to her mouth and she whispered, "Oh, my God, he's here too!" Her voice was strangled.

"Who? Who are you talking about?" Cane turned around in time to see the back of a dark haired, medium sized man entering the terrace door of the hotel.

"Do you know who that is?"

Cane stared at her blankly. "No, should I?"

"He's Magen Ben-Yanait, code name Jasmine. A top Israeli agent."

"Mossad?"

"Yes. He's been following you since you left Oklahoma City."

"Oh, come on."

"It's true. I watched him board the plane in Oklahoma City and I followed both of you from Kennedy Airport into New York. When you lost us in Manhattan, I knew then you were a professional, and he did too. I didn't see him in Munich but he was in Alpendorf."

Cane was stunned. He felt like a fool.

"I knew I was being followed as soon as I got off the plane in New York, but I didn't see you."

"I was in the waiting room when you came in, and after you, Ben-Yanait. He saw you when you stood up to get in line and nearly fell apart. He'd seen you somewhere before because he recognized you."

Cane shook his head in disbelief.

"I'll be damned. To have the Russians and Israelis on my tail, God help me!" He looked at his watch. "I've an important date. Will you excuse me?"

"Yes, if you'll tell me where you're going."

"Sorry, Company business."

"You know you'll be followed."

He laughed and pushed his chair back, fumbling in his pocket. He dropped a handful of lira notes on the table and stood up. "That's all right. You can tell from my poor but honest face I have nothing to hide. Don't forget our date tomorrow. About ten o'clock?"

"Oh, much earlier than that if we go to Venice. And we can have a breakfast picnic!"

# CHAPTER XXVII

*Rimini*
*Monday, October 13*

Cane made no effort to hide his destination. He was reasonably certain that Anya's sitter and the Israeli agent both would follow him. And that's just dandy. The skull is at the bank and it will stay there until someone from the Embassy picks it up. My responsibility ends right here, thank God! Tomorrow I'll go to Venice with my lovely spy and we'll let the future take care of itself. So Thyssen, my Nazi friend, it's back to the ash heap for you. He parked his car just off Corso d'Augusto and walked to the bank. Dr. Parlotti was already there with the executive officer. Introductions were made and the three men entered the vault. The skull was brought out of its box, placed on a table under a bright light and Dr. Parlotti compared it with the X-ray. He frowned, perplexed, then shook his head. Using the X-ray as a pointer, he touched the skull and said, "This skull here, is not Otto Thyssen's."

Cane stared at him, stunned.

"That's—that's impossible! We know it's Thyssen. It has to be!"

"I'm sorry, Signore Becker. But even a layman can tell that this X-ray and the teeth in the skull don't match." He pointed out a mouthful of discrepancies as Cane and the banker hung over the table. "They don't match anywhere."

Cane had to agree. He took a long breath and released it slowly.

The dentist knew what he was talking about. The X-ray had Thyssen's name on it and the date, July 10, 1944. There was no doubt. The two did not match.

"Well," he said mostly to himself, "that really makes it a whole new ball game."

"A ball game?" asked Parlotti, "I don't understand."

"Nothing. I was talking to myself. May I keep the X-ray?"

"Yes, of course." The banker and the dentist watched as Cane carefully replaced the skull in its plastic sack and pasteboard box.

"And now I've a favor to ask. Will you have this box delivered to me at the hotel tonight after dark. I'd rather not be seen carrying it out."

"Certainly," the banker answered.

"I'm sorry things didn't turn out the way you expected," Dr. Parlotti added.

Cane nodded. He thanked them for their help, then took the X-ray and walked to the post office. Addressing an envelope to himself in care of the American Express in Munich, he slipped the X-ray between two postcards and mailed it. It would be interesting to see Hastings' reaction to this new development.

From the post office, Cane walked around the village to the 2,000 year old Arch of Triumph Augustus built to commemorate his victories. Down the ancient thoroughfare that bore his name. He stopped across the street from the old cathedral with its ornate sculptures and rococo architecture, crossed over and went inside. In the cool semi-darkness, candles reflected the burnished gold leaf as he sat down on a side pew and considered the consequences of this new development. It sure as hell changed his plans! He had thought that he would be through. All he had to do was fit the X-ray and the skull together and that would be it. A few stolen hours with Anya and—a grimace of pain crossed his face. The vigil candles quivered in a halo of light by the altar. An old lady in a black dress and shawl slipped down the aisle, crossed herself and knelt to pray. Cane was conscious of the cathedral doors opening twice more, letting in a long stream of evening light. That would be the Sitter and the Israeli. They know that I don't have the skull, so there's no need to fear an ambush.

Cane rose slowly, walked to the altar, dropped some liras in the receptacle. He chose a candle and carried it to the vigil light stand. The lighted candles were of all sizes and from the smallest he lit his own and placed it on the lower tier.

Back at the hotel he had dinner in his room, stood on the balcony and watched the lights come on one by one across the town, in the garden and along the boulevard by the sea. When it was dark, there was a knock on his door, and he accepted the skull back into his keeping.

He locked the door, drew the curtain, filled his pipe, then lifted the skull from its box and sat down to think.

Rolling the skull around in both hands, he examined it as closely as he had at the ranch. *Who in the bloody hell are you?*

That poor guy buried at Fort Reno in Oklahoma under the name of Heinrich von Stober, Major in the 1st Paratroop Division. Well, it didn't take long to determine it wasn't von Stober, that instead it was Otto Adolph Thyssen, Nazi war criminal, and now, by God! it's not him either. Otto Thyssen had to be one smart operator. He purloined the Major's clothes, dog tags and papers. So what happened to the Major? Then faced with a return trip and knowing Frau von Stober would take a dim view of a well-known Nazi masquerading as her husband, he had to make a quick decision in the POW camp. Which of the prisoners was sacrificed so that Thyssen would come back to Germany under a new name?

To obtain a list of the prisoners from the General Services Administration and to check out everyone would take more time than he had. Did Thyssen pick a fellow prisoner, make sure he had a fatal accident, drowning, for instance, in a farm pond, since that was the official description of von Stober's death?

Pulling the papers Hastings had given him from the inside pocket of his jacket, he examined them again. The man, Thyssen, had a fortune to hide. How did that relate to the skull? Why did he leave Berlin in August of 1944 and head for Italy? Did Mussolini have a hiding place? Is the cache of Jewish treasure in the Dolomites? The Appennines? Right here in the Coriano Hills? Or did he use a Redoubt tunnel in Bavaria or a salt mine in Austria? No telling how the bastard's mind worked. It looked as if he'd left Lake Garda, gone to Rimini, had his dental work done, visited an acquaintance in the military hospital there and lifted his tags and uniform. Instead of returning to Garda where he was supposed to be he visited the front where Kesselring had a final delaying position in front of the Gothic Line. It would be easy enough, considering his position, to go anywhere he wished. Then in some dugout, changing clothes and identities, he conveniently let himself be captured. After Rimini fell to the Allies, arrangements were completed to ship the prisoners to America.

So that gets him to America and it gets someone buried, but where the hell is Thyssen now? The answer must be South America. That would also explain the vigorous interest of the Spider organization. They don't give a damn about the skull. They have Thyssen. They don't want the fact that Thyssen is alive and well to be broadcast and they sure as hell don't want anyone snooping around the Treasure of the Third Reich.

Cane walked out on the balcony and stood at the iron balustrade gazing over the casually lighted garden to the dark sea beyond where he could hear the restless whitecaps rolling from the east. He emptied his pipe, slapping it against the palm of his hand over an ashtray, the sound of it breaking the stillness. He thought of Anya. We're coming to the end of the trail. Natalya will put a period to her usefulness to the Soviet Union. If she is exiled abroad then Anya will never be allowed outside the USSR again. Could he persuade her to defect? No. She would never leave Natalya and Misha in Russia, certainly not if Natalya is in prison. It's a dead end, Anya, my love. We'll have tomorrow and tomorrow night. That will be our Rubicon.

Inside, he finished the wine, then sat down at the desk to organize

197

the facts he had on paper for Hastings.

In the hotel garden, beyond the fountain, Magen Ben-Yanait saw Cane step out on the balcony, watched as he flicked the dead ashes from his pipe and wondered where Anya was. It didn't take her long to pick up the American. Where was the goddamned skull? At the bank? In his room? A delivery had been made to him. Was that the skull? He would wait until morning to make his move.

# CHAPTER XXVIII

I t was barely daylight when Cane called Anya, who answered the phone with a sleepy, "Da?"

"Let's go."

"So early?"

"*Da!* Hurry and I'll have a made-to-order sunrise straight from Yugoslavia to go with our breakfast."

"I can't miss that. Give me five minutes. I love special order sunrises."

"I'll be in front."

The clerk on duty had a cup of coffee in his hand as Cane came downstairs. "You're leaving early?"

"Yes, Miss Petrovna and I are going to Venice. We'll be back tomorrow. Will you unlock the gates?"

"Of course. It's necessary to keep the cars locked up at night."

"I understand." Cane followed him down the steps to the drive and put the skull in the trunk. Why didn't Anya hurry! He had a strong feeling that he should get out of Rimini as soon as possible. In minutes she appeared, carrying a picnic hamper. Cane shook his head as he took the basket from her. "Faded jeans and tennis shoes. What you need are cowboy boots—you're the last person I'd expect to look like...."

"Like a Colorado cowgirl. That's me today. What the well-dressed Russian wears on the Rubicon." She settled herself in the car, but not until she brushed her hand along the fender of the Mercedes.

199

"My, but you've spent sometime at a body shop—I can't believe the difference since I saw your car last!"

"Yes. Germans take very good care of their motor cars—especially those that get tangled up in unfortunate accidents."

She looked at him sideways, grinning.

"I'm glad I ordered our food last night. I'd never have made it so early."

"Miss Petrovna, I must tell you that I refuse to glide down the Grand Canal in a gondola with a Gondolier singing O Sole Mio and you in blue jeans."

"Not to worry." She held up her straw bag. "Here I have a skirt and blouse, even jewels to bewitch you with, my dear."

The sound of the motor woke Ben-Yanait, who had spent most of the night watching Cane's window. Only when he was satisfied that Cane had gone to bed and was asleep did he go to his own room, which overlooked the parking lot and the locked gate. He rushed to the window in time to see Cane drive through the gates.

Damn! Where the devil is he going so early? Magen lost little time getting dressed and taking the stairs two at a time. The room clerk was a great help.

"Oh, si Signore, the American is going to Venice."

"Alone?"

"Oh, no, no, Signore. Does one go to Venice alone? He has the beautiful Russian with him."

"How long will they stay?"

"Only for the night."

"You're sure?"

"Si, Signore. They took no luggage." He shrugged and added, "That's what Signore Becker said."

"*Grazie.*"

"*Prago.*" Ben-Yanait handed him a multi-lira bill. "Will you let me know when they return?"

"Ah, yes. Si, si!"

Interesting. Magen pursed his lips and then smiled. So the American and the Russian were stealing a little of the Company's and the Center's time to do their own thing. He was more than likely so engrossed in the beautiful Anya that he had left the skull in his room. He sure as hell wouldn't take it with him. So today would be the day!

~~~~

The tree was a scrawny pine that had lost most of its needles. The Rubicon, what they could find of it, known locally as the Uso, was an almost invisible drainage ditch overgrown with weeds and emitting a faint but distinct odor. The remains of the picnic were on a hotel towel being investigated by a number of flies. Anya sat on another towel, her back against the tree trunk, smoking. Cane stretched full length on his trench coat, his head in Anya's lap, his eyes closed.

"I think you could have done better," she said.

"Not if you wanted to picnic on the banks of the Rubicon."

"But it smells."

"Most old things smell. Consider then the Rubicon—it probably smelled even in Caesar's day. I agree it has deteriorated. I must say, though, you do a fancy picnic breakfast. Champagne and hard-boiled eggs, chicken sandwiches and sweet pickles."

"You haven't eaten your apple yet."

"I'm comfortable. Did I ever tell you that you have a very nice lap as far as Russian laps go."

"Canyon." Anya's voice was serious enough that Cane opened his eyes and looked up at her.

"What is it? Most friends call me Cane."

"Cane, where is the skull?"

"Is that all?" He closed his eyes.

"I really want to know. Is it at the bank?"

"No." He sat up and stretched. "Do we have to talk about the skull?"

"Yes. Where is it?"

"Oh, for a kiss I'll tell you." He collected, kissed her again then said, "It's here, Anya. In the car."

Anya jumped to her feet. "Here? This car?"

"Yes, in the trunk. Did I ever tell you that you have a provocative fanny? I guess on a scale of ten you'd rate about — oh, about an eight and a half."

She regarded him darkly.

"Cane, you must understand. This is something I have to do." She pulled a small revolver from her purse and pointed it at him. "Open the trunk and give me the skull."

His eyes widened. "Have you lost your mind?"

"No. I was never more serious. You must know that I have to do this. Please understand."

Cane stood up slowly. He brushed pine needles off his pants, then reached for his coat, shook it carefully as if that were the most important thing he needed to do.

"God knows," he said, "I never spoke a truer word than when I said I'd only trust you in Heaven, and I'm not sure I would there. You know, I can take that gun away from you."

"Cane, please don't try. You know I can use it."

He shrugged.

"I know. The KGB has very efficient help. Smart in selecting their agents, too. Duty! Duty! Duty! It's tiresome thinking about it." He reached into the car, took the keys from the ignition and opened the trunk.

"Lift it out," Anya ordered, "and open it."

He gave a short disgusted shake of his head, then picked up the box.

"Take out the skull so I can see it."

Cane opened the box, unwrapped the skull and watched her through narrowed eyes as she looked at the skull, her gun never wavering.

"My, it's an ugly thing! Look at his teeth. You know that is the key

202

to the whole operation. I can tell you now. There is a micro-dot map in one of Otto Thyssen's tooth fillings. It shows where the treasure that the Nazis stole from the Jews is hidden."

Cane stared at her open-mouthed. Then he shook his head. "I'll be damned," he said, "that answers a lot of questions." Then holding her with a cold level gaze, he asked, "Why do you think it should go to Russia?"

"Because we suffered more than anyone else during the war."

"Not good enough. It belongs to the Jews."

"Then why are you after it?"

"We didn't know why you wanted it. But if you did, then so did we."

"That's a dog in the manger attitude."

"Well, it would have been simpler if I had known. I'd have pulled the teeth and let the skull go."

"Canyon, I'm going to leave you here and take your car."

"And the skull," he added.

"Right. And the skull. You're not far from the road and you can catch a lift." She looked around. "Would you clean up our mess and take the basket back to the hotel? I'm in a sort of hurry." She took the keys from the trunk and motioned toward it. "You can put the Major back now."

Cane replaced the skull in the box and put it in the trunk. He slammed the lid. "There's something I'd like to tell you about this skull...."

"Cane, I know all about it. I want to show you something." She reached into her bag and pulled out Cane's pipe.

Cane recognized it and held out his hand. "I lost it at the Marienplatz."

"I want to keep it. A very special keep-sake. When I'm old and sitting on the porch of my dacha watching the seasons change along the Moscow River, I'm going to smoke it and think of you."

"You've a tendency toward larceny, lifting things that don't belong to you. Pipes, skulls."

"I picked it up in the Marienplatz. It was a nice souvenir of a pleasant evening." She smiled. "I certainly had no idea what it was going to lead to."

"Nice souvenir is right. It's the most expensive pipe I've ever owned."

"Don't feel badly. It'll have a good home."

"And the poor old Nazi's skull. Another souvenir?"

"Cane, don't be sarcastic. As we used to say in Miss Katherine's School, this will give me lots of brownie points and with Natalya's problems, God knows I need them." A shadow crossed her face and then she added, "We won't see each other again, Cane." Her voice broke, but her hand was steady on the gun. "I'll never forget you —"

"Good-bye, Anya." Cane answered. "It's been fun crossing all those Rubicons with you and a hell of an education!"

With the gun leveled on him, she started the engine, then rolled up the windows and locked the doors. She put the car in gear, raced up the grassy hill to the road.

Cane threw his trench coat on the ground and sat down. He reached for his pipe and gazed at it thoughtfully. He felt sick. An ache that started in his throat crawled through his chest to the pit of his stomach. He filled his pipe slowly from the wadded plastic pouch.

He had trouble lighting it. The flame would go out from lack of attention, or burn to his fingers and he'd drop it cursing. Finally he knocked the tobacco out on a gnarled root of the tree. Damn, I hope she doesn't get into trouble with that skull. They—they could ruin her for bringing that in. Why didn't I make her listen to me....

He picked up a pebble and flipped it toward the river. To wait so long to fall in love. To finally find someone he would like to spend the rest of his life with, and she's a Soviet spy. A dedicated Soviet spy. Not only that but she has a daughter and a grandson who will always be the padlock that will prevent her from defecting. He leaned back against the tree and relived the night they'd spent together. The cloud of dark hair on his pillow. The light in her eyes when she looked at him.

The hard gut pain in the pit of his belly wouldn't go away. That she could leave him like that. So easily, so carelessly.

Maybe she'd been play-acting all along just as Peter had said. He stood up slowly. He gathered the empty wine bottle, the sandwich wrappings, shook the crumbs from the towels, folded them carefully and placed them in the picnic basket. He followed the grassy shoulder to the highway. In a short time a small truck loaded with boxes of tomatoes stopped.

"Si," the old man shouted vigorously, "I go to Rimini. Good to have company." Less than an hour later Cane arrived at the Grand Hotel.

As soon as he walked in the door, the manager flew around the desk. "Oh, Signore Becker, a most dreadful thing. In your room a guest is murdered. The police are there now. A terrible thing for the hotel!"

"What the hell are you talking about?" Cane asked. The crowd in the lobby separated to let him pass. He handed the picnic hamper to a bellman and ran up the stairs with the manager puffing closely behind him.

*Carabinieri* filled the room and spilled out into the hall. As Cane entered, one stopped him. The manager rushing up behind Cane nodded excitedly. "Ah, si, it's Signore Becker's room This is Signore Becker. Terrible, terrible!"

The senior officer stepped forward.

"Signore Becker, we had a call a few minutes ago that we'd find a body in your room. The hotel manager tells us he's a guest here. A Signore Weleski from Warsaw. Do you know him?

Cane stepped around a man brushing the door for fingerprints and looked at the dead man. He wasn't a pretty sight. He'd been considerably roughed up before he died. He was a young man, blond, the eyes staring open were a vivid blue. His eyebrows were bushy and bloodied. This must be Anya's associate. She had probably sent him to search the room for the skull while they were gone. But who did the job on him? Cane shook his head.

"I've never seen this man before."

"*Per piacere,* Signore, will you see if anything is missing?"

"I had nothing of value." But he gave a cursory search through his suitcase. "Why would he be in my room?"

The police chief shrugged. "We may know something after we check his fingerprints with Interpol."

"I hardly think an international thug would be interested in me. I had planned to leave this afternoon. Will this make any difference?"

"You're here on business?"

"Yes. I sell chickens to restaurants."

"Chickens to restaurants? From the U.S.?"

"We sell them all over the world."

"Oh."

"I'd planned to leave this afternoon. Do you think....?"

The question went unanswered. "We'd like to have your fingerprints so we can separate them from the ones we have!"

The manager was nervously hopping around both the body on the floor and the policemen.

"We must find who did this! Oh! the reputation of the hotel...."

"Who found him?" Cane asked.

"Someone, we don't know who, called the police, Signore," the manager answered, "not half an hour ago. It happened sometime this morning."

"Could he talk?"

"No, he was dead when we arrived," The police chief answered Cane, then asked, "They tell me you left early this morning?"

"Yes."

"Where is your companion?"

"I allowed her to take my car to Venice. I'm to meet her there this evening."

"Where in Venice?"

Cane wondered where this line of questioning was leading. "At the Gritti Palace." What was it about a tangled web of lies?

"You'll be coming back?" The *investigatore* asked the question casually, almost indifferently as he made notes in a small black book.

"No. From there I'll go to Austria, then return to the States." He watched as the uniformed officers carried the dead man out on a stretcher.

The investigating officer looked up suddenly. "We've already checked with the Polizia di Venezia. Neither your car nor the Russian lady have arrived there."

"Oh."

"I think, Signore Becker, we have more questions to ask of you. Will you be so kind as to accompany me?"

The time Cane spent at the *Quartier Generale* was a period of pure torment. There were hours of questioning. Over and over he was asked: Why did you and the Russian woman leave the Grand Hotel so early? Seriously—a *picnic*? At eight in the morning? On the bank of the *Rubicon*? Where is Miss Petrovna now? You did know she is suspected of being with the KGB? Why were you going to Venice? Why did you return alone and without your car? *Why did you kill the man from Warsaw?*

# CHAPTER XXXIX

*Moscow*
*Wednesday, October 15*

Anya sat in the Zil limousine hugging the box that held the skull in her lap. She had left Vienna that morning on a Kremlin plane sent especially for her and was met by Sacha in the black curtained Zil—reserved for very important people. She tingled with excitement. No telling what her reward would be for retrieving the skull. When Cane pushed himself into her thoughts she refused to dwell on him. He had no right to the skull. He hadn't even known why it was valuable until she told him. It belonged to the Russians. They had the information; they had the skull and the Americans should never have interfered. As for the Israelis, if she could beat Jasmine at his own game that was another feather in her cap.

But it was still impossible to dismiss Cane from her mind. She knew he would be fast in the center of her thoughts for the rest of her life.

The snow fell steadily, great flakes that curtained off the Kremlin and Felix Dzerzhinsky's statue in the square that bears his name, and the stone walls of Lubyanka prison. The snow turned the world into a fairyland of nebulous shapes and murky shadows along Entuziastov Road and across Ustinsky Bridge. Only the river stayed the same. Snatching greedily at every flake, it absorbed them as fast as they fell churning relentlessly under its multiple bridges, charcoal gray in a pristine white universe.

The limousine pulled up to the courtyard entrance where a glut of Zils and Volgas and one other limousine had tangled into a massive traffic jam while drivers shouted insults.

"Never mind trying to get closer, I'll get out here. *Spaciba*, Sacha. Thanks."

She ran through the snow, arms wrapped around her package. Melted flakes glistened on her eyelashes and her excitement heightened the color in her cheeks. She nodded to the guard who checked her package. He recoiled at the sight of the porcelain-toothed skull, then laughed with her. She took the elevator to the fifth floor and signed in. Pugachev, Karuski, Dr. Nina Bleminoff and a secretary were waiting.

It was a small room and magnified the size of the four people standing around the green felt covered table. The air smelled of stale cigarette smoke.

Beaming, Anya placed the box on the table and accepted congratulations from everyone. A glorious feeling. She clasped Dr. Bleminoff's hand.

"And finally we have the skull for you," she said.

Dr. Bleminoff had everyone's attention as she pulled the letter from her purse.

"The letter reads 'I made a cavity in his left lower second molar and secured the bit of film.' So now we find it."

She picked up the skull and looked at it.

"So much porcelain and steel. He could have buried orders for an entire army here." She adjusted her glasses and held the skull close to examine it through her bifocals. A frown creased her forehead and she picked up the magnifying glass to examine it more closely. She shook her head perplexed.

"This is the left lower second molar," she said pointing with her forefinger, then she paused and swallowed. "That is the tooth. But there is no crown on it and no filling." She glanced at the stunned faces around her.

"It's almost the only perfect tooth in the skull." She bit her lower lip nervously. Her voice was scarcely audible when she concluded, "It's not there." A defiant edge crept into her voice.

Karuski spoke first. "It has to be. Examine the other teeth. Parlotti could have made a mistake."

Anya, her face drained of color, was staring at Dr. Bleminoff. Was that why Cane had made no effort to detain her, to keep the skull? She remembered there was something he wanted to tell her about the skull and she wouldn't listen. Was that it? Her chest hurt as if from a physical blow. Her breath was short and painful. She heard Pugachev shout.

"Take the damn teeth out of the skull and check each of them carefully. Call me when you're through." He stalked out of the room and Anya hurried after him.

In his office, she closed the door behind her.

"You know this is the skull from Fort Reno. How can it be the wrong one?

"It means that Thyssen is alive. Probably in South America and the Germans already picked the treasure clean. Think of all the time and money and men, good men we've wasted on this foolish project.

"Men? You mean Yuri?"

Pugachev nodded. He looked quite old.

"Day before yesterday, the day you got the skull, Yuri was killed in the American's room at the Grand Hotel."

She gasped. "Eliot?"

"No. He was arrested, but it actually happened while you were with him. The Italians think he did it."

Her breath seeped from her slowly. "I asked Yuri to search his room while we were away. What will they do with Eliot?" The ache in her vital organs was real. She walked to the window, leaned hard against the sill and took a deep breath.

"I don't know." Purgachev followed her to the window shaking his head. "The details are sketchy. Our agent in place, a longtime Italian communist who is a maintenance man at the Municipio reported an anonymous call notified the police. Yuri was dead when the police arrived."

"But why would the American get involved?"

"He couldn't have returned at a worse time. They booked him for Yuri's murder. That's all we've heard."

Anya pressed her thumb against her lip and swallowed hard, trying to keep her composure

"Do the police think Yuri was one of ours?" she asked.

"I don't think so. He had a good cover. They'll send the body to Poland. We'll pick it up there." He shook his head in disgust. "This is damn confusing. Did the American give you any cause to suspect the skull?"

She shook her head.

"No. Yuri followed him to the bank where he met Dr. Parlotti, the son of Dr. Bleminoff's dentist. From there he went to the post office, then he returned to the hotel. He was not carrying any package. But later that night he did receive a package by messenger. That's why I was sure it was in his room." She turned to Pugachev, her lips tight, then said slowly, emphasizing each word.

"The Israeli, Jasmine, whom we know is Magen Ben-Yanait, was there."

"That should account for Yuri's death."

"When will they let the American go?"

Pugachev shrugged. "When he can prove his innocence, I suppose."

Anya looked out the window, past two half frozen pigeons on the sill, into the into the blowing, swirling snow.

"So that ends the chapter."

"No, Anya. I'm going to send you back to Munich. Make contact with someone in the consulate and find out what the hell they are up to. I have no hopes that we'll find anything in that mess of porcelain." He smiled as he rested his hand on Anya's shoulder. "You got the skull and that's what we sent you for."

Anya shivered. Thank God he didn't know how she felt about Cane. *In jail for murder!* Good God! She pushed the thought to the back of her mind and said, "Colonel, will I be permitted to see Natalya and Mischa?"

"I don't think it would be wise just now. I'd like for you to return to Munich tonight. Lisita will go with you."

"The Fox?" Anya's frustration showed. "He's dangerous; I'm not sure I can control him."

"He understands you are in charge, but more than that, he can protect you."

"I'm really afraid of him. Isn't there someone else?"

"Anya, you'll have no trouble with him. I promise you." He gave her shoulder a gentle embrace, then added, "And don't worry about Natalya. Nothing will be determined until you return."

"Poor Natalya, so young and so much to learn."

"You do realize that she's gone too far. She will have to conform or leave. I must tell you, Anya, there has been some talk about the suitability of your representing us abroad."

Anya stiffened. "Because of Natalya?"

Pugachev walked to his desk and sat on the edge, looking at her. He nodded slowly.

"I had a long talk with the Director yesterday. He thinks that if Natalya is exiled, you will defect."

Anya felt her face flush with anger.

"Comrade Ivanovich, you know that's not true!"

"Of course I do. I laid my career on the line for you a long time ago. I've trusted you in spite of your father and I've brought you along because you were the best we had. And you are still best. We simply need to convert Natalya."

"I wouldn't count on that, Comrade Ivanovich. She has an uncommonly stubborn streak in her."

"And in that I would say she takes after her Mother." His chiseled face, permanently set in grim determined lines and angles softened. "*Do svidanya*, Anya. Lisita is waiting with the car. Good luck."

Anya smiled bleakly, gave him a small salute and left. Stopping by the little room at No. 5, to pick up her coat, she saw Dr. Bleminoff carefully pinching each tooth from the skull. At the back of her mind she thought, she'll be lucky if she's not practicing dentistry in Marmansk instead of Kiev next week.

And then she gave herself up to the acute misery of thinking about Cane in an Italian jail.

# CHAPTER XXX

*Munich*
*Friday, October 17*

The upper room in the Munich consulate overlooking the parking lot was charged with tension. Hastings stood at one side of the window, his coat rumpled, tie loosened, collar wilted, glancing at Cane from time to time, lips tight, jaw clenched, his dark eyes eloquent with censure.

"Wherever did Peter pick you up? You've blown the top off the whole damn thing. Shacking up with a Red Sparrow who is a hell of a lot smarter than you! Picnicking, for God's sake, *on the Rubicon*! Framed for murder! For that we had to get the Ambassador to intervene—and goddamnit Eliot....," his voice rose to a sarcastic falsetto, "that's a *Thou shalt not* under any circumstances—you're supposed to die first!" He turned his back to Cane for a full minute, then faced him furiously, "So where is the bloody car?"

From across the desk Cane answered hotly.

"How the hell should I know. She pulled the gun, took the skull and the car. So far as I know they're all in Moscow by now." Cane's face was dark with anger. His eyes, narrowed slits, were icy. Conscious of the bareness of the room, he knew he wasn't the first agent to be blistered by the embarrassment of defeat. Anya! She'd turned him wrong side out and squeezed him dry. And no way to explain it. She'd made him out an idiot.

Hastings slammed his fist against the wall in frustration. Their eyes met for an antagonistic second, then Hastings turned and glared

214

out the window in impotent fury.

"Son of a bitch! Best damn car in the pool and you let a KGB bird take off with it. Not only that but she got the .357 Magnum and the high speed transmission radio. And that's not even the beginning. You get yourself mixed up in a hotel murder that involves the State Department. What are you—some kind of clown?"

"All right, so I didn't handle it very well. Are you interested in what I found out? The skull isn't Otto Thyssen's."

"I heard you." He stared out the window, shoulders humped, hands in his pockets. The sun rode freely in an autumn-cooled mid-day sky flecked with delicate high-flying cirrus clouds and slashed with a jet stream.

Without turning he said, "So Peter threatened to take you off, eh?"

Cane nodded more to himself than to Hastings' uncompromising back. He joined Hastings at the window.

"Yes," he said between clenched teeth. "And you have my resignation right now. I saw Peter die, and it's something I'll never forget. I loved that boy. So I'm throwing in the towel and taking the first plane back to Denver."

"No." Hastings answered softly without turning. "That won't solve anything. Peter would rather you finished the job. I understand how you feel—but the department, Chili, has decided it wants you to see it through." His anger seemed to have burned itself out. He looked tired as he turned to Cane.

"In the rose garden I told you we had a whole new ball game. Now it's the last inning and we don't even know where the goddamned ball is." He pulled out a package of cigarettes, offering the pack to Cane in a conciliatory gesture.

Cane shook his head.

"We have to have more authority to cover this. I'm going to ask for the complete file on Thyssen from the Ludwigsburg Center. That's touchy business. But I want the file here and to go over it page by page, sentence by sentence, until I know more about that man than anyone in Germany. Those indictments will carry some weight. We know he murdered two Wehrmacht officers and I believe, going through the proper channels, the Commission will let us have the complete file, since we can show reasonable proof Thyssen is living." He hesitated a moment, "Reasonable proof being, I suggest, that we have no proof of his death."

Hastings inhaled deeply, then crushed out his cigarette.

"When you showed up here with the skull, we knew nothing. Then we found he wasn't Heinrich von Stober after all, but Otto Thyssen. Now by God, if the bastard is alive, it means that he and whatever organization he is with — the Spider or any of the other spin-off groups of SS fugitives—have probably already dispersed the treasure."

Cane spoke for the first time, his anger easing.

"I'm not so sure. I don't think they would have made such an effort to eliminate Peter and me if the treasure weren't still hidden. And I'm sure as hell convinced it's the Spider group behind it all."

"You're probably right. Helmut Acton was unquestionably a member of the *Spinne* in Argentina. Revenge for his death could have been a motive for their efforts against you and Peter." He paused a second then said, "So you got to see Mossad's man."

"Yes, but that was all. Just his back as he entered the hotel." "You know, Chili, I wouldn't be surprised if he wasn't responsible for the Sitter's death. Both of them after the skull. At any rate he knows what he's doing."

"He must. Anya said he'd been tailing me since Oklahoma City."

"He's as near a living legend as you'll find. From the Entebbe rescue to anything going on in the Arab countries, he's in the middle of it if it's first priority."

"So that makes this a priority affair for us?"

Hastings nodded. "It would seem so."

Cane ran his hand through his hair, then rubbed his hand over the stubble on his chin.

"It could be. When will you have your information on Thyssen?"

"I can't say. You'll know as soon as it's ready. Until then I want you to stay in the consulate. I'll send you some magazines and books." He looked at Cane critically. "You need some clothes. I'll have Tate handle it." He pushed a buzzer and a young man opened the door.

"Tate, our friend will be spending some time with us. Make him comfortable, will you?"

After they left, Hastings leaned against the window absently looking over the walled parking compound. He pinched his chin then massaged it with his thumb, smiled and shook his head in disbelief.

"What do you know!" he said aloud, "So the map to the Nazi plunder was a micro-dot in a tooth filling. The German mind is an awesome thing."

He was still staring out the window when the parking attendant, Rudi Eich, attracted his attention by waving to a driver from his glass-enclosed stall, then raising the red and white barrier so the car could enter the compound parking. The stall was across the driveway from the white rock wall that extended along the south side of the consulate.

Another car stopped and the barrier rose again, then dropped. He watched Eich slide back the door of the booth and give directions to a couple of tourists. The attendant pointed down Von der Tanne-Strasse toward the English Gardens. The driver nodded his thanks, consulted what was probably a guide book, waved and drove off. Eich re-entered his stall and closed the door. Hastings watched a few minutes more, then stepped quickly to his desk, picked up the receiver and dialed a private number.

~~~~

Rudi Eich parked his old Volkswagen half a block from the walled house on Schorndorfer-Strasse with a growing sense of unease. He'd run errands for various consular officials since he'd taken this job as parking lot attendant four years back. But he'd never been asked to come to Ludwigsburg before. Like most Germans, it was an embarrassment to him. He looked at his watch. Half an hour yet. It had been made very plain that he was to enter the Commission gate at exactly fourteen hundred hours. Go to the waiting room, sign for and receive a package, place it in the briefcase he carried, lock it and drop the key in his coat pocket. Then he was to return to his car, drive the 300 plus kilometers to Munich and arrive at the American consulate close to twenty hours. He lit a cigarette, took a quick draw, then stubbed it out nervously.

It's a nice job, sitting in the glass cage waving to employees at the consulate, answering questions from American tourists, telling them not to miss the Hofgarten across Galeriestrasse; that the building across Von der Tanne-Strasse is the Prinz Karl Palast or the President's Palace when he is in Munich. And that the National Museum is straight ahead where Von-der-Tanne changes to Prinzeregentenstrasse in the English Gardens. A very enjoyable job. One with such authority about who enters and who doesn't. But on his day off to have to do a job like this. Of course, he could have refused. But then who knows, maybe he'd lose this job and good jobs weren't that easy to come by. So what the hell, go to Ludwigsburg and pick up the package. Not any of his business what's in it. He knew Ludwigsburg well. It was a pleasant suburb of Stuttgart, but he'd never deliberately driven by the Ludwigsburg Center for Investigation of Nazi War Crimes and felt a deep reluctance to do so now. He lit another cigarette, looked again at his watch. God, how time creeps when you have something unpleasant to do. He looked at his watch again.

He followed the shadow of the eight-foot wall to the steel gates that blocked the drive, rang the bell and identified himself to the gate attendant. In the waiting room he sat on the edge of a worn leather chair until an older man with thin gray hair and a bad limp brought him a thick file of several manila envelopes tied with red cord. Eich watched as he filled in a date on the counter register and asked him to sign for the file, which he secured in his briefcase. Fastening it with two leather straps, he locked the case, shrugged at the clerk and dropped the key in his pocket. He couldn't get out fast enough.

He heard the gates fasten behind him and without looking back hurried toward his car. He didn't see the man approaching until they collided. "Pardon!" *"Verseihung!"* *"Wiebitte!"* The briefcase had fallen to the sidewalk. Both apologized profusely. The stranger picked up Eich's briefcase and handed it to him still offering apologies. Eich took it, graciously accepting the apologies. "Quite all right! Quite all right! I should have been watching." They bowed again, smiled at their clumsiness and went in opposite directions.

In his car Rudi Eich gave a long sigh of relief. What was it about the Ludwigsburg Center that chilled him so? He should be glad they were still hunting the Nazis. But he knew that few Germans wanted to have anything to do with it.

He drove as fast as he dared through the east end of Stuttgart to pick up the Autobahn that went directly from Karlsruhn to Munich. In the fast lane he kept his accelerator at a steady 100 kilometers an hour. Only once did he slow a little to negotiate a curve through the hills of Ulm, and when he did his car exploded, rolled down an embankment, through a fence into a meadow of startled dairy cattle. Rudi Eich never knew what happened. Half a dozen cars stopped on both sides of the Autobahn to rush to his aid, but they couldn't get close. The car was a mass of flames.

# CHAPTER XXXI

When Tate knocked on his door to say that Hastings was waiting, Cane had been awake for hours. Lying on his back in the early morning darkness, his arms folded beneath his head listening to the sullen, erratic rain that peppered the consulate roof with the echo of early winter, he let the kaleidoscopic events of the past few days unravel across his mind.

Indelibly imprinted there was Anya. Anya standing beside the car holding a gun on him as he took the skull from the trunk.

Anya—lovely, slender, beautiful. Her finely chiseled face with its high cheek bones, the curve of her neck, the dark smoky eyes even then brilliant with a twinkle she made no attempt to hide, the self-assured tilt of her chin, the perverse dimple at the corner of her mouth, the irregular widow's peak and soft hairline. Well, he was pretty sure she wouldn't have shot him. Or was he? He could have taken the gun in a minute. Or could he?

Of course, she had nothing to do with his arrest. That was an unfortunate accident, but tell that to Hastings and certainly he was glad Peter didn't know. What was she doing now? Was she in serious trouble because of the skull. Oh, Anya! Anya! And the ache in his rib cage was physical.

It had been raining intermittently since midnight. The forty-eight hours had been tedious. Cane had read everything he could get his hands on, even to the fine print of a cereal box. Two days in a bare room with only time and recent memories to fight a malignant ennui is an eternity. Anya. He remembered the baggy V-neck maroon sweater she wore over a silk shirt open at the throat, sleeves pushed to her elbows, the gold watch, two antique bracelets. No rings. The same gold ear hoops she wore when he saw her first in the cemetery. Her hair plaited in a thick braid down her back. Dark tendrils curling about her temples. Those faded American Levi's with the leather patch and scruffy sneakers piped in blue and laced with faded ribbons that were totally foreign to her image. Was she dressed like that when she carried the skull into the Center headquarters?

He remembered her as she sat on the hotel bath towel spread beneath the pine tree, her legs crossed Arab style eating a chicken sandwich thick with lettuce and tomatoes and oozing dressing, then licking her fingers, grinning at him. He remembered the oversized bag that held, besides his pipe, a lipstick, passport, billfold—a gun. He remembered the faint sour odor of the Uso. Their Rubicon. Somebody said it was impossible to cross the same river twice. That was true. Even so small a ditch as the Uso.

He shook his head in disgust and threw his legs over the side of the iron cot. Damn! What a mess he'd made. He welcomed Tate's news. He brushed his teeth, shaved and, still damp from a cold sixty-second shower, pulled on his trousers and stretched into a shirt. Hastings was waiting with a thick set of papers before him on the desk.

"Come in, Cane. Sit down. How does it feel to do nothing for two days?"

"Like hell. What have you found?"

"First would you like some coffee, breakfast?"

"Only coffee, black." He sat across the desk from Hastings, crossed his legs, waited.

"It's just as well you had a rest. It might be the last for some time. By the way," his granite face softened somewhat, "your car was found at the Vienna airport. It's here now. Also the .357 Magnum and the radio. Your account is closed."

"Well now, should I thank you?" Then he asked, "How did she leave?"

"Private plane. Destination Moscow."

"She's something else—for sure an education."

"Before Peter was killed, he sent word that you thought you could get her to defect." The statement had the inflection of a question Hastings watched closely for Cane's reaction.

He shook his head.

"She's the pro. I'm the novice. No way she'd defect. She played me for a sucker all the way."

"Even with her daughter in trouble?"

Cane glanced at him sharply. "Where did you hear that?"

"You knew she had a daughter?"

"Yes, she told me in Alpendorf."

"You didn't think it important to mention during your debriefing?"

"Frankly, Hastings, so much happened so quickly I forgot about it. You think the daughter is being forced out?"

"There were four lines on an inside page of Izvestia."

"Did it give her mother's identity?"

"Of course not. We've known about her daughter as long as we've kept a dossier on Anya. It mentioned two other young women involved with her in publishing seditious propaganda. She'll be exiled."

"Anya won't defect. They'll keep her in Russia if her daughter is sent out."

"That's probably right." He leaned back in his swivel chair and sighed. "I'll say this, Chili, you've been up against two of the toughest agents in the book." Cane didn't answer. "So much for Anya Vasilievna Petrovna." He sifted through the papers on his desk. Tate brought in a tray with a pot of coffee and two cups, placing it on a cleared corner of the desk, then left closing the door firmly behind him.

"Pour the coffee, Cane, while I get these papers in order." He separated a couple of sheets of notes from the stack in front of him.

"Here's a quick resume of Otto Thyssen, including what you already have. Then we were concentrating on his career. Now we can understand some of it."

Cane read aloud, "Born April 6, 1913 to Eva and Heinrich Thyssen in Riva, Italy." He stopped. "That explains a lot, he's from the South Tyrol."

"Yes," Hastings answered. "Thyssen lived there until 1919. I'd forgotten that Austria owned all the South Tyrol, a great hunk of Northern Italy, for a hundred years or so until it was taken away when they broke up the Austrian Empire after World War One."

"I remember," Cane said. "When I was in school in Vienna, the Austrians felt as strongly about the Treaty of St. Germain as the Germans did the Treaty of Versailles. And with some 200,000 German-speaking people, Italy had a built-in problem trying to assimilate them. It's not an easy thing to make Italians out of Germans." He turned back to the notes, "So after the treaty in 1919 the Thyssen family sold their small vineyard near Riva and moved to Innsbruck when Otto was six years old."

"Old enough," Hastings interrupted, "to catch the drift of their bitterness. He went to school in Munich, met a certain rabble-rouser and hitched his star to disaster. Even so, Otto shared Hitler's successes. It's easy to see why Der Führer made him an official of the SS treasury and his liaison officer to Mussolini. Speaking fluent Italian and completely trustworthy, he was the logical one to keep his eye on Il Duce." He paused a minute to light a cigarette.

"Most of this stuff was found scattered around the Reichbank by a Russian soldier. Perhaps a bomb had blown the files out of Thyssen's office. Anyway they were picked up and taken to the house where he was billeted. When Berlin was divided and he moved from the American sector to the Russian, he left them behind. There is no evidence that they were used during the Nuremberg trials, nor even that much attention had been given to them. Too bad. There's dynamite here. Lists of the collections brought in from the camps plus receipts to couriers who brought the loot. It's not surprising the friends of Standartenfuhrer Thyssen didn't want that file investigated.

"There was trouble?"

"Yes." Hastings rubbed his chin. "Our courier to Ludwigsburg had an accident on his return. His car was blown off the Autobahn east of Ulm by a radio-controlled firebomb."

"Christ!" Cane exclaimed. "Then how did you get this file?"

"We were afraid something like that might happen, so we sent an operator with an identical attaché case as the courier. Outside the Ludwigsburg Center he managed to collide with the messenger, dislodge his briefcase and in the confusion switch them. Very slickly done."

"Was the messenger one of your men?"

"Oh, God no! He was a quasi Nazi who worked for us as a parking attendant, errand boy and we think, a sometime spy for one of the SS organizations. Shed no tears for him."

Cane walked to the window, his hands deep in his pockets. The rain beat a steady tattoo against the glass. The parking compound, filled with blurred images of cars, swam mistily below the dripping panes. The glass stall across the drive was almost invisible.

"There has to be a reason for Thyssen being in Italy just before he was captured." He lit a cigarette with great deliberation, watched the thin stream of smoke float to the ceiling. "It'll be a shock to Herr and Frau Müller to discover that her late husband is anything but late."

"I wonder, Cane, if they don't know it. If they haven't for a long time." He pushed back his chair and joined Cane at the window.

"You're suggesting...."

"Yes. What if Müller is Thyssen?"

Cane nodded. "I think you may be right. Have your checked out Müller?"

"All we've been doing the last two days. He's well covered. During the war he farmed up in Schleswig and used POWs to work it. It's all on record."

"How did he happen to leave?"

"An older brother who was an officer in the Wehrmacht had a prior claim to the farm after the parents died. Müller went to Munich to work, met Frau Thyssen and followed her to Alpendorf where they married. Everything is documented. Almost too much so."

"The Germans are fanatic about details. Could Müller's papers have been forged, and Herr Müller is our Otto Thyssen?"

"It looks that way."

"And I've got something that chinches it." Cane said. "The younger son, the one who was careless enough to run his pickup off the road above Alpendorf...."

Hastings nodded dryly. "Yes?"

"He was a dead ringer for the older son, Stefan."

"I follow you. With different fathers that would be a little unusual." The two men stood eyeing each other without speaking for a long second.

"Most unusual," Cane echoed.

Hastings returned to his desk and sat down motioning for Cane to join him. He reached into the stack of papers and withdrew a single sheet.

"I was saving the *piéce de résistance*. It was with the papers found near the Reichbank. I have a gut feeling that it's the same map that was micro-dotted in Thyssen's tooth." He handed Cane a cracked sheet of vellum parchment.

"You don't say!" Cane examined it for several minutes, then handed it back. "There's just one problem I can see. Nothing is identified except by numbers. What is it a map of, and more important, where is it?"

"I have an idea, but I can't prove anything. I'm going to leave that to you. You notice that for one thing there's a coastline facing west with a promontory marked four. It almost looks like the profile of a man's face, the promontory being the nose. Then a road proceeds to a number

23 marked with an iron cross. Another road goes east, turns north, turns again north by northeast to number 10 marked with a swastika. Directly east is the mountain marked 884 which could be meters. Then back toward the coast, but with no road to it is a death's head."

"Have you had a cartographer examine it?"

"No. We don't want anyone to see it. Now if we use the German alphabet and number it backwards — minus one — that could be the key to the names of the places on the map."

"That's not a very complicated code *if* you know where you are."

Hastings opened the top desk drawer and pulled out a topographical map of Lake Garda. "Look at this carefully and see if you can find an area of similarity."

Cane spotted it immediately and nodded. "Easy enough when you know. I'm not sure I could have come up with the answer."

"You would eventually. I've had two days to study Italian maps. That," he pointed to the drawing, "has to be a west coastline of an ocean or the eastern border of a lake. Rimini is on the Adriatic and Lake Garda is the closest body of water that fits."

"I hate to point out—it's still like finding a needle...."

"Right. So that's your assignment. Find the needle at Lake Garda." Again he pointed to the map. "Right above this promontory of Punta St. Vigilio-Number 4 for Vee—there's always been a ferry to Maderno, which is conveniently located between Sala and Mussolini's residence at Gargnano. In other words, it was easy to get from the Mussolini headquarters of the Sala Republic to the opposite side of the lake. Those particular Baldo Mountains have to be approached either from the lake or through passes from the rear. Many Germanic people live around there."

"But your needle? That treasure could be anywhere."

"I feel sure it is somewhere between C, number 23, and P, number 10, marked with a swastika. Now if we take the small town of Costermano as number 23 with an iron cross and follow the road to the equally small town of Pizonne, number 10 on the map, we have negotiated the back side of this formidable ridge. There are no roads leading toward the death's head. I think we should speculate that is where the treasure is hidden. Either in old ruins, a cave or lake. So your assignment is to head for the Baldo Mountains. For once we know we're ahead of the Russians and the Israelis."

"Okay. So I have an assignment. What am I doing there, hunting?"

"No, you're an American geologist—one Dale Lupine—doing a book on the origins of Garda—comparing the hypothesis of Antonio Stoppani who suggested the marine fjord re-emerged during the Pliocene period and modern scientists who seem to agree on the 'sinclinale benacense'...."

"Good God! Do you know what you're talking about?"

"No, but you're going to before you leave. It's a dirty shame the Russians didn't steal the skull in the spring. It'd be much simpler to go into the hills as a lepidopterist with a butterfly net. Of course, that's not too original. It's been done before."

"I'm as ignorant of butterflies as I am of geological periods. How do I get this crash course in geology?"

"From Tate. He was a geology major who can teach you enough to bluff your way through any situation in the hills. You will convince anyone who is curious that you are studying the form, arrangement and internal structure of limestone and sandstone rocks that make up the western face of the Baldo Mountains. You'll carry a hammer, a chisel and a sack, and leave your gun here."

"No way."

"A knife would be an obvious necessity. A gun, no."

"What the hell am I looking for?"

"Trails leading off the last road near Mt. Belpo or Mt. Ago...."

Cane interrupted. "Ago—needle—very apropos."

Hastings frowned, ignoring the interruption and continued, "The roads usually peter out in the squares of tiny towns with only goat trails going higher. Somewhere, someone will know something." He pushed all the papers together, neatly mitered their corners, shoved them to one side and stood up. "Good luck, Chili."

"Oh, Hastings, something else. If, although I think it's highly unlikely, if by a miracle I find this treasure, what then?"

Hastings pulled at his ear lobe thoughtfully, then answered slowly.

"It's up to Washington. I imagine they'll call in the Italian Ambassador and brief him. Actually, your guess is as good as mine. You'll keep in touch by radio."

Cane folded the copy of the map, and stuck it in his shirt pocket.

# CHAPTER XXXI

T he steep track was narrow, rutted and evil, shadowed in the early morning by the mountain it barely scarred with its convoluted twisting. Cane, in mountain gear with a backpack, a steel-spiked alpenstock in one hand and a geologist's hammer swinging from a belt loop, looked the part. He ducked his head into a vicious west wind, known locally as the Ander, which foretold changes in the weather that was all for the worst. It kicked up chiseled dust particles and debris from the limestone heights above and whirled them furiously against his face.

Above him the eroded folds of perpendicular cliffs stretched a thousand feet or more with intermittent splashes of dwarf conifers and below, barely visible through layers of mist, was Lake Garda. He had been following this half-hidden track for five hours, since well before daylight, when the old man woke him and said, "Now. Now is the time." He guided Cane to the path that led to the ruins and wished him God speed. Cane's backpack held a flask of whisky, cheese, hard bread and a radio. His lungs burned and his legs were like lead. How long would this last?

The track cut across highlands thickly covered with scrub heather and lichen stained rocks. There was no doubt in Cane's mind that this was the route taken by Thyssen when he was commissioned to hide the SS treasure. A donkey and cart would manage this very well. No wonder he evacuated the village. The treasure could have come by boat, then loaded in covered trucks and taken to Ago-Piccolo. From there donkeys and carts. Was this the same trail used by the Romans? By the barbarians? Probably. The quarry and that trail had been erased by an earthquake years before.

~~~~

It had been a week since Cane left the Munich consulate wearing a chauffeur's uniform, driving a rented limousine to the Bayerischer Hof to pick up two visiting congressmen with their wives and delivering them to the opera. A heavy mist hung over the city. The glistening pavement mirrored shimmering yellow and red streaks of moving traffic. Cane left the limousine in its reserved stall in the underground parking area and a few minutes later crossed the Maximilianstrasse, walked a couple of blocks to the tiny Platzy square dominated by the Hofbrauhaus.

A throbbing oom-pah band had the famous Schwemme—watering place—swinging with impromptu singing and dancing. It was crowded with noisy Germans and tourists. He joined a table of students and ordered a stein of beer. Scratching his neck, he twisted on the bench. Good God! Was it Anya? *It was!* Without a change of expression, their eyes held for an instant then slid past without a sign of recognition. She turned her back. He suppressed a smile. Thank God she's not in a Moscow cooler. And she's traced him here. The Center's still working! And their only lead is to follow him. A minute later he saw her leave. He stayed where he was, laughing at one of the student's jokes. He had to be careful. Anya didn't operate alone. Somewhere there was a KGB goon waiting in the wings. He glanced at his watch. It was almost time. He gave himself ten minutes to toss off another beer, then went to the men's room. It was huge and crowded, smelling of smoke and sweat and urine. Cane grinned at the pen and ink drawings above the tile urinals, zipped his pants and was still reading the raunchy cartoon captions when he felt the man brush against him.

The stranger wore thick-lensed glasses, a Tyrolian hat and jacket and sported a huge handlebar mustache. Cane followed him to adjoining stool closets. Quickly jackets, hats, glasses and the mustache were exchanged beneath the partition.

Cane emerged wearing a green Loden jacket with black braid, thick-lensed glasses that changed his appearance without affecting his vision, and a Bavarian hat with a miniature feather duster in its braided band. He felt completely at home with the thick mustache that matched his newly dyed gray-blond hair.

Back in the rowdy Schwemme, he wondered if Anya had returned. He joined a loud group of American tourists and scanned the room but didn't see her.

The stranger in Cane's chauffeur's hat and jacket left, and Cane watched a tall, loosely hung-together German follow him out. So that was her guardian-angel. He set about out-drinking, out-laughing, out-joking, out-dancing the tourists. With both arms around his friends they swayed to the rhythm of the band and once he danced a polka on a table with a waitress.

Sometime after midnight, Cane kissed the waitress, made a date for the following evening and left with his noisy, half-drunk companions. Parting with a great show of inebriated affection, he picked up a winterized Jeep parked near the Peterskirche. He drove aimlessly for several blocks, then convinced he had no shadow, he peeled off his mustache and picked up Highway Two for Innsbruck. From there he followed the Autobahn south to Verona where he made a rest stop to change identities and license plates. He drove until daylight, then checked into a hotel in Peschiera, where he stayed until the following morning. Then Cane took the lake road north.

The whole area was a semi-tropical paradise enveloped with mountains, ancient villages, overflowing with palm trees, bougainvillea, oleander and roses. Every kind of flowering plant and tree, bush and herbaceous shrub. Cypresses pointed straight to heaven, dominating cemeteries and outlining vineyards. Castles dating from God knows when topped every natural fortification, and the pink, black and rose sandstone cliffs, fringed with firs and pines, made dramatic backdrops. It was no wonder that Austria hated to give this up in 1919. It was easy to understand why those Germanic people who had lived here for centuries were here still.

When Cane reached Costermano, number 23 on Thyssen's map, he was surprised to find an impressive German military cemetery. Strange, he thought, that Costermano should be pinpointed on Thyssen's map —for that was drawn long before this cemetery was built. Located in a small sheltered valley on the Guardie heights it drew Cane like a magnet. He walked through the gardens, nodding to caretakers and visitors. For the German soldiers who died in Northern Italy it was a fitting memorial. A steel Maltese cross, eight meters high, dominated the red porphyry headstones.

Looking around him Cane felt a vague unease. Something was wrong. Ghosts of men killed in war lying uneasily in their tidy graves? Two men sharing a marble replica of an Iron Cross? A gardener with a hoe, picking sporadically at a flower border spoke, "Guten Tag, Mien Herr. You have a brother here?"

"No." Cane answered softly.

The old man looked at him closely, "You are English?"

"American." Cane didn't encourage the conversation and the old gardener moved on with his hoe edging the beds.

Cane returned to the car wondering at the depression he felt. Those ghosts—were they just from World War II or did they also include a host from the Hapsburgs, the barbarians, the Caesars?

Looking to the north Cane saw that snow had already capped the summit of Mount Baldo, the pride of the Baldo chain, and to the east was the stone spire of the Needle—L'Ago. He got back in the Jeep and turned on the ignition. Was this road past the cemetery the only way to Thyssen's treasure?

For several days Cane had wandered into and out of tiny mountain hamlets between Costermano and Pizzone, number 10 on Thyssen's map, over roads he could never have negotiated without a four-wheel drive vehicle. He spent much time in bars, such as they were, sometimes only a corner of a general store or benches in front of a post office, drinking with grizzled graybeards. He had no interest in the young. They had no memory of the war, of that part of the war he was restructuring.

With open frankness he introduced himself, explained what he was doing and why. More than adequately disguised as Dale Lupine, a geologist with a string of degrees and professional honors modestly tucked in his wallet, he labored with honest endeavor cataloging rocks and collecting bags of specimen stones. He bored anyone who would listen to his fractured Italian about the book he was writing on the Origins of Mount Ago. And he took pictures. Old men posed on benches and grinned their toothless grins, while Cane snapped them.

It was in Caprino, a dead-end village in the shadow of Mt. Belpo, one afternoon that he was stopped by a young girl with a Brownie camera. She couldn't have been more than fifteen, with great brown eyes and long blond pigtails. With a warm smile she asked Cane to pose for a picture. He laughed and shook his head, escaping into a bar. Hell no, he didn't want a picture taken! After a couple of glasses of wine and a little desultory conversation, he left. As he came through the door, the young girl waiting, snapped his picture. He frowned, annoyed. He couldn't very well take the camera away from her without creating an incident. She laughed at him with twinkling eyes.

"Handsome Americano, please for my album. Americans take picture of me, I take picture of you. Grazie." She turned and ran off.

The hell with it! What harm could a child do with his picture. Except so damn many people knew what he looked like. People he'd just as soon not find out he was wandering around Lake Garda. He pushed it to the back of his mind and continued on to Ago-Piccolo, a tiny hamlet at the base of L'Ago.

The small village was an old one set among grape vineyards, worn-out villas, ruins of past civilizations and faded, tile-roofed houses of red and orange, blue and yellow. A few scraggy trees, gnarled and wind-swept, bordered the road and rows of cypress trees marked property boundaries.

But it was The Needle, L'Ago, that dominated the village. Towering above and shadowing Ago-Piccolo by mid-afternoon, it was at once awesome and dazzling. Toward the lake the thousand-foot drop of limestone folds shaded from white to darkest gray and made, for all the world, a gigantic face in profile with a Roman nose and full beard and head of hair from the murky stands of fir and pine. Even an ear showing through the grained erosions gave character to an extraordinary natural sculpture. Directly above the village there were the ruins of a twelfth century castle superimposed on the remains of a seventh century monastery that had been build on the foundations of a first century Roman fort. The walls of the fort were barely seen outlining a great massif, but the castle keep and the crenellated battlements built high into the limestone mountain rose in perpendicular grandeur. The Germans know how to pick their spots, Cane thought, from the Eagle's Nest of Berchtesgaden to L'Ago—a very superior spot to hide treasure. Somewhere up there, marked by a skull on his map, is the Nazi plunder. Cane followed the graveled road until it came to a dead end at the village square.

A Fiat was parked, angled onto the sidewalk, in front of the bar. He pulled the Jeep beside it, stepped down and took in the town with a sweeping glance. A weathered municipal building was on the north side of the tiny piazza. Its original color had long since faded to a neutral beige, trimmed with marble facings on the windows and an oval arch at the entrance. A marble balustrade decorated with sculptured heroes in Roman dress circled its flat roof. Above was a large sign in wrought iron, MUNICIPIO. Great blocks of quarried marble were placed at intervals for benches. Two small boys sat on one of them and observed Cane gravely.

A rococo cathedral just down from the bar, amply iced with marble, stood as faded and water-stained as the municipal building catty-corner from it. A great iron bell was visible through arches in the tower and marble urns decorated each corner of its pitched red-tiled roof. The square and the small spokes of streets that radiated from it were paved and curbed with marble. Old marble. Cracked and stained, but the beauty was still there. Cane asked about the marble. "Ah, si," an old man answered. "The mountain, she is the Marble Needle."

"That's where all this marble came from, the Ago?"

"Yes, but a very long time ago, even before Napoleon"

"Where is the quarry?"

"Ah, Signore, it has not been used in half a century. It was a cave, on the other side of the mountain, too difficult now to bring out."

"But if they quarried it then, why not now?"

"The earthquake. It changed the mountain road." He shrugged. "Not worth all the money it would cost to bring the marble down. Too bad. Long ago Ago-Piccolo was a prosperous village, but now, nothing is left. The young men didn't come back after the war, so we stay around, gather our grapes and send them to Garda."

"I saw two boys at the Municipio. Why aren't they in school?"

"The school bus comes when it's not broken down. There are only six children here. Today it didn't come."

"But their parents came back after the war."

"They are Germans." The old man spat.

"Germans?" Cane asked softly, "What are they doing here?"

"They've been here since the war."

"You mean they settled here after the war? That's strange."

"No, I mean they moved here during the war. During the time they evacuated the village. When we came back after the war, they were here. Two families of them. The boys go off and get married and bring wives back here. Eventually Ago-Piccolo will be a German village."

Cane sat down beside the old man on the marble bench. "You mean everyone here was moved out?"

"It was toward the end of the war. After the King booted Mussolini.

The SS moved in one day and emptied the village.

Cane tensed. *This was it*! Thyssen had moved the Reichbank treasure through Ago-Piccolo. If he could just keep the old man talking.

"Where did you go at that time?"

"To Pescheria. I worked in the vineyards. My wife died there, so I came back. This is home." He stiffened and Cane saw a very blond young man walk toward them. He nodded to the old man, eyed Cane curiously, then crossed to the Municipio.

"That's one of them. A son. They think they own the village." He spat through a yellow-stained mustache.

"Can I buy you a drink, *mio amico*?"

The old man shook his head. "Strangers aren't welcome here. I think you should go back to Garda or wherever you came from."

"I can't do that," Cane answered. "I'm doing a book on the geologic formations of L'Ago and its origins."

The old man's eyes widened. "I would pick another mountain if I were you."

"No, this is my mountain. But I'll need help."

"It would be worth my life."

"Then I'll find the way myself."

The old man laughed.

"My house is at the end of that lane." He pointed down the marble spoke opposite. "Spend the night with me and I'll help you. Now, let's have the wine." When the young blond man came out of the Municipio, he laughed again and spat.

That night at the old man's home they ate cheese and bread and thick purple grapes and drank the old man's home vented wine. They talked far into the night about the mountain, the Roman ruins above the town, and the ancient castle. Eventually, as Cane knew they would, they talked of the marble quarry. The old man's father had worked in the quarry and he himself had spent much time there when he was a boy. But the earthquake had ruined it all, the quarry, the village.

"Why can't you dynamite the opening and work it again?"

"Impossible," the old man insisted. "The earthquake sealed the quarry and destroyed the road. It is too expensive."

"How far is it from the castle?"

"It's just below, but the only way to get there now is through the Keep. There's a circular stair that goes down to what was a dungeon. It is filled with rubble from the quake. You think your reason for going is important?"

"Yes."

"It will be dangerous."

"I know."

The old man stood up, emptied his pipe in the fireplace and said, "No one who has gone up has returned."

"Don't the authorities wonder about that?"

"The Carabinieri aren't interested in going up there. It's said to be haunted."

Cane stood up, yawned and stretched.

"I'll let you know," he answered.

# CHAPTER XXXII

*Ago-Picolo, Italy*
*Monday, October 27*

Anya and the East German Fox, Lisita, were in Ago-Piccolo wondering where Magen Ben-Yanait was leading them, but satisfied it was closer toward the SS loot.

Five days before, they had been covering the American consulate in Munich. Anya was waiting impatiently for Lisita in the underground crossing between the consulate and the English Gardens. He had cultivated a friendship with the parking attendant at the compound and spent a great deal of time hanging around cracking jokes, watching the consulate cars come and go.

It was cold in the underground. The mist that blanketed Munich hadn't lifted in two days. The wall against which Anya leaned was damp and clammy. She pulled her coat closer. Her teeth chattered. For three days she and the Fox had staked out the consulate and covered it from every angle. Cane was simply not there. Where was he?

The Fox came running down the steps. "Quick, the American left in a limousine and he told me he was going to the Bayerischer Hof to pick up visiting firemen!" They hurried up the stairs to their car and only after they had turned down Oskar-von-Miller-Ring did she question him. "What do you mean, he told you?"

He was hunched over the wheel, gripping it with both hands, a lean, taut fox-faced man as thin as a praying mantis. "I was talking to Franz, the gate attendant; when this fifty meter limousine pulled out. The American was driving. He waved to us and I said, casual as hell,

'You look in a hurry. Find me a dame, too.' He laughed and answered, 'No such luck tonight. Just to the hotel for some visiting firemen and then the opera.'"

"Something's wrong. If he said that, he wants us there. It's a trap."

"No. He thought I was German. We'll find him at the opera. Why would he take visiting firemen to the opera?"

Anya didn't smile. This was too serious. Would she stand by and let the Fox kill Cane? She shivered.

The Fox glanced at her, "Cold?"

"Yes." She explained, "Visiting firemen mean either U.S. Senators or Congressmen. If he's in a chauffeur's uniform, he's trying to slip out of town. Perhaps they aren't going to the opera. Hurry!"

They caught the limousine at the hotel and watched as Cane held the door for two important looking Americans and their wives. They were behind him as he delivered them to the opera and they followed him into the underground parking of the National Theatre. They were nearby as he walked to the Hofbrauhaus.

In the noisy smoke-filled room Anya could not help remembering the Oktoberfest. It was so long ago! Now here was Cane drinking and talking with strangers as if he'd known them all his life. That's all he is, a chameleon. He could be anybody, anytime. And I—well, I'll never forget him. Cane turned just then and caught her watching him. Their eyes held for a long second, Anya turned away and whispered to the Fox.

"He's recognized me. I'm leaving, carry on."

Outside she walked slowly to the opera parking, her chest tight and pinched. She tried to take a long breath and broke into an aching sob.

She was sitting in their car when the chauffeur returned to his limousine. She ducked in her seat and didn't look up. She wanted no more confrontations. In a few minutes the Fox joined her.

After the opera, they followed the limousine to the hotel where the Americans were deposited with all the honor due visiting celebrities and were not far behind when he turned into the consulate parking.

That was when Anya got a good look at the chauffeur and gasped.

"Lisita! That's not the American. Somehow they switched at the beer hall. We've lost him!"

"Are you sure?"

"I know that's not the American agent."

Lisita drove past the consulate, muttering an oath. "What do we do now?"

Anya made up her mind quickly.

"We go to the Alpendorf. The Müller's have the secret. It's up to you to get it from them."

~~~~

In Alpendorf, Magen Ben-Yanait was methodically going through Herr Müller's safe. He had returned to the Alpine village with one thought in mind. He had to find Thyssen and he knew the key would be found at Herr Müller's Souvenir Shop.

He parked his rented car in the same clearing and camouflaged it as he had done before. With his binoculars, he had scanned the low tiered reaches of the village. There were the fire-blackened skeletal remains of the hotel. There was the Platz with only one motorcycle parked by the fountain where a flurry of pigeons played musical chairs. And there was the Souvenir Shop. He watched as a man came out the door. Müller no doubt, Magen thought watching him. Then he caught his breath! With the photograph of Thyssen etched on his mind he knew instantly who Müller was. Well past middle age, he still was a dead ringer for the picture Miss Bush had given him at the Fort Reno newspaper office. Magen watched as he stood looking at the burned out shell of the hotel, his hands clasped behind him, a mourning band on his left arm. Then with a quick nervous gesture, he ran his fingers through his hair, turned and went back inside the store.

So—Thyssen lives! Before dark, Magen scouted his approach to the town and to the back entrance of the shop. He nodded with satisfaction.

Nothing he couldn't handle. Simply a matter now of waiting until the village was asleep.

The lock was no problem. Magen had been picking locks long before he arrived in Israel. He slipped noiselessly through a storage room and found Müller's office. The old fashioned safe was a breeze to the light-fingered Mossad agent and the papers it held caused Magen Ben-Yanait to grip his fist with excitement. A pencil clip light from a lapel clamp was focused on a packet of letters. Magen held his breath as he read the first one from Buenos Aires addressed to Müller, but the salutation was *to our faithful Standartenfuhrer Otto Adolph Thyssen whose farsightedness had led DIE SPINNE to financial success.*

Well, well. Magen sucked in his breath. He'd made a find this night! A box of gem stones, some still in their mountings, was on the top shelf of the safe and he put them aside. He examined all the papers and photographed each one. It was in the last small file that he found the map. It was a photograph of an original and Magen had no doubt that it had been drawn to guide SS survivors to the concentration camp loot. He photographed it carefully, making several exposures to ensure a perfect one. Then he replaced everything as he had found it. He looked bitterly at the box of jewels before he emptied them into his pocket and returned the box to its place in the safe.

He closed the safe as carefully as he had opened it, left as surreptitiously as he had entered, locking the door behind him. Spotting a can of gasoline beside a power saw he made an instant decision. Splashing the gasoline on the walls, he flipped a couple of matches into them. It was a five minute run to the gray German Ford and from there he could see the flames already shooting over the roof. Once he reached the highway he headed for Innsbruck and drove directly to a small camera shop in the old part of town by the railroad station.

Ringing the bell sharply twice, then once more for a longer time, he heard its faint echo somewhere in the back. Some minutes passed before an elderly woman in a gray flannel robe peeked around the door. When she saw Magen she broke into a broad smile and unfastened the chain. Leading him into the darkroom she spoke slowly.

"Do what you need to. When you have finished I'll have breakfast for you."

"Danke, Sarah." He emptied his pocket into a large glass ashtray on the work table. In the glow of the red safety light the jewels came alive. He heard Sarah gasp in astonishment at their glitter.

"See that these reach the Prime Minister." Then he closed the door behind the old woman and proceeded to develop the negatives and make enlargements of the film.

Sometime later Magen sat at Sarah's kitchen table, coffee and bread and sausage pushed to one side. He was studying the enlarged photograph of the map. There was a coast line, the point marked 4, then an inland road leading to 23 marked with an iron cross, then a road to 10, identified with a swastika. There were the graduated circles indicating a mountain with the number 884 across it. Meters, of course. Then the road ended, but toward the coast, with no road marking it, was the drawing of a death's head skull. *The SS treasure site for sure!* But where was the location of the map? Where was there a mountain only 884 meters high? Certainly not in the Bavarian or Austrian Alps. There it would be only a foothill. And it was near a coast. *So* the mountain must be in Italy.

Soon afterward the Mossad agent was in contact with Tel Aviv via the transmission set in the old lady's bedroom. Then he left for Lake Garda.

# CHAPTER XXXIII

*Munich*
*October 28*

Anya in a blond wig and oversized tinted glasses stood beside the souped-up Opel parked on the hill above Alpendorf and watched in horror as the souvenir shop of Herr and Frau Müller burned to the ground together with the stores on either side. The Müllers, in night clothes, stood with the townspeople, wringing their hands and watching a thin stream of water pour from the fire truck. The burned-out hulk of the Alpendorf Falconhof stood across the Platz, its charred rafters and timbers reflecting the fire with sharp angular shadows.

Lisita shouted to her. "It was the American who did this just to keep us from getting information from Müller. There's no way we can interrogate him today. He'll be surrounded with people."

Anya was quiet. She knew the "interrogation" of Müller would be difficult, but that was why Comrade Colonel Pugachev had sent the Fox with her. She would be no good at the kind of questioning Lisita specialized in. He had always been uncommonly successful in getting needed information. But he was right. There would be no opportunity to talk to Müller now.

The Fox turned the car around and drove back to the highway. "So, Comrade," he asked, "what now?"

"I don't know. I'm sick of the whole thing. Let's go to Verona and contact Italian Control. I'm at my wit's end. Damn that letter. Damn the stupid dentist! Thyssen is alive and he could be anywhere." She curled up with her head on the arm rest and went to sleep.

It was morning when the Fox woke her at the Brenner Pass border check. Anya stretched, opened her eyes wide and then grabbed Lisita's arm. "That car, that gray Ford with Munich plates, it's Jasmine!"

She put on her glasses and straightened in her seat. "Keep him in sight. He's the Mossad man on this job. Wherever he's going, it will lead us to the Jewish treasure."

# CHAPTER XXXIV

In the five hours since he'd left the village, ominous clouds pushed by the restless Ander had closed the top of the Needle and the violent strength of the wind on the margin of the mountain rocked him again and again. Plodding along with his head tucked into his fleece-lined coat, Cane shifted his pack and leaned harder on his alpenstock. It had been a tough five hours.

He stopped short, caught his breath and noticed a man's heel print in the soft verge of the path. What the devil! Who could be ahead of him? It was a fresh print. How many had he missed? He remembered the old man's warning. No one has returned from the mountain.

He kept finding other signs of recent passage. Other footprints. Nearby someone had sat on a rock and smoked a cigarette, then crushed it with his foot. For sure he wasn't expecting anyone to go up the trail ahead of him. Behind? Possibly.

The old man knew the secret of the mountain. Cane was sure of that. He knew why the population had been evacuated and why the Germans were in the village now. They were the Spider guards. Or Thyssen's. Or, hell, maybe the SS. That's proof positive the treasure is still up there. Somewhere.

His thoughts returned to Anya. He wondered if she knew about the treasure. Where were they, Anya and her hungry-looking sitter? The empty feeling in his gut when he thought of Anya was real. God—to see her again. To touch her face. To kiss her, just once. Occasionally he stopped to listen. But there was no sound except the unforgiving voice of the wind.

On the upper reaches of The Needle, the storm grew steadily worse. The wind whined around the limestone precipices with shrill and evil intent. Mist turned to sleet and then driving snow, whirling from every compass point. A blizzard of major proportions was in the making. Cane's lungs were about to burst and he had an ominous feeling that he might be lost. He forgot about the tracks he had seen ahead of him.

Survival was at the back of his mind. A memory came into focus —when he was playing cat and mouse in the Alpine Redoubt with the Gestapo that winter of '44. There was one big difference. He had been young then. Where were the goddamned ruins?

The steel spike of the alpenstock struck a block in front of him. That was it. The beginning of the old Roman fortifications, a wall that had crumbled through the centuries until here it was only a foot or so high. But it rose rapidly and Cane stumbled over stone and rock debris, clinging to the little protection the wall gave.

He realized he had lost the trail completely. That was all right. He simply wanted to find a shelter of sorts, anywhere he could sit out the storm. The fortune be damned.

Half an hour later he reached an arched recess built into the old wall. He stumbled to a corner and dropped his pack. God he was weak. He looked at his watch. Six o'clock. He'd been climbing a full day and every muscle knew it. He stretched on his back, taking deep breaths and exhaling slowly. His temples throbbed and his heart echoed like a trip-hammer. When he could take a breath without feeling a knife twist in his chest he opened his pack, broke off a hunk of cheese and bread, then washed it down with a searing drink of Scotch that warmed his belly. He started to light a cigarette, then shook his head. That's the reason my wind is gone, and made a vow to stop smoking. Stretching out again, he pillowed his head on a flat stone and listened to the roar of the wind through the ruins.

This then was the reason Lake Garda was so warm and tropical.

The ring of mountains closed off all this bloody weather, and its fury was vented on the far side of the cliffs. Snow filtered in and brindled the floor of the alcove. Outside it was a swirling, wind-driven monster clawing at the walls with shrill Homeric laughter that echoed in the grotto.

Cane slept. The deep, unconscious dreamless sleep of exhaustion.

When he woke the storm had passed. Opening his eyes to the unfamiliar arched roof for a minute he was confused. It was daylight. Then he remembered the storm. Outside an anemic sun, half apologetic and more than half surprised at its own survival tried to reach him through the opening. He stirred, stretched, sighed. He took a deep breath and sat up. Then his eyes widened and he straightened with a jerk.

A young, good-looking blond man sat opposite on a stone holding a revolver that was pointed at him. He was smiling, and Cane recognized him as the same German who had spoken to the old man in Ago-Piccolo. One of the guards of the Jewish treasure. Cane's backpack was open beside him, his radio was on the ground smashed. The man was eating his bread and cheese. He ran his tongue around his mouth dislodging bits of food stuck between his teeth.

Neither spoke. Cane decided now was not time to give up smoking. He picked up the package of cigarettes where he'd dropped them, took one and started to reach in his pocket for a light. The man stopped him with a wave of the gun and pitched him a pack of matches.

Cane lit it slowly, deliberately. Why the bloody hell didn't the guy speak? Was he going to shoot him now? Well, obviously not until he'd smoked his cigarette. Cane offered him the package, the German nodded and took one, and still smiling, lit it without taking his eyes or gun off Cane.

The German inhaled deeply.

"Herr whoever-you-are, we've been waiting for you. You have a great deal to answer for. Two murders, arson and the theft of a box of jewels. Quite a life of crime you've been leading, Mien Herr." He flicked the ash from his cigarette. He was speaking German and Cane looked blank. What the hell was he talking about—arson and jewelry?

"I'm Dale Lupine," he answered in English. "I saw you yesterday in Ago-Piccolo. Don't you speak Italian?"

"Mr. Dale Lupine, American geologist, Herr Cranach, Austrian writer, and God knows what other aliases," he answered in Italian, "you speak German as well as I do. You talked with the gardener at the cemetery in Costermano in perfect German. The little girl took your picture in Caprino. Oh yes, Mr. Canyon Eliot, formerly of the OSS and now with the CIA, we know you very well. We also know what you want on L'Ago."

Cane answered in broken Italian. "I'm sorry. You speak so fast. Speak slowly, *per piacere.*"

The smile left the German's face and his eyes narrowed. "Don't push me, Signore. My father and brother are on their way up and Stefan Müller and his father will be here soon. They don't want anything to happen to you until they arrive."

Cane shook his head, grinning. "*Non capisco.* I don't understand." He shrugged apologetically and added, "*Per favore, mi scusi.*"

The German jumped to his feet and swung back the gun to slap Cane with the barrel. Cane grabbed his hand, twisting it, rising as he did. He threw the German over his shoulder with a broken wrist. The German lay on the floor of the grotto glaring at Cane standing above him with the gun. "I needed this," Cane said, "Grazie."

Suddenly the gun flew out of his hand, a devastating blow on the back of his head knocked him forward and he fell on top of the German. "You stupid clown, letting him take you like that."

"Get the bastard off me! He broke my arm."

"Serves you right." Another voice.

Cane's head was bursting. He should by rights be unconscious and that's the way he played it. One of the men grabbed his arm and pulled him off the German. "Ach! You so smart American!" Then he shouted, "Papa! You killed him. What will Müller say?

One of the men felt Cane's pulse. "He'll be around shortly. Then we have questions to ask."

"Before Müller gets here?"

"Ja. Before Müller gets here." The guttural voice was obviously the father. "Jacob, get up!"

"But my arm...."

"GET UP!"

Cane heard him struggle to his feet. He felt blood seeping into his shirt. Damn, his head ached.

"Martin, tie him up."

As Martin turned him over, Cane grabbed him by the neck, pulling him in front as he came to his feet. Using Martin as a shield, he pulled out the Chinese princess cocked. The blade flew within an inch of the German's neck.

"Now shoot and be damned. Martin will go too." For a minute there was a stalemate. Martin stood stock still, his eyes glued to the purple handled knife at his throat.

"Drop your gun and kick it aside." The older man stood helpless, furious, wondering what the hell had gone wrong.

With his knife at the boy's throat, Cane ordered the father to stand by his son. Grudgingly, slowly, his eyes filled with hate he approached Cane. Cane swung a hard left upper cut at the man's chin. His head flew back with an ominous crack, then Cane doubled him up with a blow to the belly that arched his own back and scratched Martin's throat with the princess. The father crumbled in slow motion.

"Now you," Cane called Jacob. "Here!"

But the boy backed off until he was braced against the wall. Mesmerized, his eyes wide and staring, his arm dangling helplessly, he was white with fear.

Cane held his eyes a minute, then turned to Martin. He changed the angle of the knife by twisting his wrist, and struck him behind the ear with the hilt of the lapis knife. The crack of his skull echoed in the grotto and the German youth fell as quietly as his father had. Then Cane turned his attention to Jacob.

During the war, when he was face to face with the enemy, there was no question what to do. Kill. Now he hesitated to knock out a young man who minutes before would have killed him. Soft and addle-headed in my old age. He looked the frightened Jacob in the eye and said,

"You'll have a headache, but that's all." He clipped Jacob with a strong right jab to the jaw, caught him as he fell and eased him to the floor.

Gathering his pack and alpenstock, Cane retrieved Jacob's gun, stuck it in his belt and dropped the other in his pack. He retraced his steps from the grotto until he found the trail and followed it around the Roman ruins up toward the castle. He went as fast as he dared, using the steel shafted staff as a balance. The snow had drifted; in spots he sank to his knees. One thing, if it slowed him, then it would slow Müller's thugs. But Müller-Thyssen was on his way and certainly Stefan, who would be a formidable enemy.

The snow was deeper, harder to negotiate as he circled to the north. The crumbling ruins the Romans built 2,000 years ago disappeared. Then, as he rounded a cleft wall he saw the castle. The old barbarian builders had used not only the stone of the Roman walls and the masonry blocks of the monastery, but also the foundations of both to raise an altogether awesome fortress completely enclosing the massif which overlooked the Aidge Valley and the great meandering river to the east.

Cane barely noticed the wild, rugged grandeur of the place as he looked up at the ruined pillars reaching into a pale sky. Some were built into the natural rock, others formed an uneven jagged skyline that broke the crenelated border around the massif.

Trails and stone fortifications angled around the mountain. Caves were everywhere. Caves in manmade cliffs, caves in manmade walls, and caves in natural hollows. Somewhere up there the SS had stored their loot.

The track stopped abruptly, blocked by huge masonry stones tumbled about and filled through the years with enough windblown soil to support slender young pines, mountain grasses and heather. No doubt this was debris from the earthquake that had ruined the quarry. He took a path that angled in rough zigzags like a goat trail. Certainly no donkey or cart, or even men with heavy packs, could negotiate this. Unless the boulders have been dumped on purpose after the job was finished.

The sun, pale as it was, warmed the earth and the snow, melting now and slick, made for treacherous climbing. Above the rubble of stone, Cane saw what might have been an entrance. He decided to follow the old man's suggestion. Somewhere there was a spiral staircase inside the fortress. He climbed and scrambled, twisting to keep his balance, pulling himself up through sheer force of will until he reached the fortress wall, then circled it until he found a cleared area where the ramparts had crumbled. It opened into a broad courtyard, partially framed by a limestone fold of bleak mountainside and partially by the great buttressed walls of the keep. No more than half the round tower stood, but inside, just as the old man had described, Cane found the stairs.

They had been carved from stone, fitted with a layer of marble and were slick as oiled glass from the seeping wind-driven snow. Cane pulled a flashlight from his pack and followed its beam down the triangular steps. Would it never end? Round and round, his shoulder and elbow scraping the rough hewn stones for balance while he held the staff in one hand, the flashlight in the other. How could a ton or more of treasure be brought down this stairway? Answer—impossible. There had to be another way.

At the bottom, a trio of tunnels fanned from a cavern. One held a pinpoint of light and Cane turned into it. The walls were white marble and reflected Cane's flash with diamond-like sparks of mica. So the quarry began here.

He stopped at the opening overlooking a plateau thinly frosted with snow. It was rimmed on the mountainside with fifty foot pines and firs that climbed up the Needle. Opposite, the plateau angled in terraced slopes down to the quarry. It was easy to see what had happened so many years before. The earthquake had tumbled the whole excavation into a cleft below the mountain. Great squares of hewn marble were tumbled about like a giant's game of blocks. A road that had led from the quarry dropped abruptly, leaving snow-filled ruts in the marble bedrock. Following the plateau where the forest dipped to the open stretch, Cane picked a comfortable, well-hidden spot where he had an unhampered view, sat down and opened his pack. He hadn't realized how hungry and exhausted he was. He broke off a hunk of cheese and bread and washed it down with half a bottle of red wine. At least the German hadn't finished off all his food.

After he had eaten, he filled his pipe and rested, enjoying the satisfying taste and smell of the tobacco and reflecting on this wearing adventure. *Too damn old. My reflexes aren't all that good. Peter, Peter. How I wish you were with me.* He stretched, twisted, braced his shoulders. *God, I'm sore. Sore and stiff and old.* He shouldered his pack again and saw the faint indications of an old trail behind him. Curious, he gripped his pipe between his teeth, took up his staff and started up a steep incline. He followed the dim trail through heavy brush and rubble until it stopped abruptly in front of a great boulder settled solidly on a wide swath of unquarried marble. Behind the boulder the mountain rose and in front was a great expanse of marble meadow and beyond was the forest. Then Cane saw the cave.

Almost completely hidden by the boulder, there was a medieval door, reinforced with iron bands and a lock that had been hand forged centuries before. He was checking the hinges when a voice spoke softly behind him in English.

"It will only open with a key, Mr. Eliot. And I have it."

Cane spun around at the same instant pulling his gun. Two

men had guns—it wasn't even a standoff. He dropped his instantly, recognizing Müller.

"Well, well," he said, "sure and if it isn't Major von Stober himself —straight from the grave!" Stefan was standing behind his father, holding a gun, and a dark-complexioned, white haired giant of a man was behind him.

"Search him," Müller ordered, "then tie him up."

Facing Cane, Müller's face reddened.

"You bastard," he said, "believe me when I tell you this will be your longest day. Murder, arson and theft are just a part of it."

Stefan shoved his gun in his belt and moved to frisk Cane. He jerked Cane's shoulder to turn him around and in that instant Cane grabbed his wrist, lifted his knee and with a quick jerk broke Stefan's arm over it. As Stefan screamed, Cane swung his elbow back and caught him under the ear.

Müller shot as Stefan dropped, unconscious. The bullet passed through Cane's sheepskin jacket, nicking his upper arm. Cane stood holding his arm where blood seeped through the sleeve, as Müller struck him viciously with his gun. Semi-conscious and with a head that felt like it was exploding, Cane realized his arm wasn't hurting all that much. If he didn't lose too much blood, it wouldn't pose a major problem. But like Müller said, it could be a long day.

The stranger, searching, found the identification for Dale Lupine, the wallet, the map and the lapis princess. He pitched it to Müller who asked, "What the hell is this? Groggy, Cane sat up, opened his eyes, then closed them again. "My good-luck piece," he answered wearily.

Müller laughed. "Give it back to him. His luck has run out." He pitched it to the white-haired giant, then added, "Tie him up, hands to feet. I want him to see what I'm going to do to his fingers and that's just the beginning." The stranger replaced the lapis carving in Cane's pocket, then trussed him up with nylon cord.

Müller examined the map with a startled look. "Where did you get that!"

"The Ludwigsburg Center. You should know. Our man was wiped out."

Müller continued staring at the map. He seemed to have forgotten his son, even Cane. "Incredible. This is the original map that's been lost since the Russians came into Berlin. How did it get to Ludwigsburg Center?"

His arms and feet securely tied, Cane answered without looking up, "I think it was found with some Reichbank papers in the street."

The German laughed mirthlessly. "All the people who have been murdered for this map."

He wadded it up and tossed it to the ground.

"I was running some foolish errand for the Führer when the Italian bastard cleaned out the bank and brought it all to Italy. Mussolini hid it here and had a map made and sent it to Hitler. I saw it on his desk and photographed it."

"And had it micro-filmed and hidden in your tooth." Cane looked up at him.

"Yes, you bastard. So you traced von Stober and all for nothing. What brought you here, Eliot? This was none of your affair. Certainly the Jews would be interested, but not you. Why trace a man from his grave?"

"We were curious to know who was buried in that Oklahoma grave, Thyssen. You've worn lots of different hats." Cane's arm ached, but the bleeding had stopped.

"He was a good friend, but he understood I had to come back."

"No sacrifice too great for the Third Reich, eh, Thyssen? But how the devil could he drown in a POW camp where there wasn't a lake over three feet deep within miles?"

Müller looked at him coldly. "I don't know why I bother to tell you, but it was a stock tank. He was sick—not going to make it. I left him there in the tank."

"How could you get by with that?" Cane forgot about his arm.

"We looked something alike. I switched tags. Some knew, but nothing was made of it. The war was over and everyone wanted to go home." He paused and gazed at Stefan lying on the ground still unconscious and as comfortable as the stranger could make him. He looked back at Cane. "That boy better get all right quick." Then his own curiosity got the better of him and he added, "What I can't understand is how it was discovered after all these years."

"I don't know why I should tell you, but it was the Russians. A dentist in Rimini wrote a Soviet friend about a letter to be opened after his death. It told the whole story. When we checked the skull with the X-ray in Rimini, we knew then where Thyssen was."

"The X-ray!" Thyssen was shaken. "Verdamn! I searched the old man's office but couldn't find it. So they dug up von Stober."

"It didn't take long to check the picture the farmer had with the Major's wife and we thought it was Thyssen in the grave. You've led us on a hell of a chase."

"And I have the pleasure of finishing it off. Due to my foresight, I was the only person in Germany who knew where the Reichbank treasure was. And our organization has made good use of it."

"Having no conscience is a convenient thing for the SS and Die Spinne."

"The only regret I have is not doing a better job on that bastard in Rimini. I knew that when I saw him in the prison camp and he recognized me. Well, things have a way of evening out." Müller's voice was as icy as his expression. "It hurt when you killed Max," he said. "He was an old friend. But you made your biggest mistake when you killed Hans."

"They tried to kill me."

"You burned my store, broke into my safe and stole a box of jewels."

Cane shook his head earnestly. "It wasn't me. Who burned

the hotel?"

"Die Spinne. Your partner had been sentenced to death. They made sure he couldn't get out of his room Our only regret was that you weren't with him."

Cane wanted to keep Müller talking. "I'm surprised you haven't had fortune hunters here like they had in the Toplitzee."

"We've had them," Müller answered shortly, "but they've had climbing accidents."

"So, it's guarded?

"Hitler moved them in with the treasure. When they saw I had the map, they knew I was in charge."

"And the police don't bother you?"

"They understand about mountain accidents. And the latest is yet to happen. An unfortunate American geologist falls into a crevice and when the rescuers finally get to him they find every bone in his body broken. They won't know that it was all done before he went into the crevice."

He looked down at Cane with a grim smile.

"But Mr. Canyon Eliot, before you go for good you're going to be anxious to tell my good friend here, Señor Juan Illia, just where the jewels are. He's especially interested because he'd planned to pick them up today and take them back to Argentina." He ran his tongue across his lips and then added, "This is the second half million dollars they have paid for the jewels. The first you took off another friend."

"Who just happened to look like me?"

"It seemed a good idea at the time. Where's that money?"

"In the consulate safe in Munich. But I don't know a damn thing about any jewels."

Müller turned sullen and dark-faced. He kicked Cane's wounded arm, a blow that rolled him on his side, then grabbed his hair and jerked him back upright.

"You lying son-of-a-bitch, you won't know when we pitch you

from the Needle, but you'll be wishing for it long before we do it. We'll start with your fingers. Your hammer will be just the thing. Each joint smashed separately."

Cane couldn't help looking at the hammer and a chill rippled down his back. A hell of a lot of damage could be inflicted with that rock breaking tool before he lost consciousness. He watched Müller stoop and smooth Stefan's hair back from his face. He was still unconscious. His head had hit a stone when he fell and there was an ugly gash below his ear.

"If he dies," Müller said slowly, "you'll think you're in hell before you ever get there." He grabbed for Cane's hand, the hammer raised.

Cane threw his feet up and grabbed Thyssen's wrist with his bound hands, pulling him on top of him. He had no leverage except to jab the hammer the German was holding straight into Thyssen's face. His nose broken, Thyssen screamed with pain. The South American kicked Cane in the head and he rolled back, unconscious.

# CHAPTER XXXV

*Mt. Baldo*
*Monday, October 27*

Cane tried to open his eyes. He made a tentative effort to move, but the resisting muscles made him decide to lie still. He lay there, his mind vague and disoriented. Where was he? Someone was with him. Suddenly he remembered the Austrian and the hammer. He struggled, then realized someone was helping him sit up.

"It was a nasty blow you had and you've been wounded too."

Cane forced open his eyes, failed to focus, then closed them again, conscious now that his arms and legs were free. Who was with him? The voice was soothing, comforting.

"Come on, old man, take a swig of your whisky." Cane felt the liquor hot in his throat. He opened his eyes again and this time they stayed open. He saw a stranger with a friendly open face, dark hair and eyes, a warm smile.

Magen Ben-Yanait saw the questioning look on Cane's face.

"We're sort of friendly competitors. I'm Magen Ben-Yanait."

Cane closed his eyes and barely nodded. "Mossad?"

"That's right. I've watched you for a long time and have come to the conclusion you're too tough to kill." There was sincere affection in his voice.

"It was pretty close this time." Cane made a feeble effort to touch his head. "It feels like a drum and throbs as loud. Christ! It hurts to talk.

Where did you come from?"

"Alpendorf."

Cane managed a bleak smile. "Then you were the jewel thief who burned up the town? Where are the Müllers, Thyssens—that is?"

"They've been taken care of. Let me check your arm. It looks like a flesh wound."

"Let it go for now. So you stole Thyssen's jewels."

Ben-Yanait chuckled. "And you were going to get the treatment! Slow torture with a geology hammer. An ex-SS officer would know how to do it."

"Saved by the Israeli cavalry! Were you listening?"

"I was. And I had the pleasure of telling the Thyssens and the gangster from Argentina that they were on their way to Israel to stand trial for war crimes. Unlike you, I didn't come alone. We've searched for Thyssen for years. When I knew we'd found him, I didn't take a chance on his getting away. We also collected the lookouts they'd posted on the trail. You're home free, Eliot."

Cane didn't answer. It hurt to breathe.

They were silent a few minutes, then Magen asked, "Would you tell me one thing. Where is the bloody skull?"

"The Russian woman."

"So she got it away from you. Well, she worked hard enough for it."

Cane shook his head. "There was nothing in it. The skull, as you know, wasn't Thyssen."

"I discovered that when I saw Müller in Alpendorf and recognized him. I broke into his safe that night and then set the fire. I hoped he'd burn!"

Cane sat up and straightened his shoulders and looked at Magen with a curious expression. "Do you know anything about the man in my hotel room in Rimini?"

"Oh, yes," Ben-Yanait said. "I killed him, but it seemed to be necessary at the time. Sorry about your getting involved. I thought you were gone for the day."

"I rather thought you had."

"He's the third man we've killed in your quarters. Getting to be a habit." He pulled out a package of cigarettes, offered it to Cane. "I went to your room to search for the skull, although I didn't expect to find it. What I did find was this fellow from Moscow going through your things. He jumped me and I had to kill him to keep him quiet."

Cane took a lung-searing draw on the cigarette and watched the smoke evaporate. "I hear you've been following me since Oklahoma."

"That's right. Anya told you I suppose."

Cane nodded.

"A very sharp lady. We've crossed before. Well, by now she's delivered the skull to Moscow and she's probably on her way to Siberia. The KGB have a way of getting impatient with agents who don't deliver."

Cane grimaced and Magen thought it was from pain.

"Can you get up? I have something to show you."

"Just barely." Magen helped him to his feet and steadied him. Cane shook his head and tried to smile. "I'm all right, I think. A little dizzy, but that'll pass." He followed the Mossad agent to the cave and saw the iron rimmed doors were open. The air was stale. A Coleman lantern on a block of marble lighted the interior. Coils of rope and a box of winches were by the door. Beyond were meter-square wooden crates stacked to the ceiling marked in black stenciled letters as they'd come from the camps—Auschwitz, Belsen, Dachau, Buchenwald and more, all ringed with metal bands as they had been sealed in the camps by the prisoners whose belongings they were.

"My God!"

"And there are probably fifty of them. Can you imagine this?"

"No. Have you opened any?"

"Haven't had time." He took Cane's hammer and pried the seal until it broke, then split open the wooden lid. Smaller boxes, the breadth and width of a hand span filled the large one, each marked in block letters: *3 kilos*. Magen forced one open. It held kilo bars of gold. "That's from Auschwitz—a camp noted for its efficiency. They melted their dental gold and shipped a kilo a day to the Reichbank." They moved to another crate and opened it. Filled with smaller boxes, these held odd lot collections of watches, a kilo of pearls, another of loose diamonds and rubies and emeralds. "This is the kind of box I took from Müller's safe. Christ! It makes you sick."

Cane nodded. He felt nauseated.

"How will you get it to Israel?"

"I haven't a clue. Italy will claim it. Germany, too. And the Russians will show up sooner or later and put in their claim. Eliot, this has to go back to Israel."

Cane agreed.

"If we lowered it by night to the lake, could it be picked up by motor launch?"

"It looks like that's how it was done. Here's a cargo net and winches and ropes."

The men threaded their way back through the crates. At the entrance, both took lung-filling breaths of the fresh cool air. Cane sat down and leaned against a tree trunk.

"I'm so damn weak. And the contents of the cave didn't help any."

"What you need is food and whisky. Or maybe reverse the order." Magen opened his pack. They sat on blocks of marble, breaking off hunks of heavy black bread, cheese and stripping chicken bones bare, washing it all down with great gulps of strong red wine.

Cane took a deep breath and smiled at Ben Yanait.

"If food is the way to a man's heart, believe me you have mine!"

For an hour or more the men talked, rested, speculated about transporting the treasure to Israel.

"If you stayed to guard the cave, I could go to Peschiera and rent a boat," Cane suggested.

"We'll still need help. I can get a man down from Munich in a day. He's as strong as an ox."

"You have a radio?"

Ben-Yanait nodded. "Yes. He could be here by tomorrow night and start moving then."

"One other small problem," Cane said, "to get the crates out of Lake Garda...."

"These are heavy; they will have to be broken down. Then we can take the smaller boxes to waiting cars." He paused. "It will be a dicey business."

"And out of Italy?"

"We'll cross that when we get to it. Pretty young tourists or sweet old ladies in vintage cars don't have much trouble crossing borders."

Magen stood up, stretched and smiled down at Cane.

"Feeling better now?"

Cane laughed, flexed the muscle in his arm. "I could whip a bear. What was in that wine?" He stood up and followed Magen toward the cave. They had just reached the entrance when Magen gasped and dropped to the ground. Cane hadn't heard the shot. He fell to his knees to help, but the Mossad agent was dead. Blood was seeping through his jacket.

"Stand up. Turn around with your hands up," a low voice ordered in German. Cane straightened and turned slowly, then felt his guts tie themselves in a knot. Anya stood by the boulder, her eyes wide, her face pale. Beside her was a tall, extraordinarily thin man, the same one who had followed the chauffeur from the Hofbrauhaus. A nasty looking, fox-faced man with hands like hams. He was holding a gun fitted with a silencer.

"So this is the American agent who slipped so neatly through our fingers in Munich? Huh?" When Anya didn't answer, he turned to her and asked again, "Huh?"

She nodded slowly. Her eyes filmed over and she couldn't break away from Cane's level gaze.

"Well, you might as well kill me now," Cane said coolly. "It obviously doesn't bother you to shoot a man in the back." Cane walked toward them. "Hello, Anya. And you brought your sitter. He just killed a fine man. But you approve, don't you? Anything for Mother Russia. You know, you're going to have to kill me, too." He was looking at Anya as he talked, ignoring the tall Russian, until he stood in front of her.

When he made his move, his eyes still held Anya's. He grabbed the sitter's gun wrist more by luck than good judgment. The gun fired harmlessly into the woods as they struggled for it. Both men fell to the ground, Cane straining to keep the gun aimed away from him. He kneed the Russian in the groin and took a quick advantage as his grip relaxed for an instant. Cane twisted his arm but couldn't reach the gun. The Russian slugged him in the face. His head jerked back and they were rolling over and over. Now Cane was on top, then the Russian. Somewhere the gun was lost, but the sitter's muscles were like steel cords. Cane couldn't hold him. His arm was bleeding again. A surge of adrenaline gave Cane a charge of strength and he nearly had the man's arm twisted behind him. But he couldn't hold it. The Russan was younger and stronger and broke loose. Cane saw the blow coming, but he couldn't duck or dodge or feint. His head snapped back, and he thought he heard a shot.

There was a stillness about the mountain when Cane's coughing brought him to. It echoed around him as he fought to stay conscious. He reached out—groping—and felt her. He opened his eyes.

She was cradling him in her arms, trying to feed him brandy. He coughed again. It felt like his lungs were ripping open. He smiled feebly. She was crying.

He'd never seen her cry before. Then he was the protector, and his strength surged back. He gathered her to him and held her close. "Where's your sitter?"

She shook her head. When he looked over her shoulder, he understood. The Fox lay as he had been when they were fighting, a pool of blood where his face should have been. Cane took a deep breath, then held her closer and let the choking sobs drain her. Finally, there were only great heaving gasps that shook her body.

"He was—he was going to kill you," she whispered.

Cane had no way to comfort her. Anya had broken the umbilical cord that bound her to Russia, and it was traumatic. He held her until the sun had gathered the western clouds into a final burst of ragged color and disappeared. Darkness closed over them and Anya shivered.

"Anya, we must go inside," Cane whispered. "But I'm not sure I can make it without help."

She nodded and got to her feet. Cane ached all over, every muscle strained, every joint bruised. With Anya's arm for balance, he managed to stand. Supporting Cane the best she could, Anya guided him slowly to the cave. The lamp had burned out. Anya used her pencil flash to look for oil. She filled the lamp and lit it while Cane leaned against the crates.

"There's some cheese and bread in the pack," he said. "And whisky." His strength was returning in measured cycles. Now he could stand alone. Now he could move. Now his arms responded to the demands of his mind. He gathered brush and dead branches and kindled a fire. Anya handed him the bottle of Scotch and he drank quickly. "Now you." She smiled for the first time, and sipped, shuddered, and they both laughed, remembering.

"Good medicine," Cane said.

"I know. Take off your coat and shirt and let me clean your wounds. What happened to your arm?"

"A hundred years ago in a cave in a Roman wall a man shot me. But it's only a flesh wound." He winced as Anya helped him out of his coat. His shirt was caked with dried blood. Then she saw his head wound. "Oh, Cane!"

"It's been a strenuous day. I'm just a little old for this sort of thing. But I'm all right now that you're here. Ouch!"

Anya soaked her handkerchief with Scotch and cleaned his arm. "Go easy with that. I'd rather use it inside than out!"

"Be still and let me finish. This is the best disinfectant ever." She pulled off her blouse and ripped out a sleeve. "It's not sterile but it's better than nothing." She touched the back of his head carefully. "I need to clean this so no hair is in the cut. Turn toward the light."

Afterwards, they finished the bread and cheese in Cane's pack and started on Anya's. Cane quartered an apple with the lapis princess.

"Where did you get that? It's beautiful." She cupped it in her hands.

"From my grandfather. The little Chinese princess has saved my life more than once. Now I want you to have it. My two good luck girls together always."

"Cane, I love it. Thank you." She smiled, closed the knife and dropped it in her pocket. "Now I have two things to prize, your pipe and your princess."

"And you have me. There's an old Chinese saying that if you save someone's life they belong to you for always." He took her face in both his hands and kissed her gently on the lips. The lamplight danced on her cheeks. She buried her head in his shoulder and Cane held her, his hand on her head, his bandaged arm around her feeling her tortured breathing, the turmoil that twisted her thinking.

"Never mind now. The worst is over. I want you to see something." He pointed to the crates.

He showed her the boxes of gold bars. Opened, they glowed like something alive in the lamplight. She put her hand into a box of jewels, shivered and jerked back as if she had touched fire.

"So this is it," she whispered. "The ransom of six million lives." Neither of them noticed the first tremble in the cave.

Then the lamp rocked and Cane caught it. There was a definite shift of the floor.

"My God! It's an earthquake!"

He grabbed Anya's arm and pulled her toward the entrance. They worked their way as rapidly as they could around the boxes as the cave shook and the crates shifted. Stones fell from the roof. There was a crash at the back of the cave. Before they reached the entrance a rubble of rock fell on Cane. His knees buckled and he dropped to the floor. They struggled to get out before they were buried alive. On their hands and knees, desperately crawling over debris, they scrambled out of the cave into the clearing beyond the ring of boulders.

Huddled together, they heard the grinding and deep throttled roar as millions of tons of cracked and tortured marble under the influence of some mighty pressure center twisted and cracked, reared and tore at the ground under them. Boulders rolled, rock and gravel rained down. Cane lost consciousness. Lightening flashed. Thunder roared. Rain came in dizzying torrents. Anya cradled Cane in her arms, covered his head with her coat, shielded him with her body. He was bleeding, but she couldn't tell where. The rain washed it away as fast as it flowed. Where was he hurt? There was no way to tell. Still the earth shook.

Cane slipped into and out of consciousness. Anya held him close, crooning Russian lullabies.

By daylight the rain had ceased. The world had stopped its trembling. The tunnel was gone and the storeroom cave. Magen Ben-Yanait had been buried as had the Russian Fox, Lisita. The plateau was covered with rocks and masonry from the castle. Boulders had breached the walls; the keep was gone. Trees along the plateau were lopsided. There was a different slant to the quarry and a great chasm split it.

Cold and miserable, Anya pulled Cane's sheepskin coat tighter around him. Restless, muttering in delirium, he called aloud. She buried her face in his hair, kissed his cheek and when the sun, rose-tinted and warm, came up over the Aidge River far below, she knew they would survive.

Cane, shivering with fever and unconscious, was still in Anya's arms when the old man found them. He and the three Carabinieri with him unrolled the stretchers and with infinite patience carried Cane and Anya to the makeshift hospital at the base of the Needle. The village was gone. The marble streets had buckled; the Municipio had only four walls behind a cracked fountain. The statues were broken into fragments. There were no pigeons. The small bar was gone. The Jeep was crushed beneath the weight of the cathedral bell. The old man and the police ministered to the injured. Finally, help arrived in helicopters.

# CHAPTER XXXVI

*Hospital, USA*
*Monday, November 10*

The room was dark. Or was it because he couldn't seem to open his eyes? His head was ringing. It felt swollen, about to burst. The sheet beneath him was wet with perspiration. He was miserably hot. Where was he? How long had he been here? Vague memories of a floating apparition hovering around him, protecting him, wandered through his mind. He forced his eyes open, tried to focus them.

Gradually they began to define objects. A bright place on the wall was an open window. Long fringed shadows teased an upper corner. A tree? But the effort was too great and his eyelids closed. He reached for the limits of his bed. He moved his feet, his legs. He tried to turn his body and couldn't. He lay exhausted, breathing heavily. And then he slept normally for the first time in two weeks.

The sun, bright and glaring against the white wall hurt his eyes. He struggled to focus them on something—anything. He saw the window then and remembered having seen it before. At night. There were palm fronds waving across one corner. He thought he could hear a surf breaking nearby. The dull drumming—the rhythmic pulse—the in and out of the ocean breathing. The air was fragrant. He didn't hear the door open. Then a white mass at the foot of his bed materialized into a nurse with a tall tiara cap.

She didn't smile or speak. He made only a token protest when she pushed up the sleeve of his hospital gown and gave him an injection. His eyes were closed and he couldn't force them open yet he knew another person had entered the room. But in the subconscious recesses of his mind he heard the conversation in Russian! He recognized one voice. *It was hers!* A hard physical pain in his chest raked him and he shivered. He tried to pull the sheet over his shoulders and realized someone was helping. The conversation in Russian continued. He welcomed the oblivion that came when the injection took effect.

The darkness lay about him like an enveloping blanket when he woke. The window was open. The air, cool and salty, smelling of tropical flowers hung over his bed. The shadow of a palm tree whisked across the window. Cane moved his legs cautiously and when he felt no pain, turned over. His bed was freshly made, the sheets cool to his body. He took a deep breath. Where the devil was he? Threads of memory came back in snatches—the ranch in Colorado. Peter. Then after Peter, a fire. A raging cauldron of hell—a hotel, but where? It was like a nightmare and he turned his head into the pillow. But the threads kept unwinding. Anya—over and over again he saw Anya. In Munich at the Oktoberfest. In Alpendorf. In his bed at the hotel and the memory was an excruciating pain. Then there was the winter storm on the Needle and all the actors—Müller's. No—not the Müllers, the Thyssens. The man from Spider and the Mossad agent. *Our man the Israeli* and Anya shot him. No—not Anya. The tall skinny sitter. Then his mind turned into a jumbled kaleidoscope of quick flashes like psychedelic lights at a rock concert. The cave and its riches. The moving mountain and its disaster. A dream-like sequence where he floated down the mountain between up-rooted trees and scattered boulders—Anya beside him.

She had brought him here and had betrayed him. Like the sound track of an old movie he remembered the conversation. He couldn't understand it, but he knew Russian when it was spoken. Now he had to escape. From the nurse who gave him injections. From Anya. Especially from Anya.

He lay in the darkness making plans. First thing—he had to get his strength back. He sat up slowly. His heart was pounding, but he didn't feel shaky. He swung his feet to the side of the bed and then sat up. He put both feet on the floor and pressed his weight on them. He stood up.

Supporting himself with his hand first on the dresser, then on the back of a chair, he reached the window. A dark expanse of textured lawn rolled down to meet a phosphorescent sea. Frothy breakers slapped over themselves in their rush to cover the beach. Where could he be? Palm trees silhouetted against the night sky marked a beach that curved into the sea. He tried to think of a spot in Russia that could be so tropical. A Black Sea resort?

He made his way back to bed, feeling his strength returning in adrenaline pumped surges. Where was Anya? Was she afraid to face him? Had she returned to Moscow? Damn! He'd given her the lapis princess.

Conscious of his hospital gown he had a sinking feeling. Where were his clothes? He searched briefly, then gave up. Naturally the first thing they'd do to keep him captive would be to take his clothes. He would bide his time, get his strength back, then catch an orderly and make an impromptu switch. Put the Russian in his bed, climb out the window, down the palm tree, and where there's water there are boats. He twisted his shoulders, flexed his muscles. The old man wasn't dead yet.

When the door opened in the morning, he pretended to be asleep. When it closed, he found a tray near his bed with a sprig of bougainvillea beside a plate of ham and eggs and hash browned potatoes. A big pot of coffee. What kind of food was this but pure American! They were softening him up for something. Hunger overcame his curiosity. In short order, he'd cleaned his plate and finished three cups of coffee. American coffee.

No doubt fattening him up for the ordeal in Moscow when he would face Anya backed by the KGB. Was he the price for Natalya's freedom?

He pretended sleep throughout the day. And always there were the conversations in Russian. What were her plans for him? There was the food, always American. And so it was each day. And the next. And the next.

When there was a tray beside his bed, he ate. One time there was a bottle of wine. He looked at the label. Taylor's—New York! Proof that they'd go to any length to confuse him. When it was just dark, he pushed his door open and looked into the hall. He saw a young man coming toward him, dressed in a sort of olive green pants and shirt with a stethoscope around his neck. A doctor?

"Would you come here, sir?" he called in German. Then he moved behind the door. As it opened wide, he hit the unsuspecting man as hard as he could, an uppercut that shoved his head back and lifted him off his feet.

"What the hell do you think you're doing?"

Cane froze. He recognized the voice and this wasn't the first time he'd heard it in the full throw of anger.

"By God, Chili, no one can ever say you do the expected thing!" Stunned, Cane looked square into the unhappy face of Hastings. Speechless, they stood for several seconds, starting at each other.

Then Hasting stooped over the hospital aide and helped him to his feet.

"I wouldn't blame you if you transferred him to a psychiatric hospital. Their patients at least are under restraint."

The aide looked at Cane and then at Hastings.

"I thought he was asleep." He rubbed his chin as he turned back to Cane. "Is it asking too much for you to return to your bed and stay there until I can call Dr. Raye?"

Cane gave them both a long level look, conscious now of the hospital gown barely reaching his knees and open down the back. He backed slowly to his bed. There was a certain security in the white enameled bed and the hard mattress. He pulled the blanket over his shoulder and

271

didn't look up when Hastings sat down beside him.

"Why in God's name did you attack the poor guy?"

Cane answered weakly. "I thought he was a Russian."

"A Russian! Chili, if I live to be a hundred, I could never understand you. Why would you think he was Russian?"

Cane pushed back the covers and sat up. "Will you tell me where I am?"

"Where the hell did you think you were?" Cane grinned faintly. "For some reason, I forget why, I thought I was in Russia." He shook his head slowly. "American hospital, right?"

Hastings nodded, puzzled. "Right."

"Do I sound stupid asking what body of water is out there?"

"You do. But it's the Atlantic Ocean, my friend, and you're convalescing in Florida."

"How long have I been here?"

"Three weeks and over. Would you like to go back to Colorado tomorrow?

Cane's face was suddenly free from strain and he broke into a wide grin. "Do I have to answer that?"

"No. Your plane leaves at noon tomorrow. Before that, you'll be debriefed by an officer from Langley. Then you'll be free to leave. A heavy snow has blanketed Colorado. Poor guy. It looks like you'll have a white Thanksgiving." He pushed his chair back and stood up. "Chili, be kind to Dr. Raye. I don't think I'd mention that you thought his aide was Russian."

Cane smiled. "I understand."

# CHAPTER XXXVII

A cool, unseasonable mist covered Southern Florida. The airport was fogged in and Cane sat with Hastings in the small waiting room hoping the ceiling would lift so the plane could take off.

The debriefing had gone very well. Cane told them everything he could remember. His voice was completely steady as he recounted the Mossad agent's death. His fight with the Russian agent and Anya's saving his life. It was all told as dispassionately as any stale adventure.

"So she saved your life? Hastings asked.

Cane nodded without answering.

"Do you know where she is now?"

Cane shook his head.

"Do you wonder?"

Cane stood up angrily. "God man, what do you think I am—made of stone?"

Hastings shrugged.

Cane stirred restlessly.

"Don't be in such a hurry, Chili. We're waiting for some other passengers. Two just came in from Europe last night and they're flying into Miami this morning. We can't leave until they get here."

"They're going to Colorado?"

"Yes." He stood up and said, "Chili, come outside—we need to talk."

Cane looked at him curiously. Who would be going with him to Colorado?

They walked along the damp path that surrounded the small terminal for several minutes before Hastings said, "I had to wait until the debriefing was over before I could tell you all that's happened. Don't interrupt."

He pulled out a package of cigarettes, offered it to Cane who shook his head, then chose one carefully.

"Anya called me from Verona as soon as the helicopter brought you both from Ago-Piccolo. So we were able to rescue an American geologist and his wife along with other Americans caught in the disaster of the earthquake."

"Wife?"

"Don't interrupt. The wife had lost her identification, but it was no problem fixing her up with a new passport. Many lives were lost, foreigners as well as Italians. Many are still missing. Among those are two Russians, a man and woman who had been in the earthquake area. Their bodies haven't been found, but some of their personal effects were. Also missing is an Israeli mountain climber who got separated from his friends. They escaped and made their way down safely with some Germans who returned to Tel Aviv with them. We brought the Americans, Dale and Jeannette Lupine, into Frankfort and then, because it was her wish, we sent them to a Florida hospital. Lupine was very ill. Pneumonia with all sorts of complications."

"Damn it all. Get to his wife."

"In good time. Well, I returned with them. You know, we all envied him. She was so attentive, helped nurse him through a bad time. She was the only one who insisted he would live. But she also had other problems to worry about. It seems she had relatives in Russia. She was afraid she might have to go there if those relatives couldn't get out."

Cane ran his tongue across his lips but didn't say anything. His chest began to tighten.

Hastings flipped his cigarette across the wet macadam paving and continued. "It was thought they were going to be exiled because of some seditious literature that had been published abroad. When it was firmly established in Moscow Center that two of their top agents had been killed in the earthquake, Mrs. Lupine's relatives were given a choice of prison or exile. They flew in from England yesterday."

Cane took a deep breath and exhaled slowly. "Where is Anya?"

"She went to meet Natalya and Mischa in Miami. They should be here in about an hour." He smiled at Cane. "It's been real touchy. We had to keep both of you isolated until her daughter and grandson were safely out of Russia."

For the first time since that day he had returned from Europe after the war and saw his son, Cane wanted to cry. He felt his eyes water and blew his nose strenuously. He swallowed hard.

"I really don't know what to say, except—thank you. Thank you for everything."

~~~~

Three hours later, the plane was high above the clouds heading west. Cane sat beside Anya holding her in his arms and talking softly.....

"Somehow I never thought this day would come." From time to time he would take her face in his hand, turn it to his and look at her as if memorizing it. Then push her hair from her forehead and kiss her softly, and whisper, "Oh, God, Anya. I love you so....."

Or, he'd sit up straight and say, "Oh, Anya, you'll love the ranch! And it's a great place to raise a kid. Anya, I love you....."

He held her close and together they watched Natalya trying to control a dynamic bundle of three-year-old kinetic curiosity.

Sometime later Cane asked, "Tell me, Mrs. Lupine, did you speak Russian to anyone at the hospital?"

"Why, yes, Mr. Lupine," Anya smiled at him, "every day with your nurse. Her parents came from Moscow when she was young. She liked to practice her Russian on me. Why?"

Cane shrugged. "Oh, nothing." Then he raised her hand to his lips and said, "This is the longest damn trip I've ever made waiting to get you into our bedroom at the ranch....."

"I can't wait to see the ranch!"

"All in good time." Cane kissed her. "First things first."

# THE END

Made in the USA
Charleston, SC
18 February 2011